Walk On By

Walk On By

Ted Darling crime series

'trouble of a serious kind'

L M Krier

Cover design DMR Creative
Cover photo "Hollywood Park steps"
Photographer : MartinM3C2 [25 June 2010]

WALK ON BY

Fisherman's Friend is a registered trademark of the Lofthouse
of Fleetwood Ltd Company of Lancashire
Shewee is a registered trademark of Dales Distribution Ltd

ISBN 978-2-901773-08-5

Contents

About the Author

L M Krier is the pen name of former journalist (court reporter) and freelance copywriter, Lesley Tither, who also writes travel memoirs under the name Tottie Limejuice. Lesley also worked as a case tracker for the Crown Prosecution Service.

The Ted Darling series of crime novels comprises: *The First Time Ever, Baby's Got Blue Eyes, Two Little Boys, When I'm Old and Grey, Shut Up and Drive, Only the Lonely, Wild Thing, Walk on By, Preacher Man.*

All books in the series are available in Kindle and paperback format and are also available to read free with Kindle Unlimited.

Contact Details

If you would like to get in touch, please do so at:

tottielimejuice@gmail.com

facebook.com/LMKrier

facebook.com/groups/1450797141836111/

https://twitter.com/tottielimejuice

For a light-hearted look at Ted and the other characters, please consider joining the We Love Ted Darling group on Facebook.

Discover the DI Ted Darling series

If you've enjoyed meeting Ted Darling, you may like to discover the other books in the series:

Acknowledgements

Thanks to all those who helped with this seventh book in the DI Ted Darling series. Book 8 is planned for release later in 2017.

Beta readers Jill Pennington (Alpha) Emma Heath, Kate Pill, Alison Sabedoria, Karen Corcoran, Jill Evans, Shelagh Corker.

To Kate the Cow

(you know who you are)

Just love your comments and stickers

– long may they continue

Chapter One

'Afternoon, Ted, Magnus here. Before I forget, congratulations on the promotion. About time too.'

'Hello, Magnus, and thanks. Long time since I've heard from you. How's life on the posh side?'

'Wilmslow's getting so I can't afford to park here, never mind live here,' the inspector from Cheshire Constabulary grumbled. 'I'm just giving you a call as we've had a fatal stabbing on our patch today, and rather an unusual one. Do you have an Inspector Galton at your nick?'

'Galton? No. Not sure I can think of one anywhere, off the top of my head. You're sure it's Galton? Not Dalton? Or Walton?'

'Have you got one of those?'

'No, sorry, not one of those either. I'm not being very helpful, am I? It's just that they're more common names. What's it about?'

'Well, here's the strange part. A woman's been robbed in a car park on our patch. We're not sure why it escalated as it did but she was then fatally stabbed. All her possessions seem to have been taken, so it's not immediately clear why she was killed, unless she knew her attacker, perhaps.

'A woman in her sixties, we think, although we don't have a definite ID yet. My team are out working on it now. It does seem as if everything of value has gone, bag, phone, possibly her car, but we're not sure yet. That's just how it looks from the initial reports. And we don't have a name for the victim either, at this stage.

'She didn't die at the scene, only it was a close thing. She actually bled out in the ambulance on the way to hospital. But before she died, she told the paramedics that she was working undercover for a Detective Inspector Galton, at Stockport nick.'

'A civilian? In her sixties? I'm struggling to think of anyone who would use someone like that undercover, especially as it seems as if it was for something dangerous, or at least potentially so.'

'Hang on a sec, Ted, just got another call ...'

Ted could hear him talking briefly in the background, then he came back on the line.

'That was my sergeant. They've got a likely ID now, and the woman's definitely from your patch, Ted. I know it's ours to take, but with all the odd aspects of it, I wondered if you fancied coming over, just initially, to see what you can make of it. Maybe give me a few pointers? I have to confess it's way outside my experience. I know you've headed up a lot of murder enquiries, with some good results. It's not something we get much of here. Our daily round is more of the white powder sort, and handbags at dawn between the WAGs. I'd really welcome your expertise, especially with the link to your patch. Just to make sure I don't make a total tit of myself with the basics on my first murder enquiry.'

'Something like this sounds a bit outside my experience, too, with phoney police involved, if that's what it is. But I'm happy to come over and take a quick look, if you think it will be of any help. It would give me an excuse to abandon the paperwork for a bit. And in case there is any connection to us here that we might need to follow up. I'll just have to clear it with my boss first, stepping onto another force's territory.'

'Ah yes, I heard you got the Ice Queen, for your sins. You must have been very bad in a previous life, Ted. See you shortly then?'

'Half an hour or so, Magnus. And, surprisingly, she's not as bad as her reputation. Almost human sometimes, in fact. Although things are a lot different to when I had Jim Baker as my boss.'

Detective Chief Inspector Ted Darling headed up an experienced team of officers who investigated Serious and Serial crimes in Stockport and other divisions within the Greater Manchester Police Force area. He grabbed his trenchcoat as he headed for his office door. It was pouring down outside, had been doing for days now and there was no sign of an end to it. He looked round the main office to see who was available to go with him. There may be nothing in it for them, but it was worth checking out at first hand, in case there was any involvement. He hated having to pick up a case later on when vital clues might have been missed by an inexperienced team. It would be an interesting one, by the sound of it, even if it turned out not to be one for them.

Ted's eyes fell on one of his two Detective Sergeants, Rob O'Connell. Young, keen, recently promoted. It might be the ideal case to put him on.

'Rob, how do you fancy a quick run over to Wilmslow, to see how the other half lives? It's a fatal stabbing, a woman in her sixties. There may be nothing for us, except that the victim is from our patch and she's mentioned an officer, supposedly from Stockport, so I've been asked to go over and take a look. Can you get my car and I'll meet you outside? I'll just let the Super know where we're going and why.'

Superintendent Debra Caldwell – the Ice Queen, as everyone called her, not entirely fairly, as Ted now knew – listened attentively while Ted gave a brief summary of what details he had so far.

'Interesting. Even if the victim is from here, the death itself is down to Cheshire, I would have thought. But I agree, you should go and take a look for yourself, to see if you can get to the bottom of this undercover idea. There may be nothing to it.

Wires may simply have been crossed somewhere. But I don't like the possibility that someone clearly put this woman in serious danger. We need to get the full facts on that, for a start, and we need to find out who this so-called Inspector Galton is. While you're out, I'll try to find out if there's some sort of covert operation going on involving our patch that we've not been made aware of, which would of itself be highly irregular.'

'I've already put Océane on to searching the Scams Book to see if there's anything current involving bogus police officers. Steve's contacting other stations to see if there's an Inspector Galton anywhere, or if anyone else has had anything similar. It's an unusual name, I've not heard it before. I'll know more when I get over to Wilmslow. I'm taking Rob with me; it'll be an interesting one for him. It's nothing I've come across before.'

She nodded her agreement.

'It certainly won't be a wasted trip, even if it provides nothing more than a training exercise for DS O'Connell. Good personal development. And I'm sure your input will be very helpful to Wilmslow. Please keep me posted. I'm likely to be working late this evening so you'll probably find me still at my desk on your return. Yet another budgetary planning meeting to prepare for. I'm constantly having to make the case to retain our current staffing levels. The powers that be want higher detection rates with fewer personnel hours.'

Ted felt a wave of sympathy for her. Number crunching was never his favourite activity.

'Do you ever miss Firearms?'

They'd both previously had careers in Firearms which they'd given up for family reasons, she because of her sons, Ted because of his partner, Trevor.

'Do you?' she countered.

'It all seemed a lot simpler, back in those days. Certainly a lot less paperwork. I think about it sometimes. I'm not sure whether I miss it or not. Right, I'd better get going and see if I can help to get some justice for this victim.'

Rob had the car ready outside the entrance, the engine running and the heater on. He glanced sideways at the boss as Ted lowered himself rather awkwardly into the front passenger seat.

'You all right, boss? You look like you're in pain.'

'Just a bit of muscle strain, nothing serious,' Ted told him.

'Martial arts stuff?'

'Something like that,' Ted said evasively.

He wasn't about to let the team know that Trev was teaching him to ride. Ted had had his first long hack out at the weekend on a safe but rather broad cob called Walter. He'd enjoyed himself, more than he ever thought he would on a horse, but the breadth of his mount had left him aching.

Magnus Pierson had given Ted directions to a small car park behind a row of shops, all now taped off. Rob parked the official car as close as he could get and he and Rob identified themselves at the entrance to the crime scene. The uniformed officer who took their names called Pierson over.

'Hello, Ted, good to see you. I could certainly do with your input on this one.'

Ted made the introductions between him and Rob O'Connell then asked to be filled in. His experienced eyes were travelling round the scene, missing no detail, as he listened.

'I've had officers out round and about to see if we could find out who she was and what she was doing here. She didn't give a name to the ambulance crew, she was too busy trying to tell them about this so-called Inspector Galton, and she didn't say much more before she died.

'As she'd mentioned Stockport and as she was found lying bleeding on a car park here, I thought we'd start with the assumption that she was from your area and had driven here. I've put all my available officers, which doesn't amount to a lot these days, on to seeing if we could get a trace on her and we got lucky at a jeweller's shop nearby. Someone answering her description had been in not long before she was found and bought a Cartier watch. Sixteen-and-a-half grand's worth.'

'Sixteen-and-a half grand for a watch?' Ted echoed in surprise.

Pierson laughed.

'You're in Wilmslow now Ted, not Stockport. Small change here. Wilmslow folk would probably spend that much on the nanny for a birthday present. Anyway, she paid by credit card. We've got the details and the purchaser was a Mrs Freda Ashworth, lives in Marple. We're trying to track down next of kin for a positive ID.'

'Who found her?'

'Another shopper, coming back to get their car. She was on the ground, bleeding heavily. Luckily, it was someone sensible enough to phone an ambulance straight away. It's getting depressingly common for people just to walk past and do nothing.'

'What makes you think she had a car, apart from assuming she did?'

Ted tried to keep any note of criticism out of his voice. He just didn't like assumptions, not in his line of work. It could slow an enquiry down, especially in the early stages.

'There's no marked out parking spaces here, as you can see, but she was lying in a car-sized gap between two other vehicles. And there was a tyre track through the not inconsiderable pool of blood. Even with people being inclined to look the other way, I didn't think anyone would be callous enough to drive off and leave her there bleeding if they weren't involved in the crime.

'We deduced that whoever stabbed her took her car and drove off, leaving the tyre track through her blood. We can see from the tracks that the car came out forwards, and fast, so it had been backed into the space, and it just missed running over her as she lay there. It could have been her attacker's car, of course. We're just checking for details of any vehicle registered to her, so we can see if hers was parked somewhere else.

'Initial reports from the hospital say she had no personal possessions with her at all. No handbag, car keys, house keys, nothing.'

'I'd like to talk to the people in the shop myself, if that's all right with you? As a starting point.'

'Absolutely fine. I called you over because, like I said, it's not something I've come across before and I know Serious and Serial is much more your thing than mine.'

'Rob, next stages?' Ted asked.

Rob was doing well since his promotion and Ted was keen to give him every opportunity to show his initiative.

The DS turned to Inspector Pierson and asked, 'Have you sent anyone to her home address yet, sir?'

'Next on my list, sergeant. It's not all that long since we got the details, and we've been checking them out. I didn't want to get it wrong. This is my first real experience of a murder enquiry. The last thing I wanted was to start off by telling the wrong person their other half was dead.'

'Boss, I think we should send someone from our nick round to the address, as soon as possible. Not just to look for next of kin but if whoever it was took everything, including the car, there's a good chance they have the keys to the victim's house, too. Do you want me to get someone on to watching the property, in case anyone turns up there?'

Ted nodded, pleased. Rob was thinking along the same lines as he was. Pierson looked impressed as Rob got on his mobile to organise it.

'It's glaringly obvious you two know much more about this sort of thing than I do. I'd better brush up on my "Every Boy's Book of Managing a Crime Scene." If you don't mind, I'll tag along with you to the shop, to see what I can learn from you.'

'Just a couple of things, before we do that. Is this the nearest car park to the shop where she bought the watch? I take it there was no sign of that anywhere?' Ted asked.

'No sign of the watch or anything else. Nothing on her at all, according to the hospital. And no, there's plenty of parking nearer to the shop than this, and easier to find. You'd have to know about this parking to get here. There's no signage pointing to it.'

'CCTV?'

'None currently operational. This area is mostly used by people working in shops and offices nearby rather than by Joe Public doing their shopping. There was a camera, on the back of that building there, but it was vandalised recently and hasn't been fixed yet. So you're thinking ...?'

Ted's eyes followed the direction Pierson was indicating.

'Nothing yet, until we have more details. So can we walk round to the shop now, see what they have to say?'

It was a short distance to the nearby shop, which they covered briskly, Ted asking more questions as they walked.

'What can you tell me about the injury? Knife wound? Any indication of what sort, how many wounds, anything like that at this stage?'

'All I know so far is that the victim was stabbed. I haven't heard anything further yet, other than the fact that she was DOA at the hospital. We'll know more after the post-mortem, of course.'

'Macclesfield Hospital?'

'No, in the end they took her to Stepping Hill. There'd been a major incident, with victims being sent to Macclesfield, so the ambulance crew were told that would be quicker. That means she came from your patch, and she died back there, officially.'

Ted laughed.

'That sounds like a good attempt at buck-passing, if ever I heard one. Any CCTV in the shop?'

'Yes, and with a good shot of the person we think is our victim. We went off the description the first responders gave us. Fortunately for us, she was wearing a distinctive bright red coat.'

They watched the CCTV through first at the shop, before questioning anyone. An ash-blonde woman in a red coat, possibly in her early sixties, approached the counter and appeared to ask for a specific item, which the assistant went and found for her. The woman was on her mobile phone the whole time, and the transaction didn't take long. She paid by credit card, then left with the expensive watch neatly wrapped and in a small paper carrier bag.

'Can we find out what she was saying?' Ted asked.

They asked to speak to the young assistant who had served her. Ted asked her if she remembered anything of the conversation.

'The lady was on the phone when she came into the shop and she was talking on it all the time. I thought she was perhaps a mum, buying a gift her son had asked her to get for his girlfriend. You know, something like that. But then as she was getting ready to leave, she said something I thought was a bit odd. She said, "your officer hasn't made contact with me yet, so I'm just going to find him." Just for a moment, I thought about a Trading Standards Officer, or something like that, but that seemed strange. The watch was perfectly genuine. We don't sell counterfeit goods here.'

As the three of them walked back to the crime scene, Ted said to the others, 'I think it's a racing certainty that the person she was talking to on the phone was our so-called Inspector Galton. Now all we have to do is to find out who he really is and where we can get our hands on him. Or her.'

Chapter Two

Magnus Pierson left his team to it, promising Ted that he would be copied in on all the witness statements and any other relevant information they gathered. The fact that the victim was certified dead on Ted's own patch meant it was likely to be his friend Professor Nelson who carried out the post-mortem examination, so she would forward him her findings if he asked for them. He still didn't see how the murder enquiry would be theirs, but the apparent scam which led up to it might well be, if it had originated in Stockport.

Back at Pierson's station, in its pleasantly leafy surroundings, a world away from Ted's usual urban working environment, the three men made a detour via a hot drinks machine before crowding into Pierson's small office.

'Sorry about this muck, gentlemen,' Pierson told them as they took seats at his desk. 'It's barely drinkable, but it's all I can offer you. We've been banned from having kettles in our offices. Health and Safety. Apparently we're responsible enough to be police officers, but not to avoid scalding or electrocuting ourselves.'

'They tried to do that to us but I've claimed exemption on the grounds that I drink green tea and the machine doesn't provide it,' Ted replied, grimacing as he took a sip of his hot drink. It had been labelled as tea with sugar. It could have been anything.

'So, now, first thoughts on what we have so far?'

'I'll give you my initial ideas. Rob, feel free to add or

contradict anything. Whoever it was and whatever their reasons, someone was clearly telling Freda Ashworth what to do in that phone call. Both on the phone and, I suspect, well before she got here. I don't imagine that it's a coincidence she parked in the particular place she did, if that was her car. Not when it wasn't the nearest place, and certainly when the CCTV covering it had suddenly been put out of action.

'I think she was set up to buy the watch. It was an expensive purchase – by my standards, at least – but not outrageously so. Not enough, presumably, to set alarm bells ringing with her credit card company. I strongly suspect, when you check that out, she will have contacted them herself to inform them she was about to make a sizeable purchase, just to make sure it went through.

'I haven't heard of this particular scam before but I would imagine, from what you say about this Inspector Galton character, that someone has contacted her and told her some fairy story about unusual activity on her credit card account. I would guess that she was fed some line about if she made a large purchase it would stop anyone else buying something on her card. The fact that she mentioned making contact with an officer suggests to me that her bogus policeman set the whole thing up. Where to make the purchase, where to park and so on.

'She went along in all innocence to hand over the watch to what she thought was a police officer. For some reason, I imagine she got suspicious at the last minute, perhaps refused to hand over the watch. It's very rare for a scammer to go as far as killing, from the limited amount I know of it. They're usually simply after quick money and as little personal contact as possible.

'That would be my reading of it, at least. Rob, what do you think?'

'About spot on, I'd say, sir.' Rob was keeping it formal in front of another officer. 'And the reason the attacker took her phone was, of course, that it's our only means to date of tracing whoever the bogus copper on the end of it was. Which is why I suspect that whoever is involved will have gone straight round to her house, with her keys, to give it a going over in search of her laptop, if she has one. Just in case she's been emailing someone about her supposed undercover operation for Stockport police. Although if this is a clever scam, it is just possible she was told to bring it with her, for some reason which sounded plausible.'

Pierson was looking impressed.

'So how do we go forward from here?'

Ted chuckled.

'Nice try at buck-passing again, but we don't, for now. It happened on your patch, so unless the powers that be rule otherwise, it's down to you. I'm happy to help, unofficially, in any way I can. But without an official edict from higher up, you're on your own with this.'

Ted's mobile rang at that moment. He took it out of his pocket and glanced at the screen. His partner, Trevor, calling. He excused himself and went out into the corridor to answer it.

'Hey, you. Are you going to be working late tonight?'

'Looks likely. I'm over in Wilmslow at the moment.'

'Wilmslow? That's a bit off your patch.'

'I know, and it's a strange one. But yes, by the time I've finished here, then gone back and briefed the Ice Queen, I've no idea what time I'll be back.'

'So do you mind if I go out with Mark tonight? He's going to look at a bike and wanted my input. If you're going to be late we might as well make a night of it and have a meal out somewhere.'

Mark was a friend of Trev's from the karate club, who shared his passion for big bikes.

'Go for it. I'll pick up a takeaway for myself at some point, if I feel like eating something. Just don't take your bike if you're planning on having a few.'

'No, mother,' Trev laughed as he rang off.

'Boss, Mike just phoned,' Rob told him as he went back into the office. 'He's been round to Mrs Ashworth's house. Nobody at home, but he's spoken to a neighbour. Mrs Ashworth was a widow, lived alone, with a cat. The neighbour has a key, if we need to go in at some point. He didn't want to do anything without your say-so as it's not our case, officially.'

'Your call to make, Magnus, and ideally it should be your team who go over there. It's the likely starting pointing for your murder investigation. But I can talk to my boss and I'm sure we could cover it if you need us to and if it would help. I've got a DC, Sal Ahmed, who's worked in Major Fraud before. He'd be a big help to you, if my bosses and yours can perhaps agree on a joint operation. Something will need to be sorted out, and soon, for the cat, if nothing else.'

Ted had six cats at home. He didn't like to think of one alone in the house, waiting for its owner to return and feed it.

'We'd best be getting back now, though. Keep me posted on what you want us to do.'

It was getting late by the time they got back to their own station. Most of the team had gone. Just Ted's DI, Jo Rodriguez, was still in the small office he shared with DS Mike Hallam, finishing up and getting ready to leave. Rob grabbed his things and went on his way, leaving Ted and Jo to catch up before Ted went down to talk to his boss, to see whether the case would need to become a joint operation between them and Wilmslow.

'What else have you got on at the moment?' the Ice Queen asked him, lifting her coffee jug in offering, to which Ted shook his head. He preferred not to take a caffeine hit later on in the day.

'I daren't say it but for now it's all quiet on the Western Front. It sounds as if the scam originated on our patch, and Mrs Ashworth was certified dead here, too, so I suppose there is a case to be made for us at least being involved in a joint operation. DC Ahmed is our expert on any type of fraud, so I imagine this would be right up his street.'

'I'd have to talk to our top brass who would talk to those in Cheshire, but it looks like a possibility. I would perhaps ask Superintendent Baker to oversee it. He's got the experience.'

Ted looked at her and smiled.

'A bit of pass the parcel on the paperwork and budget, by any chance?'

To his surprise, she laughed, guiltily. She was usually so stiff and formal at work that it seemed out of character.

'I can see why you have such a good detection rate. You're very perceptive. You also have an excellent record on murder enquiries, so it would seem to make sense for you to be involved. I'll make some calls and let you know. Meanwhile keep me up to date on any other cases you have which might affect this matter.'

'So with the prospect of this joint operation coming up, which will involve some of us, has anyone got anything else in the pipeline that I don't yet know about and ought to?' Ted asked his team at their usual morning briefing the following day, after he'd filled them in on what he knew so far on the possible scam originating on their patch.

He usually had his finger on the pulse of everything which was going on but, just occasionally, a team member would find something and start looking into it before they brought it to him, to see whether they should continue.

'Boss, I wanted to talk to you about some happy slapping I've seen on social media, from our patch. I think it's something we need to be looking into, but I don't know if we've had any reports about it officially yet.'

'I'm going to need a bit of help with that, Jezza,' Ted told her. 'You know I know next to nothing about social media and I have no idea what would be happy about anyone getting a slapping. Please enlighten me.'

'Okay, basically, it's starting to be a bit of a thing. It usually happens with gangs of younger people, often girls. One of them, who's usually the leader or making a bid to be, will pick on the weakest member, or just someone else at random, and start to slap them round a bit. The others watch, film it on their mobiles, then share it on various social media sites, like Snapchat or Facebook.

'I've seen some recently that's been posted by girls from our area, school-age girls, and it's pretty nasty. They hang out in parks and open spaces, where they're less likely to get seen than if they did it at school.'

'People must see it going on, though, surely, in public spaces? And nobody does anything?'

'Boss, we're talking packs of wild animals here. They're vicious, really. Anyone who does see anything just keeps on walking and looks the other way, if they've got any sense. I was just thinking that I might possibly be able to get close to some of them. Find out what's really going on. They'll often steal from their victims, mobile phones, that sort of thing. I'm wondering if some of them might be stealing to order.'

Ted held a hand up.

'Stop right there, Jezza. Firstly, you're not going anywhere near anything like this until full risk assessments have been done. Secondly, if the motive is theft, and stealing to order in particular, why put themselves at risk of being seen on social media?'

DC Jessica – Jezza – Vine, was certainly Ted's most headstrong team member. She was good at her job, outstanding in some areas, but she took some careful handling. With her drama training, she could blend into any situation to suit, and was adept at any number of accents. She could also look older or much younger than her actual years. She'd fooled all of the team, Ted included, on one memorable occasion. But once she got an idea into her head, it was like trying to stop a whirlwind.

'Boss, with respect, firstly, I've studied the videos I've seen and my kickboxing would be more than a match for anything I've come across. None of them use weapons, just bare hands. Secondly, it's just a theory about the stealing to order. They may not care if they're caught or not. Let's face it, as young offenders, they might get away with just a slap on the wrist anyway. But we need to look into it, for sure, if it's happening under our noses. We risk copycat crimes with this sort of thing.'

'We could try initially asking Uniform to provide a presence in any areas where we know it's been going on,' Ted suggested.

'Boss, are you serious? We all know that the latest round of cuts have left precious little for anything in the way of crime prevention. This is the best way ...'

'All right, come and see me in my office after I've spoken to the Super and we can at least talk about it, but that's all I'm promising. For now, go through the videos you've been looking at and see if you can positively identify locations. You'll need to put a proper full written proposal forward for me to take to the Super at some point, but I'll mention the idea to her shortly. I need to know first where we're up to on this joint operation idea.

'Steve, any luck in tracking down anyone called Galton or anything which might sound like it, in any nearby stations?'

'Nothing, sir, not finding any officer called Galton, certainly not in our area,' the team's youngest member, DC Steve Ellis told him. 'I've identified some Daltons and Waltons further afield. Do you want me to start ringing round to see if they know anything?'

'I'll tell you what you can do first. Track down the ambulance crew who took Mrs Ashworth to Stepping Hill and talk to them. Check that they definitely had it as Galton that she was trying to say. It could be one of those Chinese whispers things, where a name gets changed with repetition.

'Océane, anything similar listed in the scams bible?'

'Nothing identical, boss, although a lot of stuff about calls from supposed credit card companies and banks along similar lines. I've printed everything out for you to look at when you have time. I can't find anything anywhere, yet, where the victim has finished up being killed by the scammers, or even where there's been any type of physical violence or threat of. That seems to be a new and a worrying departure, if that is who killed her.'

'Right, before we put in any more time on it, I'll go and talk to the Super to find out if we're having any official involvement in the scam aspect or not, or whether it's one for Fraud.'

Ted was happy to accept a coffee from his Superintendent in the morning. It was always good quality. He noticed the Super had also studiously ignored circulars about Health and Safety and Small Appliance Testing regulations to keep her own machine.

'So, there's been lengthy discussion between all the powers that be and we are all systems go for a joint operation with Wilmslow on all aspects of the case, both the scam and the killing. It has also been decreed that, since you have the expertise, you will lead on the murder enquiry while your team work on the scam itself. Liaise with Wilmslow for extra officers as you need them, particularly for the legwork there. As I thought, Superintendent Baker will oversee the operation, so the headache over the budget is his and not mine.'

'DC Vine just raised something with me which is going to take a lot of consideration and planning,' Ted told her, and proceeded to outline what Jezza had said in the briefing. 'I've told her to put together a proposal but not to do anything until it's been signed off. She can be a bit headstrong but she's right in a sense, in that if anyone can get near to these delightful young ladies without arousing suspicion, she can. It's not something I know much about. I had to get her to tell me what happy slapping is, and social media is an alien world to me.'

'With two teenage boys, I know all about Snapchat and the likes, and I never cease to be amazed at the sort of thing which finds itself on there. I agree, if we have this going on in our area, we need to do something about it immediately. I just don't want any of our officers put at avoidable personal risk in the process.'

Chapter Three

'So, Jezza, talk to me. Tell me first of all how we justify putting you in amongst these delightful girl gangs on the basis of the seriousness of the offences.'

'I've made a start on the written proposal you asked me for, boss, and I've emailed you links to some of the attacks where they've been posted online. You can see for yourself that it's a long way from being just a bit of pushing and shoving. If we don't do something about it soon, I can foresee one of them getting out of hand and someone getting seriously injured. Or worse.'

They were in Ted's office, sitting on either side of his desk. Ted had called her in at the end of the morning, when he'd caught up with what needed doing. He'd made a detour from the Super's office to the front desk on his way back up from the ground floor. He'd noticed that Bill, the usual desk sergeant, was not on duty. It was so unusual that he went to find out where he was.

'He called in sick this morning, sir,' Bill's replacement told Ted. 'Bronchitis. His doctor's signed him off for a week initially. It must be bad. You know Bill never misses a shift normally.'

'I'll try and get up to see him later on, if I get the chance, just to make sure he's all right and there's nothing he needs.'

Ted turned to his computer screen and pulled up the links Jezza had sent him. She sat in silence while he watched, frowning. The footage was disturbing. Ted saw what Jezza had been getting at. It was a pack mentality, everyone from the alpha down turning on the weakest member. He didn't like it, not one bit, but he wasn't sure if allowing Jezza to get close to those involved was a justifiable risk for the level of crime it represented.

'I'm a long way from agreeing to this, but start by telling me how you envisage it working, so I can make an informed decision. You can hardly hang around the parks looking like a teenage thug then drive off in a limited edition car back home to your nice flat.'

He said it with a degree of irony. He didn't want to throw cold water on her idea from the start, but he did want to make sure she had thought of all the implications. He was sure she would have. She was a thorough and a competent officer.

'I've thought of that, boss. I'd need to change lifestyle quite a bit, but it would be worth it, if I did succeed in mopping up this lot, surely?'

'Can we not simply ID them from the videos, round them up that way?'

'We'd get some of them by doing that, for sure, but not all of them. And I can see them closing ranks and keeping quiet, so some would slip through the net and just go on to do the same thing somewhere else. I also highly doubt the victims would tell us anything, and certainly would refuse to testify in court against their attackers. You know we don't have the resources to watch them full-time. It shouldn't take me long, just by hanging round with them, to find out who's who, then we can round up as many as possible.'

'And what about Tommy, if you're going undercover?'

Jezza lived with her autistic younger brother. Any change in his usual routine always risked trouble as it could provoke a total meltdown in his behaviour. He had been getting better lately, as he gradually got to know other members of the team his sister had joined. He was now usually comfortable in having some of them to look after him when Jezza was working. He was also slowly coming to accept that his sister was seeing someone, Nathan. It was developing into a steady relationship and most of the time, he was fine with that.

'I'd have to stay away for a bit, but that would be no problem now. Tommy gets on really well with Maurice and Steve. They're on board for staying over with him. And Nat spends a lot more time at my flat these days. Tommy even likes him and gets on with him.'

'So you've discussed this with your boyfriend and with two team members before even putting the idea to me?'

'I knew you'd want a proper written report, boss, so I had to find out if it was remotely feasible before I brought it up,' she countered.

'You're going to need a controller. And preferably someone who stands at least a chance of controlling you in the field.'

'Thought of that, too. It should be you, and we have the perfect cover to meet up every week. Keeping in mind that I'm going to be looking like a teenager, fifteen, sixteen at most, I can join your kids' self-defence group. That gives me a valid reason to see you every Wednesday evening, and I'm sure we can find time, either before or after the session, for a catch-up. We can even do some sparring. That should be interesting.'

She was grinning triumphantly at him now. She'd clearly been giving the idea a lot of thought.

'Accommodation?'

' What about one of the safe houses? A flat, basically. I know some of them can be a bit of a doss, and that would be even better. Perfect cover. And it would keep your budget down.'

Ted leaned back in his chair and studied her. Once Jezza had the bit between her teeth, there was no stopping her. Something like this would need clearance from the Super and possibly even higher up. But it might work. He just never liked putting one of his officers at risk.

'And you're sure Tommy would be all right with it? If we commit to an operation like this, we can't risk it being aborted if you have to drop everything and go back to see to him.'

'Obviously I won't be able to have my own phone with me undercover, but I could keep it, or a throwaway, at the safe house, with essential contacts. That way I could phone him whenever I get chance, touch base with him, at least. And you know we're all one big happy family now. Maurice is seeing Megan, and Tommy gets on with her and her son, too.'

Ted wasn't usually keen on relationships between team members. They could sometimes spill over into the workplace and cause problems. There were currently two. Divorcé DC Maurice Brown was seeing single mum DC Megan Jennings. Maurice had twin daughters, who lived with their mother but saw him most weekends. Megan had a son, Felix. They were keeping their relationship away from the work setting so Ted was happy enough to let it ride for now.

Young Steve was spending rather a lot of his off-duty time with their computer expert, Océane, and not just because of their shared love of World of Warcraft. And Jezza herself was in a recent but steady relationship with Nathan Cowley, who'd been a witness in two previous cases. So far, they were all being professional and it was posing no problems to the dynamics of the team. It did give Jezza, who was great friends with Maurice and Steve, an extended childcare circle to help her out with Tommy when necessary.

'And I'd need to keep contact with at least one of the team, someone I could pass off easily as someone other than a police officer. Virgil is the obvious choice, and we've worked out the perfect cover story between us, for if I have to call him up.'

'Is there anyone you haven't talked to about this, before discussing it with me?' Ted asked dryly. 'I will consider it, Jezza. And I will put your proposal to the Super, as soon as you've finished it and given me a copy. In the meantime, you do absolutely nothing to start on this until you get my authorisation. And that includes not discussing it with anyone else until then.'

Ted's mobile interrupted them. He looked at the screen and saw that it was one of his two immediate bosses, Detective Superintendent Jim Baker calling.

'I need to take this, it's the Big Boss. Are we absolutely clear on that, DC Vine?'

'As crystal, boss,' Jezza told him pleasantly as she left his office.

'Ted, I'm on my way over to you. We need a meeting about this joint operation with Wilmslow. Just the basics, nothing heavy, so can we meet in The Grapes in half an hour?'

Ted had been planning on working through lunchtime with a sandwich at his desk. But he would need a catch up with the Big Boss about the new case, so it might as well be over a drink at the nearby pub the team liked to frequent. He cleared his desk of what he'd started then walked the short distance and ordered a Gunner while he waited for Jim. He didn't drink alcohol, sticking to his preferred mix of ginger beer, ginger ale and lime.

He stayed at the bar, chatting to Dave, the landlord. A quiet, somewhat timid voice from behind him asked, 'Chief Inspector Darling?'

He turned, warily, not recognising the voice and wondering who would know him by sight. He was confronted by a young woman with a thin, earnest face, framed by long mousy hair, with large, purple-framed glasses, their thick lenses slightly magnifying anxious-looking pale blue eyes.

'Erm, I'm Penny. Penny Hunter. Alastair's replacement.'

Seeing Ted's blank look, she went on, flushing slightly, 'From the local paper. I just wanted to introduce myself. Alastair said you used to come in here together sometimes so I've looking out for you, so I could introduce myself.'

She thrust a hand towards him and Ted shook it. It was limp and moist in his grip. It concerned him that someone had come up behind him without his being aware. His martial arts training was usually more effective than that.

'Yes, of course, sorry, Penny, I was a bit distracted there. Was there something I can help you with, in particular?'

'No, no, nothing, really. I just, erm, wanted to say hello. Alastair said you'd always had such a good working relationship, so I just wanted to say how much I'm looking forward to taking over.'

'Can I offer you a drink? I'm just waiting for my boss to join me but ...'

'No, thank you, but no. I just wanted to say hi. So now I'll be going. Bye for now, then.'

She scuttled off towards the door and Ted heard Dave chuckle from behind the bar.

'Well, she's certainly a change from Pocket Billiards. She doesn't look like she'd say boo to a goose. I wonder what sort of a newshound she's going to turn out to be.'

'Well, as long as her table manners are slightly better than Pocket Billiards' were, that will be something,' Ted laughed, just as Jim Baker walked in.

Ted got him a drink and they went and sat down in a quiet corner of the bar, Ted with his back to the wall, facing the door.

'Right, now we know you're taking a part in this case, have you got anyone round to search the victim's house, yet?' Jim asked.

'Got some of the team on it now. I didn't want to start until I knew we were involved. I know what you and the Ice Queen get like with hours and budgets. I got Rob O'Connell's fiancée Sally to send the RSPCA in yesterday to collect the cat. The neighbour has keys, but they couldn't take it in, they're allergic to cat hair.'

'Bloody typical of you, make sure the cat is all right first. You and your bloody moggies, Ted,' the Big Boss growled, but it was good-natured. 'Right, so hopefully we should soon have something to go on. Her computer, perhaps. Then you can turn that over to your CFI and see if we can find out where this cock and bull story of a police undercover investigation came from.'

'It's my feeling we won't find a computer there, unless she had a desktop. With a sophisticated scam like this seems to have been, I'd guess she would have been told to take her laptop with her, if she had one, to the meeting place where she was supposed to hand over the watch. I imagine that she was told it would need to be forensically examined to catch the scammers. And she, of course, wouldn't have known it was the scammers themselves she was dealing with, not the police at all.'

'Do the public really fall for things like this, though? Surely people are getting more aware of this kind of thing. I know we don't know much about it yet but surely the victim would have been wary of the whole thing, of being asked to help police in this way? It sounds so far-fetched.'

'We don't know who we're dealing with, but if it was a sophisticated operation, with authentic-looking warrant cards and the whole works, then yes, I think people can and do fall for such things. We've both heard often enough of these phone scams where the victim is given a number to call back to check credentials, but it's actually the scammer who stays on the line the whole time.'

Jim drained his pint and stood up to go.

'Are you not staying to eat?' Ted asked him.

'No time. I'm on my way to a meeting, so I just thought I'd swing by for a catch-up. We'll need to have a proper team briefing tomorrow at some point, with you and someone from Wilmslow, but I'll fix that up. Might be simpler for us all to meet here in Stockport. What about the victim? What do we know about her? And is there anything from the post-mortem yet?'

'All we know so far is that she was a widow, living alone. Bizzie Nelson will be doing the PM but they're backed up there at the moment, so she can't fit it in until tomorrow at the earliest.'

'Right, well, keep me updated on anything your team find, and I'll see you tomorrow, at some point. This sounds like an interesting one, and something which needs stamping on, swiftly.'

Ted was right about the computer. His team turned over the victim, Freda Ashworth's, house carefully from top to bottom but they didn't find a computer anywhere. Mike Hallam, who was leading the search, phoned him from the house.

'She clearly had a laptop, boss. There's a desk here with a mouse and keyboard, connected to a USB hub which had obviously been plugged into one, from the way things are positioned, but there isn't one here. No laptop, no mobile phone, nothing like that.

'We did find a very detailed hand-written diary though. The last entry mentions going to buy the watch, and then meeting one of this Inspector Galton's officers to hand it over. I've only glanced at it for now. I'll bring it in and get someone to go through it in detail and transcribe it for us, perhaps.'

'I might have left when you get back, Mike. I want to go up to Marple to check on Bill. He's off sick and that's not like him. He's on his own so I just want to go and make sure he's all right and has everything he needs. I'm on the mobile if you need me for anything, though. If not I'll catch up with you in the morning.'

Ted had known Bill since he'd first started at Stockport. They went for the odd drink together from time to time. Bill was a widower whose wife had died young. There'd never been anyone else and he was a lonely man. He lived for his work, his only company an irascible sulphur-crested cockatoo called Father Jack, which swore horribly, like his namesake in the old television series.

Ted stopped on the way to buy a bottle of ginger wine. He

knew Bill liked the odd whisky mac. He would be bound to have Scotch in, but perhaps not the ginger. He parked outside the small terraced cottage in Marple Bridge.

The sergeant was some time coming to the door and Ted could hear his hacking cough as he moved slowly down the hallway.

'I was going to ask how you were, Bill, but you sound dreadful. I'm sorry to drag you to the door, but I just wanted to see if you needed anything. I brought you this.'

Bill was breathless and wheezing.

'Come in, Ted. Nice of you to come, thanks. Come through to the kitchen. You can make us both a brew.'

As soon as Father Jack heard a visitor, he started shouting, 'Feck! Arse!' at the top of his voice. Ted had visited many times and was used to the bird.

'Hello, Jack, and the same to you.'

He stayed long enough to make them both a cup of tea and listen to Bill's unconvincing claims that he was all right. He saw himself out, after impressing on Bill to phone him at any time, day or night, if he needed him for anything.

Ted was, as ever, driving carefully within the speed limit as he came up the hill into Marple. He noticed that he had a black car tailgating him, but there was no way it could overtake, even if the traffic had been lighter. It was an annoyance but, for the moment, nothing more.

As he started to head down Dan Bank towards the traffic lights, although there was oncoming traffic, the black car suddenly pulled out and started to overtake him, squeezing him close to the edge of the road. It stayed parallel to him, cutting him up, forcing him to take defensive action. An oncoming vehicle was flashing its lights and sounding its horn in warning as the black car cut in, almost touching the side of Ted's Renault.

Ted had done advanced driving courses, back in his uniform days, with the odd refresher since. Without those skills, he was sure he would have been run off the road to roll down the bank. As it was, he just managed to keep his car on a straight course, although the passenger side scraped up against a tree or two, making a tortured screeching sound, until he succeeded in bringing it to a halt.

The black car continued on its way, driving far too fast, running the lights at Dooley Lane just as they were turning to red, then speeding away out of sight. Ted stood no chance of getting a number. He couldn't tell anything other than that the car was a black VW Golf. He had a feeling he'd seen it somewhere, recently, but he couldn't bring to mind where.

The car behind him also pulled in to the side and stopped, its four-way flashers coming on, and the driver jumped out, running to Ted's door, shouting anxiously, 'Are you all right, mate? What a bleeding nutter. He could have killed you.'

Ted switched the engine off and took the keys out, then got out of his car to check on the damage, hoping it would still be drivable.

'I'm fine, thank you,' Ted assured the other man as he walked round to the passenger side of his battered vehicle. The bodywork was deeply scratched, a bit bent in places, but nothing which should interfere with its ability to be driven.

'I don't suppose, by any chance, you happened to get the other driver's registration number? I was too busy trying to avoid rolling down the bank.'

'Sorry, mate, no, it all happened very quickly. I was watching your car, hoping you'd be all right. Are you going to call the cops? Not that they'd come, probably, useless bastards.'

Ted sighed as he took out his warrant card.

'I am a police officer, actually. I wonder if I could take your details, please? A witness statement would be useful. It's damage only, so I don't need to call anyone out, as long as I report it. So, your name, please?'

Chapter Four

Ted decided he would drive by his usual garage, the people who had sold him the Renault, to see how soon they could fix it up for him. He was a good customer, especially as his bad luck with cars kept him going back for replacements and repairs, so they told him to leave it with them. They promised to sort it out for him as soon as they could, but they were just closing for the day. They locked it away safely and said they'd let him know when it was ready.

For the time being, he'd have to rely on his official car, but for this evening, he'd either get a lift home with one of the team, or jump on a bus. If he had time, he might even walk. He liked walking; it helped him to think, although the persistent drizzle wasn't very inviting.

He stopped by the front desk to report the incident involving his car and the black VW, and to mention his visit to see Bill.

'I'll make sure someone calls round there every day, sir, just to keep an eye on him,' Bill's stand-in, Sergeant Wheeler, assured him. 'You really don't have much luck with your vehicles, do you? Is there much damage to yours?'

'A bit of panel-beating and a respray, I imagine, but at least it was still drivable. It may have been just bad driving, boy racer, that sort of thing. But I had the feeling I've seen the car before somewhere. It felt personal, if you know what I mean. Like the driver was trying to run me off the road rather than just being in a tearing hurry to get somewhere.'

'With an arrest record like yours, you're bound to have made a few enemies, sir. Watch your back, and mind how you go, now.'

The team members were just winding up for the day when Ted went back up to the main office. He told them what had happened to his car, and said he'd need dropping off that evening and picking up in the morning. He didn't want to take his official car home with him. There'd be no room for it in the small garage with Trev's precious motorbike in there and he didn't dare leave it parked outside because of some of the neighbours near where he lived. He knew their records.

'And you think it may have been deliberate, boss?' DS Mike Hallam asked him, as they headed to his car. He lived near to the boss so it made sense for him to chauffeur him.

'It will sound as if I'm paranoid but it seemed like more than just bad driving. How did it go at Mrs Ashworth's? Have you had time to start reading the diary?'

'I'm taking it home with me tonight, boss. It's going to be very helpful. It looks as if she noted down absolutely everything. Very meticulous. The neighbour mentioned that Mrs Ashworth had worked as a secretary-cum-personal assistant and it shows in the detail she recorded. Thank goodness she was the old-fashioned sort who still kept a paper diary and didn't just put everything on her computer.

'I'll swing by just before eight in the morning, if that suits you, boss? Ring me before, if you get a shout, of course, and I'll come and get you.'

Trev was at the kitchen table, books and papers spread everywhere, his laptop open and on. He looked up with a smile as Ted came in.

'Hey, you. I didn't hear the car.'

'That's because it's in intensive care,' Ted told him, bending over to kiss him. 'This all looks very studious. What's it about?'

'What happened to the car? And this is TEFL stuff, after I

talked to Mark last night.'

Seeing Ted's puzzled look, he continued, 'Teaching English as a Foreign Language. I did a bit of it when I had that year in Japan. Mark volunteers at a centre that helps refugees and immigrants to learn English so they can integrate better and have more chance of finding work. It made me think. I have all this education, all these language A levels, and I'm basically just a lazy sod who doesn't do anything much to make a contribution to society. So I'm going to update my qualification and do the same thing. Is that all right with you?'

'Of course it is. Good for you. I'm proud of you. You'll be really good at it and you'll enjoy it, too. Knowing you, you'll pick up a few more languages while you're doing it.'

'The downside is, I've been so wrapped up in this I haven't made us anything to eat yet. Sorry. I'll knock something up quickly. But first tell me about the car. What happened?'

Ted gave him the carefully edited highlights, not wanting to worry his partner. He started tidying up while Trev began preparing their meal.

'You be very careful. There must be quite a few people with a grudge against you by now, and I don't want anything happening to you. Promise me you'll take care and watch your back.'

'Morning, Super.'

Ted had seen the caller display and knew it was Jim Baker calling, not long after Mike had picked him up and he'd arrived in his office to get ready for the morning briefing.

'Ted, if you breathe a word of what I'm about to tell you, I swear I'll have you back on the beat,' the Detective Superintendent growled menacingly.

'You know by now that you can trust me, Jim. Unless you're phoning to confess to committing some crime or another. Then it might be a bit tricky.'

'I'm in hospital,' Jim began, then as Ted started to ask

questions, he interrupted him. 'It's fine, now. I had to have an operation, but I'm okay, although they're keeping me in for a few days. The official line is I've broken my ankle, which is true. I'm going to tell you what really happened but if you laugh, Ted, you'll be issuing fixed penalty tickets for the rest of your career. No one else knows this, so if it gets out, I'll know it came from you.

'Bella wanted me to go line dancing with her. You know, all that country stuff. Not my scene at all, and I'm no dancer. But she was mad keen. Bought me the fancy cowboy boots and everything. They cost a fortune. Trouble is though, I've got two left feet, and I'm not light on either of them. And those bloody things have heels. I've never worn high heels in my life. Anyway, I fell over, off the little raised platform thing we were on, and broke my ankle. A bad fracture/dislocation, they said, and the blood supply was compromised so I had to have surgery to sort that and pin it. And they had to cut the boot off because my ankle was swelling so badly.

'So I'm bloody stuck in here for a few days, and I need keeping up to speed with whatever's going on. And it means, of course, that I won't be able to head up this joint investigation, at least not for a few days. Well, we can keep in phone contact and you can run things by me. I just won't be able to do anything officially until they let me out. And until I come off the painkillers, which have turned me into a zombie and keep sending me to sleep. Just don't you dare tell anyone what really happened, if you know what's good for you.'

Now he knew his boss and good friend was all right, Ted was having trouble keeping the laughter out of his voice.

'Your secret's safe with me, Jim. I won't breathe a word to anyone. I wouldn't be such a heel.'

'Ted, I'm bloody warning you ...'

'I'll try and get in to see you later today, if I can get away. Meanwhile, look after yourself and good luck. You know. Like they say in the theatre, break a leg.'

'Ted ...!'

Ted was laughing aloud as he ended the call. Then the phone on his desk rang. Kevin Turner.

'Hi, Ted, have you heard what happened to the Big Boss? Line dancing, in cowboy boots? Can you imagine it? I'd have paid good money to see that.'

'How did you know about that? He's just this minute phoned to tell me and I'm sworn to secrecy.'

'You know nothing like that stays secret for long in a town this size. One of my lads is married to the paramedic who took him to hospital. She recognised who it was from the name and the description he'd given her from when the Big Boss worked here.'

'He's going to think the leak came from me and as soon as he has a good leg to stand on, he'll be round here to kick me right round the office.'

Both men were laughing now, then Ted heard Kev break off and, in response to a voice in the background which he couldn't quite hear in detail, he said, 'Yes, ma'am.'

There was a pause, then he continued, 'Ted? Did you hear that? That was the Ice Queen, summoning the two of us to her office in ten minutes' time. And I have to say, Her Royal Highness does not looked pleased. Not at all. Now, I know I've been a good boy. My conscience is clear. So what have you been up to?'

'Nothing, that I can think of. Certainly nothing she might have heard about. I'll swing by your office to pick you up, for moral support. But it's your turn to go in first, this time.'

Ted went to tell the team that he had to be elsewhere and to ask Jo to start the briefing without him. He'd catch up with them once he found out what had rattled the Ice Queen's cage this morning.

'I think the priority needs to be to get that diary transcribed as soon as possible, so we might know exactly how this scam worked and what was going on. There could be vital details in it.'

'Boss, if it helps, I can actually copy type quite quickly and accurately,' Megan Jennings put in. 'I decided to learn when I was still making my mind up on a career path.'

Mike Hallam immediately got to his feet, crossed the office and put the diary on her desk. It was a smartly bound A4 book, the type often used for hand-written accounts.

'Sold to the first and only bidder. Thanks, Megan, that will be a big help. It would take me ages with two fingers and that might be a productive use of your time. Can you start from the most recent entries, please. They're likely to be the most relevant to the case.'

'Right, I'll be in the Super's office but I sense it might be best to say interrupt me for dire emergencies only. Jo, over to you.'

For once, even Kevin Turner wasn't clowning around as he usually did when he and Ted got the royal summons. All he would say was that their boss had been tight-lipped and in an extremely bad mood. It didn't bode well, especially as neither of them had a clue as to what it was about.

They knocked dutifully and waited for her summons to go in. Ted could see straight away what Kev had been getting at. He'd seldom seen her look so angry. The coffee was ready but she plonked it down in front of them much more forcefully that usual.

'Gentlemen, please sit down. There has been, please excuse the expression, the most monumental cock-up. I've been on the phone half the morning already to the top brass. I'd just hasten to reassure you, before I go any further, that although heads will roll, they won't be from here.'

Ted and Kevin exchanged a quick look. It was so rare for either of them to hear anything like that from the Super.

'You've heard that Jim Baker is out of action?'

Ted thought he'd better just check that she was up to speed with that development.

'Thank you, yes, I heard as soon as I arrived this morning. In light of what I'm about to tell you, it actually makes no difference in the greater scheme of things. In fact, I'd wager that Superintendent Baker might well prefer a cosy hospital bed to the hot seat in this enquiry.

'In a nutshell, it appears that the Fraud Team from Central were aware of this ongoing bogus police officer scam. The one in our division is gang related. Several of those behind the operation are already known to the police. In the interests of fairness, I should point out at this stage that none of the suspects has any record for serious violence.

'They had their eye on one in particular who was known to be in our area. Sam Kateb, full name Samir Kateb. Originally from Algeria, moved to France with the whole extended family, then to the UK. He's often the front man as he's well spoken, articulate and charming. Speaks several languages fluently. When I say they had their eye on him, they had him under full surveillance, including his visits to our patch.

'They even saw him have a face-to-face meeting with an unidentified woman who we're now sure was our victim. A decision was taken to concentrate on him, rather than the target, in the hopes of picking him up when he went to collect whatever he'd told the target to buy, which we now know was the watch. He may not, of course, be the killer. It's thought he probably isn't as he has no form for violence of any sort. Quite the reverse. He is the consummate gentleman.'

She paused to take a drink of her coffee. Ted and Kevin took the opportunity to do the same thing. Ted couldn't believe what he was hearing. If a team from another division had been carrying out covert surveillance on their territory, they should have been notified, as a courtesy, if nothing else. But the idea that they could have let a suspect like that slip through their fingers and possibly go on to kill would have serious and far-reaching ramifications.

'As you can imagine, gentlemen, there are currently a great

many internal enquiries going on into how this appalling mess was allowed to happen. This means that senior officers are a bit thin on the ground to take over from the unfortunate Superintendent Baker to head up the joint operation. And it is now going to be far larger than before as it will have to include Major Fraud, or what is left of their team once the axe has ceased to fall.

'In addition, it was felt at the top level, that it needs to be someone from outside the area, to be sure that the whole sorry affair is handled impartially. They envisaged finding someone who could oversee both the joint operation and the various internal enquiries. That way, the force may manage to emerge with at least some shred of integrity left intact.'

She paused to allow them all another drink, then without saying anything, got up to top up everyone's mugs.

'They've settled on an officer who's previously served with the GMP but has been with the Met for a few years now. You gentlemen might even have encountered him. Chief Superintendent Roy Marston. He'll be taking command tomorrow and we'll be attending the first briefing of all the senior officers who will be involved. Those who have survived, that is.'

Ted had a sudden leaden feeling in his stomach which had nothing to do with the excellent coffee, even if he had gulped it too hot and too quickly. He and Marston had history, and not in a good way. From back when Ted was a Firearms sergeant, in charge of a team, assigned to a case on which then Inspector Marston was SIO. They'd gone toe to toe in a dispute when Marston had tried to interfere with Ted's deployment of his weapons team. In the end Ted had called in his own senior officer who had backed him unreservedly and given Marston a public dressing-down. Ted knew he was in for a rough ride with him in overall charge of this investigation.

'I haven't met him myself, yet, but I know of him by reputation. I know he's a hard and exacting taskmaster, which is what is needed. I also know he has a reputation for calling briefings at any time of the day or night, his way of making sure that everyone on his team is in a fit state to work at all times. I'm looking forward to the challenge of working with him.'

'I'm bloody not,' Ted muttered, as he followed Kevin into his office after the Ice Queen had finished with them.

Kev looked at him in surprise. It was almost as rare for Ted to swear as it was for the Ice Queen.

'You know him, then? I know of him, but no more than that.'

'I came across him when I was in Firearms. We had a right bust-up. My boss backed me over him, in public, too. He's not likely to have forgiven or forgotten. He's also massively homophobic and I doubt that's changed.'

'You've got rights now, though. Not like the old days. If you're getting aggro of that sort, you can complain to someone.'

Ted's laugh was hollow.

'He hates me because I had to call my boss in when he was trying to interfere with how I was deploying my team. No one without firearms experience is qualified to do that, but he wasn't having any. No matter how tough things get this time, I can hardly go running to teacher again, if I want to stay on the case. Especially as my senior officer is now a woman. He'd love that.'

Chapter Five

The Assistant Chief Constable (Crime), Russell Evans, made a short appearance at the first joint briefing. He would be overall in charge of the operation, but because of the problems so far and the need for transparency, the day-to-day running would be done by the officer sent up from the Met, Chief Superintendent Roy Marston. Ted's old Nemesis.

The ACC introduced the new senior officer in charge, then left them all to it. It didn't take the incomer long to show his colours, as soon as the door closed behind Evans.

'Right, everyone. Mobiles off, ears open, mouths shut.'

Marston stood, legs apart, rocking from heels to toes, surveying those present. He was not tall – Ted put him at no more than four inches bigger than he was – and he was carrying rather more weight than he should have, which made him look smaller somehow. His receding hairline was offset by a thick, bristling moustache in a face so smooth that there was something almost feminine about it. The nose spoilt the look. Broken and badly set at some time, so it splayed across his face like that of a boxer.

Ted could almost picture him on a military parade ground, swagger stick under one arm, barking at his soldiers. Except he knew he was a career copper, fast-tracked through promotion, hotly tipped for the next Assistant Chief Constable vacancy which came his way. Ted could never really work out why, except that he knew the man was without doubt highly intelligent, had sailed through all his exams and promotion boards and didn't care how many faces he trod on as he headed for the top. Ted doubted that Marston had forgotten the history between them, or that the bad feeling it had caused had mellowed over the years. He feared it might even have grown through festering.

'You've all been called to this briefing because each of you will be in charge of one aspect of this investigation, answerable directly to me. I'll be assigning tasks shortly. I know who you all are, obviously, but it's a big team and some of you might not know one another. So when I address you for the first time I'd just ask you to make a gesture to identify yourself.

'But first of all, this is a big and a complex operation and I want to make sure we start off with the right focus. Now, I've picked out five possible operational names from The Book. I'm going to write them up on the board here. You'll find pen and paper in front of you, so I want you each to write down your choice and pass them up to me.'

Ted imagined Marston had recently been on some box-ticking course or another about involvement and engagement. To him it felt like a waste of precious operational time. He thought he'd made his sigh too quiet to notice, but perhaps the way he'd changed his posture, folding his arms and leaning back in his chair, had drawn Marston's attention to him.

'Am I boring you already, Darling? For those of you who don't know, this is Detective Chief Inspector Darling, from Stockport.'

'No, sir, not at all. You're quite right of course, it's essential that we pick the appropriate name for such an important operation.'

Marston glared at him for a moment longer, looking for any hint of sarcasm or impertinence. Then he turned to the board and started writing. Kevin Turner, sitting on Ted's right, gave him a sharp nudge with his elbow and grinned at him. Ted wasn't sure but he thought that the Ice Queen, sitting demurely on his other side, lowered her head to hide a smile.

'Right, so Operation Croesus it is,' Marston said, once he'd counted the pieces of paper. 'That's very apt, because of the financial angle, but we mustn't lose sight of the fact that a woman has died as a result of it. Darling, you're in charge of the homicide investigation. But you report every aspect of it to me, and above all, you don't move to an arrest without my say-so.

'I don't want this first briefing to turn into an inquest into what has gone wrong with the case so far. You all know by now that errors have been made. Disastrous errors, which certainly contributed to, if not directly caused, the death of a civilian who got caught up in the scam. Superintendent Don Williams, from West Yorkshire, is in charge of that part of the case, so I'll just ask him to outline very briefly what we know so far, and what lessons can be learnt from previous mistakes. Don,' Marston nodded to a uniformed officer sitting in the front row.

'Sir, from what we know so far, Fraud decided to concentrate their efforts and resources on keeping one of the known gang leaders, Samir Kateb, under observation rather than the prospective target who had been identified. With the benefit of hindsight, it was probably the wrong decision. Kateb has no record of violence of any sort. Quite the contrary. He's the front man, charming, plausible, absolutely no menace about him. It's unlikely he ever intended going near the victim in person for the actual hand-over, which is why he will have told her that she would be handing the item over to one of his so-called officers. Who that was, we don't know, but clearly someone in a different category altogether, as we're assuming from the information we have to hand that it's this second person who killed Mrs Ashworth.

'Even if Kateb had been pulled in for questioning, at that early stage, the operation was fully set up and would almost certainly have gone ahead without him. And without the victim's mobile phone and computer, which would have been removed from the scene, there would be absolutely nothing to link him to the killing, which almost certainly shouldn't have happened. The gang just got careless with who they chose to carry out the pick-up.

'Kateb will no doubt have been using throwaway SIM cards for his contact with the victim, so there will be no link to him that way. The surveillance which was carried out shows him arriving to meet the target a few days before the incident. There was no CCTV at or near the café where they met – it will have been specially selected for that reason – and it was impossible for the surveillance team to get a photo of them together. Kateb deliberately chose a table right at the back of the tea room, which was not in clear sight of the team outside. We just have a few shots of the woman entering the café, one of several to do so, shortly after Kateb had been photographed entering the premises. He was careful always to keep his face out of sight of anyone watching him. We now know that it was the victim whom he met because of the distinctive red coat and from a passport photo of her which DCI Darling's team found during the house search.

'Finally, sir, can I just say that before anyone starts asking how can anyone fall for a line about an undercover operation or anything like that, this is a very polished, professional scam. Kateb will have had a forged warrant card which could well have fooled some of us in here, even on close inspection. His cover story will have been flawless, more than enough to convince this unfortunate woman, intelligent though she might have been, to believe him and trust him completely. That's what makes him and his gang so dangerous. The only thing which is different here is that it escalated into violence. That leads us to think that they were using someone new and untried, or at least not tried in difficult circumstances, who lost control of the situation and pulled a knife.

'It's also our belief that he won't be around for us to find or to question in the future. He will simply disappear. Whether that's alive or dead is anyone's guess, until and unless we find a body.'

'Thank you, Don. So, Chief Inspector Darling, all you and your team have to do is find who it was who did kill Mrs Ashworth and make sure they're brought to book. That should be a stroll in the park for someone with your track record. Please tell us now what progress you have made thus far on that angle.'

'Sir, no phone or computer were found at Mrs Ashworth's house but we've recovered a hand-written diary which the victim kept from there, which will hopefully give us details about how she became involved in this affair. One of my officers is working to transcribe it now and I'll ensure that the relevant contents are circulated as soon as possible.'

'I would have thought you'd have been able to give us at least the bare bones of it by now, Darling. I think you might have to start prodding your team into a bit more action, to keep pace with an enquiry of this magnitude.

'Remember, too, everyone, that it is just possible, because of the complexities of this operation, that we may have to allow some of this gang to remain at liberty, under close surveillance, properly carried out this time, until we wrap up the case. But Darling, I want you and your team to get the killer out of the picture as soon as possible. By that I mean identified and placed under reliable round-the-clock surveillance until I give the word to arrest them. We can't risk another incident like the previous disaster. That is unless you can establish definitively that they have been removed by the gang themselves.

'I just want to impress upon everyone here that this operation, Operation Croesus, takes priority over everything else. Everything. And that includes your private lives. Tell your husbands and wives, your girlfriends and boyfriends ...' he let his gaze linger slightly longer than necessary on Ted as he said it, 'to forget about seeing much of you for the foreseeable future, until this case is wrapped up, including all the loose ends.

'Be aware, too, that I will, as and when necessary, be calling briefings, which will all take place here at Central Park, at any time of the day or night, as necessary. I expect you all to attend, when summoned, and to be in a fit state to take part.'

He went on to assign tasks and lay out the roles and responsibilities of each of them. Then he handed round written details of who was in charge of what aspect of the case. He was a good administrator, Ted had to concede to himself. His personnel management skills could certainly have done with some work.

As Marston broke up the briefing, he added, 'You can all go now and get on with your individual assignments. Darling, I want a word with you. You wait behind.'

The look the Ice Queen gave Ted was one of concern. It was glaringly obvious to all present that there was something going on between Marston and Ted of which they didn't have the full picture. As Ted's boss gathered up her coat and bag, she told him that she and Kevin Turner would wait for him in the car.

As soon as the door closed behind them, Marston turned to Ted.

'You and I need to sort out a few basic ground rules. I don't reckon you at all, not as a copper, nor as anything else. I think you're a cocky little sod who just got lucky on a few cases. I think all this PC crap gives us positive discrimination. I know you have friends in high places watching your back. But I think that's because you're the token queer of any rank in the force and they don't want the bad PR of having to get rid of you.'

'Sir, you've just made discriminatory reference to my height and to my sexuality. I think you might be well advised to think carefully about what you're saying.'

'Why, what are you going to do about it?' Marston's voice was a sneer. 'Run and tell teacher? You've done that before.

But there's just you and me now, so I can say what I like and I tell you now, I'll be watching you, the whole time. And the first slip-up you make, and you will make one, I'll have you, Darling.'

'You might perhaps need to be careful of how that sounds, sir. And you might also want to consider that I could be recording this conversation on my mobile.'

The other man's eyes narrowed as he tried to work out if Ted was bluffing. Ted was surprised at the intensity of the hate in them. Then Marston held out his hand.

'Give me your phone.'

'Not going to happen, sir.'

'I'm your superior officer, and I'm ordering you to hand over your phone. You know you can't make covert recordings and expect to use them.'

'You may be my senior officer, sir,' Ted put heavy emphasis on the word and its distinction, 'but you don't have reasonable grounds to order me to.'

Marston fell quiet for a moment. It was a similar stand-off to the time before, only this time Ted had no intention of calling anyone else. They needed to sort this between them. Now. Marston fired his parting shot.

'Like I said. I'll be watching you. And the first chance I get, I'm taking you down.'

'Then I'd better be absolutely sure I don't give you that opportunity,' Ted said levelly, then left a pregnant pause before he said, 'sir.'

Once they got back to Stockport, the Ice Queen asked to see Ted in her office. She switched her coffee machine on as soon as they walked through the door. What had been on offer at Central Park had been lukewarm and indifferent.

'I take it there is history between you and the Chief Superintendent, and not in a good way? Is it something I should know about?' she asked him as they sat down.

Ted shrugged dismissively.

'You know how it can be, with people who know nothing about Firearms, trying to tell those of us who do how to run an operation. It's a long time in the past.'

She was looking at him shrewdly.

'But I'm sensing that he hasn't forgotten it, and perhaps doesn't consider it as unfinished business between you?'

'It's fine. I'm sure we'll all have enough to do without letting old, historical niggles get in the way. I would really like to get away in time to go to the dojo tonight, though. A bit of time spent throwing Trev round the mat is always good for me, after a day like today.'

Ted made light of it, but the Super was astute enough to see that it was what he needed to do.

'None of us is indispensable. You need to do what is necessary to get you through this case. Please also promise me that if you encounter any form of discrimination, intimidation or bullying of any kind, you will inform me.'

She saw Ted's expression and insisted.

'You know that we cannot allow any such thing to go on. I'm well aware that you are more than capable of taking care of yourself. But if we turn a blind eye to it happening at your level, we're condoning it going on, perhaps directed at others not as strong as you are.'

'Hard day at the office, dear?' Trev laughed as he slid into the passenger seat of the courtesy car Ted's garage had lent him. The bodywork job on his own car was not yet finished and Ted hated not being independently mobile, especially with Marston's reputation for calling briefings in the middle of the night.

Trev had found himself on the mat more times than he cared to count during judo training with Ted. He was taller and heavier than his partner but Ted outdid him every time on speed, timing and technical ability. Ted would usually head to his Krav Maga club when he was as wound up as he currently was, but he hadn't the time to go there. He'd missed the juniors' self-defence but had driven to the gym near Davenport in time for his own training session.

'Sorry,' he said tersely. 'I'm a bit under pressure. Ghosts from the past, that sort of thing. Jim's replacement on this big enquiry wouldn't have been my first choice and I'm certainly not his favourite copper. It's just stirred up a few memories, that's all.'

Trev laid a concerned hand on Ted's arm as he drove.

'If the stress is getting to you, promise me you won't bottle it up like you usually do. Go and see Carol for more counselling if you need to. Please, Ted.'

'Snakebite for you, Skipper?'

Ted was the last of the team to arrive at the pub. The others had already changed out of uniform and headed straight there. Ted had stopped for a shower. He felt he needed it. It was he who had taken the killing shot. It was his job but it still left him feeling tainted.

'Here, get that down your neck, Skip. You earned it today.'

One of his team mates handed Ted the brimming pint of strong cider mixed with lager. He needed no second bidding. His first big swallow made a sizeable dent in his drink.

The team members were in high spirits. The operation had gone like clockwork. A man was dead, true, but that death had probably saved several other lives and that was what mattered for them all. An operational success.

'Good job today, Ted. Don't forget you need to a day or so off, then see the shrink and get yourself cleared as fit to come back to the team.'

It was Ted's boss who spoke, leaning against the bar and tossing back single malt as if it was water which was in scarce supply.

'I'm fine, boss. Just a job. No need for any of that.'

The other man drained his glass and set it on the bar. He'd got the first round in, as was his custom at the end of a successful job, but he wouldn't linger. His lads didn't need him cramping their style if they got a bit lively later on. He couldn't blame them, after a day like that.

'You know it's the regulation. So you also know that it's not a suggestion, it's an order. See you do it. I'll see you when you're back afterwards.'

He went on his way, nodding to his team as he left them to it. They were already starting to get noisy as glasses were drained.

Ted had lost track of how many snakebites he'd had. He knew he should get going. His dad would be waiting for him. He suspected he'd have done his usual trick of sending the carer packing too early. He'd be needing help getting changed and ready for bed. The prospect appealed a lot less than another snakebite.

When he was finally ready to leave, Ted wisely opted to leave his car behind in Openshaw. He could easily get a bus part way back then walk home. In fact, he felt like a run. It would help clear his head, focus his mind after a gruelling day with the prospect of more to come.

He found his father on the floor. He could see that he'd pissed himself and from the smell, that wasn't all. An empty Scotch bottle lay beside him and he was crying, tears and snot running down his face as he lay whimpering.

'Dad, for God's sake, you've got to stop doing this.'

Ted tried to keep the anger out of his voice as he bent down beside his father, pulling the wheelchair close.

'Put your arms round my neck. Let's get you up and into the bathroom.'

His father wasn't a big man but, paralysed as he was, it was a dead lift, and an awkward one.

'I really don't need this today, dad. Why didn't you let the carer get you changed and ready for bed at least?'

'I'm sorry, Ted, I'm sorry. I'm a burden to you, son, I know that.'

'You're not a burden. You're my dad. Just ...' Ted sighed, before he continued, *'I had to shoot a man today, dad. I just don't need this.'*

'Why don't you shoot me, Ted? I don't want to live like this any more. Just bring your gun home and leave it for me. I don't want to be a nuisance. I just want to die, Ted. I just want to die.'

'Shut up, dad! Shut up!'

It was only when he shot bolt upright in bed, scattering disgruntled cats, that Ted realised he had shouted the last words of his dream out loud. Even Trev, who could normally sleep through anything, stirred sleepily and reached out an arm to see what was wrong.

'It's fine, don't worry, Just a bad dream. Sorry I woke you. Go back to sleep.'

'Counselling, Ted. Promise me. If the nightmares are starting again, go back for more counselling.'

Chapter Six

Ted gave up on trying to sleep and went in to work. He needed to come up with some solid lines of enquiry to get Marston off his back so he might let him get on with his job. His work was one of the few aspects of his life that Ted was usually confident about. He knew he was good at it, even if he had occasional wobbles about his ability to do it. That was normal. It was what drove him on to do better. He always shunned any sort of fuss but he had been recommended for various commendations, which he always refused to accept. It wasn't a case of getting lucky or being shielded by the top brass, he knew that. He was a good copper.

The cheap jibe about positive discrimination had really rankled. Although the force had officially cleaned up its act, when Ted had first joined he'd had a hard time of it, being short, gay and called Darling. He doubted he would have stuck it out without his martial arts training. On one memorable occasion it had saved him from getting his head flushed down a toilet.

Megan Jennings had done a good job of transcribing their murder victim's diary. She'd not been exaggerating when she said she typed fast. Ted had circulated what she had already done via Marston for Operation Croesus, as well as within his own team.

He'd brought back from the briefing a list of Samir Kateb's known associates and had put Jo on to getting them checked out, although none of them were from their patch. The gang was based in Central Manchester but operated over a wide area. That checking would have to be done quietly and discreetly. Marston had made it clear he didn't want Kateb or the rest of the gang spooked unduly before the team were in a strong position to pull them all in with the hope of a solid conviction. They were likely to be wary for the moment, with the way their operation had gone so badly wrong on this occasion.

Ted would need to talk to Magnus Pierson at some point in the morning. He'd asked him to put his officers on to checking CCTV all round where the stabbing took place, to try to pick up any trace of who the attacker might be. They now had the details of their victim's car, which had disappeared from the scene. It had been picked up on a couple of cameras, arriving in then later leaving Wilmslow, but there had been no further sightings of it anywhere since. Ted guessed it would have been quickly whisked away to have the plates changed and may well already have been sold on or otherwise disposed of.

Ted's mobile rang. Magnus Pierson. Another early bird.

'Morning, Ted. I know you'll want a catch-up at some point today but I wanted to try to grab you at a quiet moment to ask what was that all about, between you and the Chief Super yesterday? I hope I'm not disturbing your breakfast, by the way.'

'I'm at my desk already, as I assume you are. Nothing to worry about, yesterday. Just Marston flexing his muscles. We've got a bit of history, although it's nothing that need concern anyone else. But you and I are both going to have to push our respective teams a bit on this one. In a sense we have the hardest part, a suspect with no ID in an operation with no prev-ous history of violence. Shouldn't take us more than a day or two.'

'I wish I'd got a slightly easier one to start with. I've begun by sending my officers out asking more questions at the shop where she bought the watch and the ones nearby, to see if we can get any hint if someone was watching or following her there. Then we'll work back from there to where she was stabbed. I hope that's right? Unfortunately, the only footage we have of her car doesn't really give us anything on who was driving it as it was leaving, only that it was a single occupant.'

'You're doing fine, Magnus. Don't worry. Any flak is likely to head my way if there are any slip-ups from our end. I'm just going through her diary now, to see if there's anything there of use to you and I'll let you know if there is. Unfortunately, although there's a lot about Kateb, she only talks about being told to buy the watch, go back to the car and wait for this supposed officer, who would identify themselves with a warrant card. And equally unfortunately, it doesn't tell us if said person was going to be a man or a woman.'

When he rang off, Ted put his kettle on. He'd not bothered with any breakfast before he left home. He'd grab a cup of green tea and an energy bar while he read through the rest of the diary extracts before the morning briefing. The last entry made by Vera Ashworth was a poignant one.

"Today is going to be so exciting. It's the day I have to go to the shop and make the purchase. I've spoken at length to Inspector Galton on the telephone. He's gone over all the details with me very carefully, to make sure that nothing goes wrong. I can't believe I'm doing this!

"I really was doubtful of the whole thing when he first phoned me up. I felt sure it was just some sort of a scam. But when I met him and saw his police badge, I was reassured. Especially when he gave me that other number to call, to speak to his boss for confirmation. He was charming, and clearly good at his job. He knows exactly what he's doing.

"All I have to do is park where he told me to, go and buy the watch, then go back to the car park. His officer will meet me there. He didn't tell me if it would be a man or a woman, he said it would depend who was available and nearest. He did say several of his team would be watching me to make sure it was all perfectly safe, and he would stay on the phone to me the whole time to make certain that everything goes like clockwork. I'm to ask to see the officer's badge, hand over the watch and get a receipt. I also have to show them my laptop, which I must remember to take with me. He said the officer would have a way, from that, to go into my credit card account and immediately block it. Then they'd arrange the refund of my purchase.

"This time tomorrow, I'll be going back to my rather mundane life of the WI and yoga classes. But what an adventure I shall have had as a police undercover agent. It's a shame I've been sworn to secrecy on the whole thing, even when my part is over. It would have made a wonderful tale to tell. I may just be very naughty and tell Malcolm the bare bones of it, once it's all finished."

'Right, everyone, Operation Croesus is our main focus for now, unless anything else turns up in the meantime. Who has anything new?'

'Boss, I've been ringing round a few old Fraud contacts to see if I could get any sort of an inside view on who our killer might be. It seems to be so far outside the normal pattern for this gang that everyone is baffled. It's partly why they were a bit slack with surveillance. There was no indication that it would escalate into something like this, so they really have no leads at all,' Sal told them.

'The PM on Mrs Ashworth is scheduled for first thing this afternoon,' Ted continued. 'I had an email from Professor Nelson confirming that. She'll be doing it herself since death was certified on her doorstep. Jo, can you take that, please. I'm trying to keep myself available at all times in case the Chief Super calls another briefing. The Professor knows what she's doing, of course, but can you press her for as much information on the knife wound as possible, please. It might give us some indication as to whether the attacker knew what they were doing, which might suggest whether or not they have previous form for knife violence. That could potentially open up a line of enquiry.

'Inspector Pierson is sharing with us all the CCTV they can find both before and after the killing. It's just going to be hard, relentless slog to trawl through it all to try to spot anything – anything at all – which stands out as unusual in any way, and to follow it up.

'Right, anyone got anything else to mention?'

'Boss, the happy slappers ...' Jezza began, but Ted was already shaking his head.

'I need everyone available on Croesus for now, Jezza. It's a big case and a serious one. It has to take priority over lesser assaults and crime prevention. Can't you just liaise with Inspector Turner about identifying those in the videos and getting them rounded up?'

'Boss, I seriously am worried that it could escalate into something much nastier. I've identified some of the locations in the videos. What if I just go round those, dressed the part, and see what I can see? Or do we just have to wait until a teenager ends up dead?'

Ted sighed to himself as he looked at her, considering. It was really one for Uniform, if Kevin had any spare officers to put on it. It would be a bit of a plod but they should, at least, be able to round up some of the ringleaders that way. But Jezza's intuitions were good and he agreed with her. He would never forgive himself if he did nothing and a young person was killed or seriously injured. With her ability to change her appearance and blend in, Jezza could get closer to the action than anyone in uniform. If he could trust her to do so without putting herself at risk.

'You have half a day today to see what you can come up with. You do it with the express purpose of making a case to take it further. You also do it without at any point putting yourself in danger. And you stay in contact with someone on the team the whole time. Have you clearly understood all of that, DC Vine?'

'Understood, boss. I'll just go and change.'

Ted was back in his own office after the briefing when his desk phone rang, with an outside call being put through to him.

'Is that Inspector Darling? This is the hospital, Emergency Department. We have your mother, here, Mrs Annie Jones. She didn't want us to bother you but there is rather a long wait at the moment so we wondered if you might perhaps be available to come and sit with her?'

'What's happened? What's wrong?'

Ted was already jumping to his feet and grabbing his coat.

'I can't tell you very much at the moment, I'm afraid. She's conscious and talking but she's been attacked, in the street. We're just waiting for her to be seen before I can give you any more details. She really didn't want us to call you, but I persuaded her to give me your contact details.'

'Please tell her I'm on my way. I'll be there as soon as I can.'

The main office was a hive of activity, everyone with heads down or on the phone, working on what they'd been allocated. Ted could see through the glass door that Jo was in his office, going through paperwork at his desk. He went over and stuck his head round the door.

'Jo, cover for me, can you. I've just had a call from the hospital. My mother's been taken in. She's been assaulted, but I don't know anything further for now. I need to be there.'

Jo looked up, his face concerned.

'Sorry to hear that, boss. Of course. You go, I've got it covered here. I'll only bother you if it's completely unavoidable. I hope she's okay.'

Ted did, too. His mother hadn't been a part of his life for much of it. Since he'd got to know her again recently, and discovered why she'd left when he was a child, they'd grown close. There was still a slight awkwardness there, certainly on Ted's part, which might never totally disappear. But he hated the thought that she was hurt, especially the idea that someone had assaulted her. She was in her mid-sixties now, small and slight, like he was. He couldn't imagine who would do something like that. She certainly never looked like someone it would be worth mugging for cash or valuables.

Parking at the hospital was a nightmare, as usual. Ted used his police sign on the dashboard, although he hated doing it, hoping it would at least save him from being clamped, then sprinted for the emergency department,

He found his mother without having to go to the reception area. She was on a trolley in a corridor, looking pale, fragile and older than her years. Bruising was already forming on the side of her face, around raw cuts and grazes which looked sore, and she had one arm up across her body in an elevation sling. Her face lit up as soon as she saw him.

'Oh, Teddy, I told them not to bother you, *bach*. But it is lovely to see you.'

Ted bent over the trolley and kissed her gently on the undamaged side of her face.

'Don't be daft. You're my mam. Of course I came. How do you feel? What happened to you?'

With her undamaged hand, she gripped tightly on to one of his and tears started to her eyes as she began to speak.

'It was horrible, Teddy. I'd been shopping in Marple. I'd just come out of a shop and my mobile rang. It was my friend Aldwyth, in Garnant. We started chatting. I was speaking in Welsh, of course. A man was going past and he stopped to listen. Then he started to shout at me to go back to my own country. Shouting and swearing.

'He pushed his face right into mine. He'd been drinking, I could smell it on his breath. I was scared. I didn't know what he meant. I started to explain to him, in English, that I was speaking Welsh. He started pushing me and calling me a filthy

Polack, telling me we were all coming over here to steal jobs and I should get out of his country.

'I tried again to explain but he pushed me really hard and I fell over. I banged my face on the pavement. It was dreadful, Teddy. There were people all around but most just carried on walking by. Nobody stopped to help me. I suppose they were afraid to get involved.

'I tried to get my phone, to call 999, but he stamped on my wrist and kicked the phone away and started jumping on it. I saw some people with their phones out so I thought surely someone would call for help. Then I realised some of them were just filming me, not helping at all.'

Tears were running freely down her face now and Ted could feel that she was trembling. He leaned closer and put his face against hers, tasting the salt of her tears. He murmured softly into her ear. Long-forgotten words from his childhood, when she had comforted him as a child.

'Isht nawr. Dere mami. Fydd popeth yn iawn.'

When she had recovered enough to continue, she said, 'Two young men came along at that point. Well, only lads they were, really. But they were tall and they looked strong. They stood up to the man, made him move away. Then they helped me. They were the only ones who did. They were so kind, Teddy. They called an ambulance and stayed with me until it came.'

'Mam, why didn't you get them to ring me? I'd have come straight away.'

'I didn't want to bother you. I know you're always so busy and your work's important, *bach*. Then my phone was broken and I couldn't remember your mobile number. The hospital were very kind. They insisted on calling you at the station. There's a long wait to see a doctor.'

'Has anyone seen you yet? Have you had any pain relief? Your wrist must be hurting, and your face looks sore.'

'Oh, it's fine, *bach*. They're very busy. There are people

here much worse off than me, I'm sure. And I feel much better now you're here.'

She gave his hand a gentle squeeze. Ted groaned softly as his mobile decided to ring just at that moment. He looked at the screen and his heart sank. Marston. That didn't bode well.

'I'm going to have to take this, mam. I'm really sorry. It's work.'

She smiled understandingly as he moved away.'

'Where the hell are you, Darling? I've been trying to track you down and getting bullshit excuses from your DI.'

'Sorry, sir. I'm at the hospital with my mother. She's been brought into the emergency department.'

There was a pause. Ted could almost hear the brain cogs turning.

'Is it life-threatening?'

'I don't know yet, sir, there's a long wait to be seen. She's been assaulted.'

Another pause, then, 'Well, you have ten minutes to find out. Then another thirty minutes to get to Central Park for a briefing if it's not.'

Marston cut the call. Ted took a short-range punch at the nearest wall; only years of serious martial arts training enabled him to stop the blow a hair's breadth before it connected. He knew it wasn't compassion from the other man in at least giving him the option. Marston was a political animal, too much a career cop to risk the bad PR of ordering him in only for his mother to die whilst he was at a non-urgent briefing.

Ted speed-dialled a number, then as soon as it was answered, said, 'Trev? Sorry to bother you, but I really need you. Now.'

He explained briefly what had happened then added, 'I know it's a big ask but can you come to be with Annie? I want to stay, of course I do, but that risks Marston kicking me off the case. I'll make it up to you, I promise.'

'Tell Annie I'm on my way. Don't worry, I'll keep you up to date. Leave your phone on silent so I can contact you if I need to. And yes, I shall ruthlessly extract payment in the near future. Go. And try not to worry.'

Chapter Seven

Ted was quietly seething on the drive back from Central Park, once again sharing an official car with the Ice Queen. Kevin Turner had been excused this one as his role was largely to supply support to Ted's team as needed. The briefing had been something and nothing which could, in Ted's opinion, have been dealt with in a circulated email rather than wasting officers' time yet again.

The Chief Super had made a point of publicly asking after Ted's mother and giving him permission to leave his mobile phone on to take any call which would give him news of her condition. To anyone who wasn't aware of the history between them, it would have seemed compassionate. Trev had sent him a quick text to say that he was with Annie but she was still waiting to be seen by anyone so had still not had any pain relief nor a diagnosis.

The briefing had been about a press conference Marston had arranged for the following day. It had been decided at high level to make a statement concerning the scam and the death of someone as a direct result of it. The powers that be wanted the public to be warned about bogus police officers or anyone else contacting them about alleged suspected activity on their credit card or bank accounts.

They also wanted the public's help in trying to find the killer. At the moment they had little to go on, so any sightings at all could prove vital. Ted doubted there would be any forensic evidence from the crime scene to help much, and there was no sign of a murder weapon. He and his team really would be starting from ground zero on this one.

'I will be leading the conference, of course, but I want you, DCI Darling, to be there as well. I want to show everyone watching the news or reading reports in the newspapers that we are taking all aspects of the enquiry, particularly the callous killing of this poor woman, extremely seriously. I think it would be a good idea to have someone with your excellent record on show to the public. That is, of course, as long as your poor mother is making sufficient progress. Just in case, perhaps you would brief your DI to be ready to stand in? Or perhaps Superintendent Caldwell, you could step in if needed? Sometimes the sight of a uniform of rank adds gravitas to such occasions. And I must say, Darling, I admire your dedication to the case in coming here from the hospital.'

Once they were back in the car for the return trip to Stockport, the Super turned to Ted. Her expression was once again one of genuine concern.

'That all seemed perfectly pleasant and supportive in public. Am I right in thinking I sensed undertones of something else entirely? But first, do you want to phone Trevor, to check how your mother is doing?'

Ted shook his head.

'He'll call me when there's some news, thank you. I came to the briefing because Mr Marston made it pretty clear that unless my mother was at death's door, it was in my interests to do so. And before you say anything,' he cut in as she opened her mouth to speak, 'I'd really prefer to leave it there for now. And no, that doesn't mean I'm condoning his behaviour.'

'I don't pretend to understand your motives but I will respect your wishes. For now.'

'I owe you an explanation. And this is all with no disrespect intended and no gender stereotyping meant. I had problems with the Chief Super before and I had to call in my boss, Matt Bryan. You may have met him? Very good copper. Smoked himself into an early grave with the stresses of the job. You know what it could get like in Firearms.

'I called him in to back me against Marston when he was interfering with my deployment. Putting officers' lives at risk. Matt Bryan was old school. A real hard-nosed, hairy-arsed copper. You've seen how that incident rankled with the Chief Super. With the greatest respect, now Jim Baker is out of the picture, you are my senior officer. Can you imagine what he'd make of me calling in a woman to fight my battles for me?'

Ted was saved from finding out if his remarks had been taken the wrong way by his mobile ringing. The screen told him it was Trev calling. He excused himself and answered it anxiously.

'Hi, it's good news; Annie's going to be fine. Physically, at least. No signs of significant head injury, but she does have a fractured wrist and some nasty bruising. They're discharging her shortly. I came on the bike, of course, so I'm going to call her a taxi and follow it back to ours. She can't possibly be on her own for the time being, especially with her wrist in plaster. She's too shaken up, for one thing, so she can stay with us until she feels better.

'Are you at work? Can you talk?'

'Not really, but thanks for that. Tell her I'll get back as soon as I can to see her, even if I have to go back in to work afterwards.'

'I will. And don't worry, I'll take the rest of the day off work to look after her. Love you.'

'Same here,' Ted said awkwardly, acutely uncomfortable about having a personal conversation in front of his boss.

'News of your mother? How is she?'

'Luckily, apart from a fractured wrist and some bruising, she should be all right, but Trev says she's still very shaken. As soon as we get back to the station, I'll see what progress has been made on finding her attacker. I'm not asking for any preferential treatment because she's my mother. I'd like to think we'd do the same for anyone who was the victim of a racially aggravated assault like this one. What has the country come to, with all the racist stuff?

'I've let Jezza go to do a recce on these so-called happy slappings today, as well. It's a similar thing, in a sense. My mother said there were people filming her on their mobiles while she was lying on the ground, instead of doing something to help her.'

The Ice Queen shook her head in disbelief.

'What are we coming to indeed, when people are capable of such acts, and they become spectator sports? The only glimmer of hope is that, presumably, some of these distasteful videos will appear online somewhere at some point and we might be able to find them and trace the attacker that way. Assuming uniformed officers attending haven't been able to see any of the footage to identify the attacker already.'

'I was planning to put Océane on to finding whatever she can online. At the moment we haven't anything for her to work on for Croesus, so I might as well see if we can use her to help wrap up some of the assaults. I don't even know how long it took first responders to get there, so any onlookers might have been long gone, complete with film footage.'

'I'm fully in agreement with that. In view of the constant restraints and pressure to reduce personnel, it is essential that we can show that every single member of your team is fully employed on cases all the time.'

It was later than Ted would have liked before he got home. There was no sign of his mother, but Trev was at the kitchen table with his TEFL work strewn all over everywhere. Whatever he was doing, Trev somehow always managed to make a mess. It was usually Ted who tidied up after him.

'How is she?' Ted asked him, pausing to kiss him, then bending to stroke each of the six cats in turn as they came to greet him, purring their pleasure.

'In bed, sleeping, poor thing. She was so shaken up, Ted. It was awful. She was trembling and weepy and couldn't really do anything. She just let me help her get cleaned up, then I made her some tea and put her to bed. Luckily, the painkillers they gave her are strong and she went out like a light, so I've left her to it for now. I just keep popping up to check how she's doing.'

Ted leaned in to hug him.

'I am so sorry I couldn't be there for her myself. I'm a rubbish son, and a useless partner. I let you both down. And I've not even been able to go and see Jim yet.'

'Don't be daft. Annie understands, and so do I. And I don't mind at all, I honestly don't. I love her too, you know. She's been more like a mother to me in the short time I've known her than my own ever was in fifteen years.

'One of us will need to nip up to her house and get her a change of clothes and some toiletries. I can do that quickly now, if you like? I've eaten, and it won't take me long. How was your day?'

Ted made a face.

'I've got to appear at a press conference tomorrow morning and you know how much I hate that.'

'I'll choose you the best shirt and tie to wear. I can't take another day off tomorrow, we've got too much work on. But I'll nip home at lunchtime to make sure Annie's all right, and we can hopefully both watch you on telly together, if it makes the lunchtime news. She'll love that.'

Trev was interrupted by his mobile. Ted sat down at the table and started looking idly through Trev's coursework. He could never understand how someone so academically brilliant could work amongst such chaos.

'Hi, Shewee,' Trev greeted his younger sister by her nickname, then grinned at Ted. 'Oh, sor-ree. Siobhan. Well, of course, if Henry doesn't like your nickname, I shall stop using it immediately. So Henry is still an item?

'No, of course I understand you're just good friends. And no, neither of us thought for a moment that you were sleeping together.'

He winked at Ted as he spoke. They had both met his sister's wealthy, horsey friend and were both convinced his interest in Siobhan was not of the kind she hoped it might be.

'Seriously, though, you're still young, there's plenty of time to find the right person. It may not be Henry. Just don't let him try to change you too much. If he likes you, he'll accept you as you are.

'Ted's fine, he sends his love. Good luck in the event at the weekend. I'd come if I could but I'm looking after Ted's mum. She had a bit of a fall and broke her wrist.'

'So, we're not allowed to call her Shewee any more?' Ted asked when he rang off.

'Henry doesn't approve. Having totally changed the way she looks and dresses, he's now decreed what she can and can't call herself. I really hope little sis is not going to have her heart broken. She still thinks Henry cares for her, but she's clearly just the token girlfriend to take home to show his parents he's interested in girls. I think you and I both know that's probably not the case.'

This time the wheelchair was tipped over as well, partly across Ted's father as he lay in a pool of his own urine. Ted tried to keep all trace of impatience out of his voice as he went across the room to right them both.

'How did you manage to tip the chair over as well? You need to be careful. You could have bashed your head on the fireplace. Or is that what you were trying to do?'

'I want you to get me some cannabis.'

'Cannabis?' Ted echoed, as he helped his father to lock his arms around his neck so he could heft him back up and into the chair. 'You know I can't do that. I'm a police officer. What do

you want cannabis for, anyway?'

'The pain. You have no idea how bad it can get. The regular medication barely touches it some days. I've heard that cannabis can work miracles. I want you to get me some.'

'Well, we'll go and see your doctor, see if you can get it on prescription. I've heard it may be possible. Have you had anything to eat today? You've not touched the sandwiches I made you, I see.'

'I hate cheese and Branston.'

'Since when?'

'Since I decided that there must be some things I can make up my own mind about. Are you going out tonight?'

'You know I am. It's my judo evening. I'll get you cleaned up, then I'll make you something to eat before I go out. What do you fancy?'

'Boiled eggs and dippy soldiers. Stop treating me like a child, Ted. I'm still your father, even if I'm not much of a man.'

Ted picked up an empty bottle from the floor and took it through to the kitchen before wheeling his father to the specially adapted bathroom at the rear of the property.

'You really need to do something about the drinking, dad. Why don't you try going to AA again?'

'And why don't you try not being so judgemental? Why do they call it Alcoholics Anonymous, anyway? There's nothing anonymous about saying, "I'm Joe, I'm an alcoholic. My wife left me because I can't get it up on demand now I'm a cripple and my son patronises me and treats me as if I was five".'

Ted put a gentle hand on his father's shoulder.

'I'm sorry, dad. I don't mean to.'

His father lifted a shaking hand, put it over Ted's and patted it.

'I'm sorry too, son. That was uncalled for. I know I'm a burden to you. I get so sick of these four walls and four wheels. Would you take me with you tonight?'

Ted hesitated.

'*You know I like to walk there, get limbered up on the way.*'

'*I can still wheel myself. You just need to give me a bit of a hand for the kerbs, in places. Or are you ashamed of me? Is that because I'm a cripple, or a drunk?*'

Ted had helped him out of most of his clothes and was manoeuvring the wheelchair and the slide board to get him across to the seat over the bath.

'*That's not fair, and you know it.*'

His father was crying now. Tears seemed to come so easily to him recently. The stereotypical lachrymose alcoholic. The weight was dropping off him, too. That visit to the doctor wasn't going to wait much longer.

'*I'm sorry, son. You're right, that wasn't fair. I'm being a selfish old sod. Tell me about your day. Did you have to shoot anyone today?*'

Ted smiled.

'*Not today. Luckily, it doesn't happen every day. And I will take you tonight. Of course I will. It will be nice for you to have a bit of an outing. We can go for a drink with some of the other members afterwards. But just one for you, and a couple of snakebites for me, all right? And don't forget, I'm taking you away for the weekend next month, to the shooting championships.*'

'*You're a good son. You should be taking your boyfriend, not an old wreck like me. I don't deserve you. I really don't.*'

This time Ted woke without crying out, though his heart was racing. He had the strange dream sensation of falling from a great height and landing with a jolt. It had not been enough to make Trev do more than sigh in his sleep and snuggle down even further under the duvet.

Ted checked the time on his mobile phone. He decided he might as well get up and go into work even earlier than he'd planned. He knew he was not going to find sleep again easily. He slid soundlessly out of bed, pulled on his sweats and padded to the spare room. He opened the door quietly and put his head round to see if his mother was all right.

'Teddy?' she asked, her voice sounding anxious.

In the street light filtering through the curtains, he could see her trying to sit up, struggling to switch on the bedside lamp, movements made awkward by the plaster cast on her wrist. Ted went across to do it for her.

'Sorry if I woke you, mam. Did you sleep all right? I'll make you a cup of tea.'

'I was already awake, *bach*. *Dere*, come and sit with me for a moment, if you've got time. I want to talk to you.'

'How are you feeling? Is it painful? What can I get you? And don't worry, I'm making sure that the person who did this to you is caught and brought to trial, as soon as possible.'

She moved her injured arm to lay her hand awkwardly over his, weighed down by the plaster.

'I slept a bit, but I've been awake a lot, too, thinking. And I've made a decision. That man kept shouting at me to go back to my own country. So that's what I want to do, Teddy, *bach*. I want to go back home, to Wales. Not just for a visit. I want to go back to live there.'

Ted was surprised at the depth of feeling her news invoked in him. His mother had not long been back in his life and now he risked losing her once more.

'But you've made your home here. And you've got me now, and Trev ...'

'Stockport was never my home, *bach*. I was here because of Joe. We got the chance to rent that specially adapted house, which was perfect for his needs. Then I stayed for my mam, because she was well settled here, and because I always hoped I'd find you again. And now I have, and I know you're doing so well in your work and you're very happy with Trev. You managed without me before, and you'll go on managing.

'It's not that far for you to come and visit me, whenever you can. And we can keep in touch by phone, all the time.

Trev's promised to help sort me out with a computer and emails and that thing where you can see people while you talk to them. Skype, is it?'

Ted felt another slight pang that his mother had clearly discussed her plans with Trev before him. Then he mentally reproached himself. He wasn't there enough for her to talk to him, even when she was hurt and clearly needed him.

'Aldwyth has been going on at me ever since my mam died to go back home. She's even said I could share her house, now she's on her own. We get on well, always have done, always stayed in touch, and it would help both of us, financially. I could sell mam's house, have a bit of money put by. And it's high time I retired. I could afford to do it, if I did all that.

'So it's time for me to do exactly what that man told me to do. I'm going to go home, Teddy.'

Chapter Eight

Ted was not thrilled to find himself alone with Marston for the pre press conference briefing. He had assumed the Press Officer would be there as well, as was standard procedure, but was told she would be joining them later. He didn't relish the prospect of it being just the two of them but there was nothing he could do about it.

'Right, turn your mobile off. I don't want us to be interrupted. Or recorded,' Marston began.

In private, he didn't even make a pretence of asking after Ted's mother. Ted did as he was instructed, then left his phone on the table in front of him, in plain view.

'You seem to have made bugger all progress on the killing so far, but we don't want to tell the public that. I'll start the conference off and field most of the questions. You sit there trying to look as if you know what you're doing. At some point some bright spark is going ask if we're confident and anticipating an early arrest. I'll bat that question over to you. You can tell them you're using every resource available, you're all over the case and you're definitely confident of an early result.'

'With respect, sir, wouldn't it be better to give a more guarded response? We're going to look a bit foolish if we don't deliver after a promise like that.'

'Not we, Darling. You. You're the one who's going to make that promise, on camera. You're the one on whose head the shit is going to descend from a great height when you don't pull it off. And I don't think you're going to. I think your friends in high places are finally going to see what I saw long ago. You're not up to the job. You've just been lucky up to now.'

Ted wasn't worried. No one who knew him, and that included the Chief Constable, would think that such rash boasts were his own words. Marston was trying to set him up for a fall and it was in danger of backfiring on him, if he was not careful.

'Whatever you say, sir,' he said evenly.

Marston's face darkened but whatever retort he was about to make was interrupted by a fortuitous knock on the door and the Press Officer coming in, with her bundle of documents. She looked surprised to see both men already there, clearly in discussion.

'Sorry, Chief, did I get the time wrong? I thought I was early, but it seems I might be late,' she said apologetically.

Her form of address to Marston was not lost on Ted. Chief was usually reserved for Chief Constables or their deputies. Some senior officers with ideas above their station insisted on it for the rank of Chief Superintendent. Clearly Marston was one of them.

'No, not at all, Jayne, DCI Darling and I were just catching up on old times. Please, take a seat. Do you two know each other?'

Ted was the old-fashioned sort. He'd stood up as soon as the young woman came into the room. He knew that some women, probably with more modern ideas than he had, didn't like it but he couldn't help it. It was the way he'd been brought up and he made no apology for it. He smiled as he shook her hand.

She sat down with them as they went over how the conference was to unfold. Ted noticed that Marston gave an entirely different version of the line he'd outlined earlier when it was just the two of them for what Ted's input was going to be.

Press conferences were the stuff of Ted's nightmares. He hated fuss, hated being put on display. He usually spent his time scowling. He knew this time he was going to have to pull something out of the bag, live on camera, that would reassure the public whilst sticking as near as he dared to what he'd been told earlier. Marston was determined to hang him out to dry, clearly, unless he boxed clever. Ted was not a political animal. He was a copper, plain and simple, and a good one, despite the Chief Super's views. These smoke and mirror games were well outside his comfort zone. He wished Jim Baker was there to watch his back, as he usually did. It made him feel even worse that he'd not yet been able to go and see his boss and friend.

There was a good turnout for the conference. Clearly the idea of a scam escalating into a killing had caught the interest of the media. Marston went confidently through his introduction and summary of the case so far. He was good at it, Ted had to acknowledge that, although he viewed him as more of a PR person than a proper copper. He could see the local reporter from Stockport amongst the pack; Pocket Billiards' replacement. She looked even younger and more timid than when he'd first met her in the pub.

Marston finished what he was saying, dealing skilfully with questions on the bogus police side of the enquiry. Then he introduced Ted and threw him to the wolves in the form of saying he would answer any questions on the murder investigation.

All Ted could think was that at some point, Trev and his mother were going to be watching his performance. He kept his mind focused on that, looked into the cameras and tried to make his expression as composed and sincere as he could. To his surprise, it was Penny Hunter who leapt in with the first question and it was a gift to him.

'DCI Darling, is it true that you have a one hundred per cent clear-up rate in murder investigations to date and is that why you've been chosen to head this part of the enquiry?'

'Thank you for the question, Penny. I head up an extremely experienced team in Stockport. Thanks to their hard work, yes, we do have a good record. It's this dedication and determination which makes us hopeful of a good result in this case.'

Ted felt Marston shift in his seat next to him. He knew that he wanted Ted to sound more confident than that.

The questions started to come thick and fast.

'Do you have a suspect yet for the killing?'

'At this early stage in the enquiry, it would not be helpful to go into such detail. As soon as there is more information, you will all be kept informed.'

Another weight change from Marston in his chair. He was clearly furious that Ted wasn't following the direction he had given him but there was nothing he could do about it under the scrutiny of the press. Questions were still being thrown at Ted and he was desperately playing ping pong, trying to answer them in the best possible way.

When the question the Chief Super had been hoping for came, he cleared his throat pointedly. Now Ted would have to tread with extreme caution.

'Are you confident of making an early arrest for the killing?'

'We are always optimistic of an early conclusion to any case. As I've said, we have a dedicated and experienced team working on this, with all the resources at our disposal. I would hope to have further news for you all soon.'

Marston wound things up then, as the press started to leave and he and Ted stood up, he took hold of Ted's arm in a vice-like grip.

'You and I need to talk some more.'

'And we will, sir, very soon. But now, if you want me to make some progress on this case, as I've just promised on camera, don't you think it's about time I went and did some proper police work?

Quite how he removed himself so effortlessly from the grip, Marston was not sure. One minute he was holding him by the arm, the next Ted was on his way out of the door.

Jo was holding the fort when Ted got back. Jezza was at her desk working, she told him, on her proposal for going after the happy slappers. Océane was helping her, looking for local incidents on any online sites. Ted asked Jo to join him in his office to bring him up to date. He was in serious need of green tea after the morning's ordeal.

'Boss, I've got some of the team tracking down friends and neighbours of the deceased and talking to them. We're trying to find out if, by any chance, she confided in anyone about what was going on. The rest are out and about round the café where we know she met Kateb, just in case anyone saw someone else, perhaps with Kateb before or after they met up.

'The CSOs are helping with putting up posters around both locations, with the photo and details of Mrs Ashworth and the e-fit of Kateb. I can't think of anything else we can usefully be doing at the moment, unless you can? I'm going through all the CCTV from around the scene again.'

Ted made drinks for them both and put them on the desk, sitting down opposite Jo.

'Let's check CCTV from near where she lives, too, to see if we can pick up her trail going to Wilmslow. I think it's unlikely but we could just get lucky and spot someone tailing her. Have you heard from Magnus how they're getting on over there?'

'They're still looking at all the footage they've got and doing the same as us, putting up posters to see if anyone saw anything. Nothing so far, though. This is going to be a tough one, I imagine. So how did the press conference go, boss?'

Ted made a face as he took a drink of his tea.

'The strangely upbeat me you will see on the screen is not necessarily representative of my levels of optimism on this case, at this stage. Not that I don't have confidence in the team,' he put in hastily. 'It's just that we really are starting out from nothing on this one. I would feel happier if I didn't keep get hauled off to fairly pointless briefings all the time, but that's between you and me.'

Jo nodded his understanding as he finished his coffee and left the boss to it.

If Ted hated appearing on television, his aversion to watching himself there was even stronger. He was even more disconcerted to be summoned to the Ice Queen's office to watch the lunchtime local news with her to see his performance. Watching himself, he decided he didn't believe a word he was saying, any more than he expected most viewers would.

'Well, that was very ...' the Super hesitated over an appropriate word, then finished, 'optimistic.'

'Not quite how I would have preferred to play it, as you can imagine, but I was under instructions. What I'd really like would be more time to get on with being a copper and less on attending briefings.'

'It goes with the rank, unfortunately, Chief Inspector,' she responded dryly.

They were interrupted by Ted's mobile.

'It's Jim Baker. Would you mind if I took it in my office?'

When she nodded, Ted left the office and picked up the call as he headed for the stairs.

'Who are you and what have you done with Ted Darling?' the Big Boss's voice rumbled in his ear. 'What on earth was all that bollocks about being optimistic and hopeful? Not like you at all. Am I to assume that you were merely a glove puppet spouting someone else's words? And that's not bloody like you either. What's wrong?'

'You noticed, then?'

'Of course I noticed. I'm a bloody copper. Certainly not a line dancer.'

'I was following a script. And that was after I'd watered it down from what I was supposed to be saying.'

'For God's sake be careful, Ted. You're playing with a shark there. I know there's history between you and Marston but he's a clever man, powerful and ruthless. And he always covers his arse.'

'He certainly does when he's around me,' Ted retorted with a hollow laugh.

There was an awkward silence. Jim Baker always became embarrassed when Ted alluded to anything to do with his sexuality. They were great friends but Jim's beliefs made it difficult for him at times. Ted decided to fill the moment, asking how Jim was and apologising for not visiting him.

'Don't be daft. I know what it's like with a case like this and I don't envy you. It's not going to be easy, unless someone gives you a tip-off or you get a breakthrough from forensics. Anyway, they say they're going to kick me out before the weekend so at least I'll be back home, where Bella can look after me. She's mortified about the whole thing. Thinks it's all her fault. At least she won't want to take me dancing again, that's something.'

After he ended the call, Ted read through all the notes on his desk to catch up with events. He would need to eat at some point. He was looking for an excuse to take him out of the office for a while. He needed to be doing some hands-on policing, to touch base with the enquiry, instead of the endless round of briefings and meetings. He found what he was looking for by way of a good excuse and went to find Jo again.

'Jo, this friend of Mrs Ashworth, Malcolm Worrall. Has anyone been there yet? If not, can you show me as attending, please? If I don't get out into the real world soon I'm going to go crazy.'

Jo scanned the lists on his desk to check, then added Ted's name alongside that of Malcolm Worrall. He'd been identified as a close friend of the deceased.

'All yours, boss. If anyone's looking for you, do you want me to cover for you?'

'If you can. If I'm going up to Marple anyway, I'd quite like to drop in on Bill again, if only for ten minutes. But I'm on the mobile if you or anyone else needs me urgently. And can you get everyone together for a catch up at the end of the day? Just so we know where we're up to with everything before the weekend.'

Ted went via the nearest bakers. He knew there was no point offering Bill his own favourite, smoked salmon and cream cheese bagel. But he wanted to make sure he was eating something hot and filling, being stuck on his own, so he picked up a hot meat and potato pie for each of them. He'd give himself ten minutes to eat it with Bill before going on to interview Mrs Ashworth's friend.

As Ted had suspected, Bill hadn't eaten and there was no sign of any food preparation happening. He did look and sound better, though, and was clearly itching to be back at work. Ted devoured his pie as fast as the heat would allow. He wished he could have stayed longer. He knew how much Bill needed company. But he had a murder case to solve and the pressure was on.

Ted's own car was back from its repairs so he'd taken that, rather than his official car. Parking wasn't always easy close to Bill's house and he'd had to leave it on the opposite side of the road, further down. Just as Ted was stepping cautiously out from between two parked cars to cross the road, a black VW came roaring round the corner and shot past, close to where Ted had been seconds earlier, before his martial arts instincts made him leap back to the safety of the pavement.

It was gone in a flash, before he could see anything but the first two letters of the registration number, either MM or MN, it was impossible to tell. It didn't advance him much anyway, as both were Greater Manchester. The make and colour of the car could have been mere coincidence. Ted's instincts told him it was more than that. It worried him that the car had obviously been tailing him again, without him noticing. His current situation with Marston was distracting him too much. He desperately needed some Krav Maga sessions. Nothing sharpened him up as much as that. It was just a matter of finding the time.

He didn't have far to go to the home of Malcolm Worrall, the friend of their victim, Vera Ashworth. As soon as Ted pulled up outside the small but neat and pleasant semi-detached bungalow, he could see the adapted entrance, with the wheelchair ramp. It reminded him of his father's place, the one that was found for him after he broke his back and was paralysed in a mining accident. Ted really didn't want any more reminders of his last years with his father right now. He was not proud of himself over how he'd behaved towards him at the end. But this was work and he was a police officer, who'd asked for this interview. So he would go in and get on with it.

He rang the doorbell, his police card in his hand. The door opened to reveal a well-dressed man in a motorised wheelchair which he operated with the fingers of one hand.

'Mr Worrall? I'm Detective Chief Inspector Darling.'

'I saw you earlier, on the television. Do please come in. It's about Vera, I take it? Please come through to the kitchen. I was just making myself a cup of tea, if you'd like one?'

Ted had only had chance to gulp half a cup with Bill so he accepted gladly and sat down at the kitchen table as instructed. Worrall's hand and arm were the only parts of him which appeared to work efficiently but he was clearly adept at coping so Ted didn't patronise him by offering to help. He knew how independent his father had been earlier on after his accident, before the drink ruined him, and how he would have hated any such presumption.

While Worrall was busying himself with the kettle, an enormous long-haired cat sauntered into the room, eyeing Ted up suspiciously. Worrall noticed and told him, 'Maximus is very wary of strangers so he probably won't stay, but please don't take it personally.'

'He's magnificent. Is he a Norwegian Forest or a Maine Coone? I'm never sure.'

Worrall put an adapted tray across the arms of his wheelchair, with the two mugs on it, expertly manoeuvred his chair and delivered them to the table.

'I see you're knowledgeable on cats. He's Norwegian. And he seems to have accepted you readily enough, so I'm assuming you have cats of your own?'

'Six,' Ted smiled. 'Just moggies though, nothing pedigree. So, Mr Worrall, you were a friend of Mrs Ashcroft. What can you tell me about her, please?'

'We used to play chess and Scrabble together regularly. We met through work, before she retired and I had the stroke which reduced me to what you see before you. What I can tell you is that she was an intelligent and sensible woman. Quite the tactician at chess. I would suggest that whoever successfully managed to draw her into this type of a scam, as I saw outlined in the televised press conference earlier, must have been extremely plausible and convincing. I wish you luck in tracking them down, Chief Inspector.'

Chapter Nine

Ted was much more alert on the drive back to the station, constantly checking his rear view mirror and looking all round for any further sign of the black VW. He didn't notice it again, but when he got back, he went straight to Kevin Turner's office, to see what the chances were of tracing it.

When he went in, Kevin stood up and approached him, went round behind him, made a show of lifting the back of his jacket, then looking him over.

'What are you doing, you idiot?' Ted asked good naturedly as he sat down.

'I'm wondering where the ventriloquist had his arm during that press conference. It may have been your mouth moving but it certainly wasn't your usual words coming out. And what was with all these pleasant looks to camera? You usually look as if you want to kill all those present.'

'I was under orders,' Ted said tersely, not wanting to go into detail.

'Seriously, though, Ted, are you getting anywhere so soon?'

'Seriously? No. I've just been talking to a friend of the victim who said that if she was conned then it was a very sophisticated operation. He told me she was an intelligent woman, not easy to take in. I'm hoping some of the team may at least have a few leads, but I'm not getting my hopes up yet. But that's not what I wanted to talk to you about.'

He explained about his latest encounter with a black VW

and gave Kevin the few details he had.

'Not a lot to go on, but I'll ask around and put in a call to Traffic in case it's shown up anywhere else. Any ideas who might be behind it?'

'The team and I have had some good arrests lately, so I suspect there's a few people who've crossed me off their Christmas card list. It could be to do with the Sabden House case. I imagine the dodgy councillor has plenty of even more dubious friends, and we're still working on building a case against him. Perhaps he thinks trying to put the frighteners on me might deter me. If so, he doesn't know me at all.'

'Just watch your back, Ted. In both instances. You may be annoying at times, but at least I'm used to you and your funny little ways. I don't want to have to break in someone new in CID.'

When he went back to his office, Ted found Jezza's report on her findings about the happy slappers waiting for him on his desk. It was, as he would have expected from her, a detailed and thorough presentation. He didn't have time to look at it yet, so he put it in his briefcase to take with him. He'd go through it when he got home, or over the weekend, which he was likely to have to spend at his desk.

The rest of the team members were drifting back in for the planned briefing to round off the week. Ted fervently hoped at least one of them would have something positive to report.

'Before we start, can I just ask if any of you have spotted a black VW which looked as if it might be tailing you, or observing you? You know I was run off the road by what I thought was probably a boy racer. I spotted what appeared to be the same car again today. I had to jump out of its way pretty sharpish when I was trying to cross the road.

'You all know I hate assumptions but I'm going on the basis that this might be someone connected to a recent case. They may be targeting me specifically but there's always a chance any of you could also be on the list. So watch yourselves, please. Report anything unusual as soon as you see it. No heroics, from any of you. And before any of you say anything, I include myself in that.'

It raised a smile from everyone, at least. Ted could sense that the team members were feeling dispirited with no real direction to go in yet.

'Right, I've been talking to Mrs Ashworth's friend, Malcolm Worrall. He tells me she was intelligent, not easily taken in. She would often joke with him about the latest Nigerian email scams she'd received. You all know the type. "My late husband left me several million pounds and if you help me recover it I will give you half".

'She hadn't told him anything at all about this one. I think we can safely assume that she was sworn to secrecy by Kateb as Inspector Galton. Some story about not jeopardising the enquiry, I imagine. She does mention in her diary that she was looking forward to telling Malcolm a bit about it when it was all over, although it was all confidential. All she did tell him beforehand was that she was going to see someone about some problem with one of her cards, but she didn't tell him which one. He told me he assumed it was her bank card and she was going to the bank, since you can't normally visit credit card providers, as far as I'm aware.

'So, where are we up to on known associates of Kateb? How has this gang gone from successful and lucrative scams to a murder like this? Jo, what news from the post-mortem? Was Professor Nelson able to give us anything useful from the knife wound?'

'Boss, the PM confirmed a single penetrating wound to the abdomen causing catastrophic blood loss. Professor Nelson said it would inevitably have been fatal without prompt medical attention and there appears to have been a delay between her being stabbed and anyone coming to her aid.

'I've circulated details, including the dimensions of the

knife. Professor Nelson says it could well be a flick knife with a long, thin blade. It's what she described as a typical stab and run wound. Just a single blow, designed to cause maximum damage, allowing the attacker time to get away. And as no mobile phone was found at the scene, it's likely the attacker took it with him, preventing Mrs Ashworth from calling for assistance herself.'

'Right, known associates? Who's on that?'

'Me, boss,' Maurice Brown told him. 'But can I just ask something first. At the press conference you were sounding as if we were getting somewhere. Do you know something about the case you're not sharing with the rest of us, for some reason?'

Ted sighed to himself. It was a reasonable question. He could see how it would look that way.

'The top brass move in a mysterious way, Maurice, their wonders to perform. I hope you know by now that I keep all of you in the loop at all times, unless there are special circumstances which prevent me from doing so.'

'Fair enough, boss. Negative on all known associates so far, and I have checked them all. None of them with any record or even suspicion of anything like this.'

'One possible slight lead from Inspector Pierson in Wilmslow though, boss,' Rob O'Connell put in. 'Someone has come forward to say they saw a car pulling out very fast from the car park where Mrs Ashworth was found. From the time and the make, a dark blue Peugeot, it's almost certainly her car. There's only a vague description of the driver. The witness saw it turn right and drive off at speed. They just walked on past as they were heading for another car park so they didn't actually see Mrs Ashworth lying on the floor.

'Inspector Pierson's team now have a bit more to go on, as they know the direction it left in, so they can try to track it on the way to where it was first picked up on CCTV and we may get something more from that.'

'Good, that's something. Right, we need as many people as possible working on this case over the weekend. Perhaps half on and half off each day?'

'I've already sorted the rotas, boss,' Rob told him. He was proving to be an excellent DS.

'Boss, I put my proposal on your desk ...'

'I saw that, Jezza, thanks. I'll take it home with me tonight and let you have my decision as soon as I can find the time to read it.'

'It's just that there's been another posting on social media. I'm seriously worried it's going to escalate ...'

'I hear your concerns, Jezza. Pass what details you have to Inspector Turner and see if Uniform, particularly the CSOs, can ID anyone in the footage. That's all I can promise you for now. And of course we can't make the suspects' images public because of the likelihood that they're young offenders.'

Seeing her open her mouth to continue, Ted said firmly, 'That's all on that topic for now, thank you, DC Vine. Anything else, anyone?'

'Boss, a possible breakthrough,' Océane began. 'I finally found something posted on social media which I assume, from the dateline and the delightful racist vitriol, to be the assault on your mother. Clearly you, or someone who knows her by sight, needs to ID her from the film.'

Ted had been perching on a desk as usual. At her words, he shot to his feet and moved over to her work station.

'Er, it's just that, I found it quite distressing to watch, boss, and it's not someone I'm related to,' she said as tactfully as she could.

'I'm a police officer first, before being a relative of the victim,' Ted retorted, more sharply than he meant to. 'Show me, please.'

Whoever was filming had clearly started as soon as the attacker began to shout. Ted saw his mother talking in Welsh on her mobile phone and heard a loud and aggressive voice shouting at her. She'd clearly given him the edited highlights of what was said as there was a lot of swearing. Most of it centred around the assumption that she was speaking Polish and telling her to go back to her own f-ing country. He could see how shocked and upset she was at the words and it tore at his heart to see his own mother like that.

The person filming panned out so the attacker came into clear view. He was a big man, towering over Ted's mother, who was now looking terrified and trying to back away. The man shoved her hard, in the chest, a couple of times, shouting all the time, before she overbalanced and fell heavily on to her side. Her cheek smashed against the hard surface of the pavement, causing tears to start to her eyes.

Ted could see that as she had said, other people were also filming, some of them laughing, none of them going to help her. He decided not to watch any more. He was not sure he could retain control of himself in front of the team if he had to watch the man stamp on her wrist and break it.

'Send it to me, please,' he told Océane, his voice ominously quiet. 'Have you sent it to Inspector Turner yet?'

'I only just found it, shortly before the briefing started, boss. I'll do that now. I'm so sorry. Your poor mother. It must have been dreadful for her.'

Ted nodded his thanks but didn't trust himself to speak further. He let the team go then went back to his office. He desperately wanted to go to his Krava Maga club and spend some time attempting to kick the crap out of someone. Instead he contented himself with writing off yet another waste-paper basket by kicking it all round the room. Then he finished up the paperwork on his desk and headed home. He put his head round Kevin Turner's door on the way but he'd already gone. He'd catch up tomorrow for news of his mother's attacker, now Océane had the footage.

He found Trev and Annie sitting companionably side by side on the sofa, feet up on the rests, purring cats piled on top of them. Trev had a protective arm lightly around her shoulders and they were both engrossed in an old black and white film. Trev was clearly not long home, his hair still damp from a shower. Ted leaned over the back of the sofa to kiss each of them on the cheek then went and sat in the armchair, watching them together. It made the day feel marginally better.

Trev picked up the remote and lowered the volume. He could see straight away that Ted had had a hard day. He looked weary.

'*Popeth yn iawn*?' Trev asked him, then, seeing Ted's look of surprise, he laughed. 'I thought I'd learn Welsh. Annie's been helping me.'

Trev was like a sponge for languages. He seemed to absorb them effortlessly through some sort of osmosis. Even the complexities of the Welsh language were unlikely to pose him any problems.

'I was so proud, watching you on telly, Teddy *bach*,' his mother told him. 'You looked so handsome. I can tell all my friends when I go home to Wales about my policeman son. And I've decided to go soon. On Sunday, in fact.'

'So soon? But how will you manage, with your arm in plaster?'

'I'm going to stay with Aldwyth. The plaster is part of the reason, *bach*. You've both been so kind, but I need help, with things like having a shower, and I'm sure it would be awkward for all of us for me to have to ask either of you to help.'

'I can get a carer to come in, mam. I'm sorry, I should have thought of that. I'll get someone. Don't worry. I'll pay for them.'

'It's not just that, Teddy. It's the *hiraeth*. It's time for me to go home.'

Ted remembered the Welsh word for which there was no real English translation. So much more than homesickness; a physical longing for the homeland.

'But how will you get there? I'm working this weekend,

otherwise I'd happily take you.'

'I've got to work tomorrow for at least part of the day, after skiving off a bit this week,' Trev put in. 'Leave me the car and you take the bike, so you're mobile. I can run Annie up to her house tomorrow to get whatever she needs, then I'll take her on Sunday and come back the same day.'

Again, Ted felt a pang of something he couldn't quite identify that his mother and Trev had clearly discussed it all in detail before they told him. He knew he was being unreasonable. He wasn't there enough for them to include him in the plans. It seemed to be happening so fast and he felt powerless to do anything about it.

'Is everything all right at work?' Trev asked him, when they were finally alone together in their bedroom. 'I know you're having a hard time with your new boss, but is there more to it than that?'

'I'm feeling guilty that I've not been able to do more for my mother. She seems closer to you than she is to me. She certainly seems more at ease with you helping her in the bathroom than me. I had to interview a man in a wheelchair today and it brought it all back a bit. I was a useless son to my father and now I feel I'm letting my mother down, too.

'And it's just the same old stuff at work as usual – a hard case and not much progress.'

'Ted, you're an absolutely rubbish liar. That's one of the reasons I know you would never cheat on me. You'd never be able to keep it a secret. And stop beating yourself up all the time about your parents. You've always done whatever you could within the constraints of the job. There must be more to it than that.'

'I wouldn't cheat anyway. Why would I?' Then, seeing that Trev was not going to let it drop, 'I saw a black VW again today. Like the boy racer who ran me off the road. It might have been a coincidence. I'm getting it checked out. It's nothing to worry about.'

'I always start worrying most when you tell me there's nothing to worry about. And Annie was right. You did look handsome on television. And more than a little sexy. By now, she will be spark out after her painkillers, so ...'

Afterwards, Trev found deep and peaceful sleep as soon as they turned the light out. Ted was condemned to a night of fitful tossing and turning, what little sleep he did manage to find punctuated by vivid dreams from the past.

Ted was perched on a barstool, sinking his third pint. Or possibly his fourth. He'd rather lost count. He was in a good mood. He was through to the finals of the rifle championships the following day and he was enjoying the company of fellow coppers, some of whom he only saw on occasions like this.

His boss moved up quietly behind him, put a hand on his shoulder and leaned close, speaking directly into Ted's ear.

'Ted, your dad needs you.'

Ted turned his head, his eyes taking slightly longer than they should have to come back into focus as he changed position. He'd left his dad at a table on the other side of the room, talking to Arthur. They'd met before. Arthur was a retired Firearms officer, the one who'd trained Ted at Claytonbrook, who always turned out to support his former colleagues. It gave him a valid excuse not to be digging the allotment his wife had insisted he get after he left the force, and which didn't hold his interest.

'He's fine. He likes talking to Arthur.'

Inspector Matt Bryan was a tough boss; hard to please, but fair. Ted would normally have picked up that the remark was an instruction, but he was feeling pleasantly relaxed.

Bryan took hold of one of Ted's arms in an iron grip, took the glass from his other hand and put it on the bar. Then he forcibly pulled Ted off the stool to stand upright. He moved his face even closer so Ted could feel the warmth of his breath, smell the perfume of a gin and tonic and the strong aroma of cigarette smoke.

'Listen to me carefully, sergeant. He is not fine. He's pissed himself and he's crying. Arthur didn't know what to do so he called me over. It should have been you but you haven't even glanced at them. Now you get your arse over there and you sort your father out. Then sort yourself out. You're half cut already and you've got the finals tomorrow.

'There's no place on my team for a pisshead. If you're not in a proper state to at least shoot straight tomorrow, but preferably to bring home at least one trophy, you'll be off back to a desk job by Monday morning. Are we clear on that, sergeant?'

'Clear, sir.'

Chapter Ten

Ted was in early on Saturday morning. He'd taken his mother up a cup of tea, with just a cloud of milk, as she liked it, before he left. There was seldom any point trying to wake Trev at that hour, except in an emergency. Ted was under strict instructions to try to get home at a decent time so they could all enjoy an evening meal together before his mother left for Wales the following day. It could be the last one for some time.

He knew none of the team members working that day would be late. Rob O'Connell had organised things well, allocating available bodies where they were most needed. He'd put himself and Sal down to go over to Wilmslow to catch up with Magnus Pierson and see what help they could offer there.

Ted hoped for some quiet, uninterrupted desk time to try and get on top of things, but he promised himself he would find the time to at least phone both Jim and Bill, to see how they were doing. As instructed, he'd left the car for Trev and come in on the bike. His leathers were hanging on the coat rack behind the door.

He looked up in surprise when his office door opened without a knock and Marston strode in. Ted rose slowly to his feet. He still stood for women and for senior officers, even though both practices were rapidly going out of fashion of late. He did it even when he had barely an ounce of respect for the ranking officer. He indicated the spare chair and Marston sat down without preamble.

'Right, I want to see all the paperwork on this case. Notes, logs, statements, anything you have. I want to find out at first hand why there's been no progress at all on it to date.'

'No problem, sir, that's exactly what I'm working on today. It's all up to date and in order.'

Ted was thankful that he was always meticulous about paperwork. He'd been paranoid about it on this case, knowing Marston would jump on any chance to fault him for the slightest procedural error, no matter how insignificant to the case.

'What's your direction for now? Why have there been no leads of any description so far?'

'We have a new line of enquiry now, sir. A witness who saw the deceased's car being driven away. Two of my officers have gone over to Wilmslow today to work with Inspector Pierson, to see if we can get any sort of a description of the driver. Or any additional CCTV footage, now we at least know what direction the car was driven away in.'

'And where is the car? Why hasn't that been found?'

Marston made it sound as if it was Ted's personal responsibility that the Peugeot had dropped off the radar and not been seen anywhere after the last fleeting sighting.

'The most likely explanation is that the plates were switched as soon as it was practical to do so. I've now asked for all sightings of any dark blue Peugeots, not just based on the number plate registered to Mrs Ashworth as the owner.'

Marston didn't appear to be listening to him. His head was down, over the paperwork, and he was scanning through it rapidly, clearly ready to pounce on the slightest discrepancy.

The partition walls of his office were paper-thin so Ted could hear footsteps coming up the stairs. The first of his team arriving in to work, he assumed. He was surprised when, once again, his door opened without a knock. This time it was his own Super who swept in. She was tall, taller than both men, and she looked even taller than usual dressed as she was in her Kevlars. She was another biker, who rode a Ducati 999. She had her helmet under her arm and dumped it on a corner of the desk. Once again Ted half-rose before she waved him back down.

'Gentlemen,' she greeted them, unzipping her jacket and hanging it on the rack next to Ted's leathers, revealing a close-fitting turtle-neck underneath.

'I wasn't expecting to see you this morning, ma'am,' Ted told her, finding the spare chair for her and putting it next to the Chief Super.

She eyed up his casual attire; comfortable walking trousers, a long-sleeved polo.

'Evidently,' she said, irony in her tone. 'Sir, everything which happens in my station is my responsibility, naturally. When I was informed just now that you were paying an unscheduled visit,' there was a note of reproach in her voice, 'I thought I'd better come in and see if my presence was required. I was just taking the Ducati out for a spin, which is why I'm dressed like this. I was about to come in anyway for a quick check on things when I received the call.'

'Your presence really is not necessary, Debra. I just wanted to catch up with Darling to see if we can't move this enquiry along as it seems to be going nowhere at the moment. To check we're making the most profitable use of everyone's time.'

She was making no move to leave. On the contrary, she seemed to be making herself comfortable in her seat, reaching up to adjust the band which was holding her long black hair in a doubled-over pony tail. Ted couldn't ever remember feeling more grateful for the presence of his stiffly-formal boss. He knew her being there was infuriating Marston. But he would know that summoning her had nothing to do with Ted. He hadn't had the opportunity. He wondered who had tipped her off. Whoever it was, he owed them a pint.

'I'm sure that will be the case, sir. I have every confidence in DCI Darling.'

'But what about this?' Marston jabbed an aggressive finger

at a sheet of paper he was looking at. 'You went in person to interview the victim's friend? That's a job for a DC. A DS at most. It's a complete waste of costly time for someone of your rank to be out doing mundane jobs like this.'

'I beg to differ, sir, with the greatest possible respect. DCI Darling is extremely good at talking to people. It's one of his greatest assets. If he felt it worth his time to go and talk to this person, I'm happy with his decision. Most of his hours come out of my budget anyway, even on this case. I'm more than willing to bear the cost of an hour of his time, if he felt doing this interview himself would advance the enquiry in some way.'

Ted was fascinated, watching the Super fighting his corner for him.

'And has it?' Marston asked testily. 'Did it give you some sort of a breakthrough?'

'Actually, sir, it gave me an idea which I was going to run past you. Mr Worrall confirmed for me what we had already been led to believe, that Mrs Ashworth was nobody's fool. Hard to deceive. Superintendent Williams already mentioned at the initial briefing that the quality of the forged warrant card Kateb was using would have been high. So have we traced the maker?'

He could see straight away that it hadn't yet been followed up, so he pressed home his advantage.

'Once Kateb had met Mrs Ashworth himself, he would know she wasn't a pushover. She'd want to see a badge from his supposed officer who was going to pick up the watch from her. And that would mean one as convincing as his own. Clearly, even if we do succeed in finding the forger, there's no guarantee they'll talk and they may not have the real name of the other bogus officer. But we might just get lucky, if we can track down the maker and perhaps even find a photo, which would be the first concrete lead to date to the killer's identity.

'Some of my team have good street contacts and they're

asking around, but I don't know offhand of a forger of this standard on our patch. I would imagine it would be one for Fraud or City. Shall I contact them or will you, sir?'

Marston's face was turning an alarming shade of deep red, his expression dangerous. Ted held his gaze levelly, until he pushed back his chair and stood up. Ted did the same, getting ready to show him out.

'I'll pass that on. It's a start, but just make sure you come up with something a bit more than that. Preferably the murder weapon at least, if not the suspect.'

As he shut the door behind Marston, Ted turned to the Ice Queen with a smile and said, 'I know you once said never even to propose a high five in your presence but could I at least offer a virtual one in thanks for your support there?'

To his amazement, she returned his smile and held up a hand, palm outwards. He tapped it cautiously with his own.

'Now, I think I've earned some of your green tea, don't you?' she asked him.

As Ted went to put the kettle on, she continued, 'You'll be wondering why I was called in. The Uniform branch here think highly of you. As much as anything, because of your kindness and concern for Bill, especially while he's off sick. As soon as Mr Marston arrived unannounced, asking for you and clearly spoiling for a fight, I was called by the front desk.

'I was going to drop in briefly before I went out for the day so I came straight here. I appreciate all you've said about the situation between the two of you and I know you can look after yourself. But I deplore bullying in any form. I simply will not have it directed at one of my officers.

'So for now, when I've finished my tea, I'll get back out there on my little adventure. Robin and the boys have gone sailing and I'm very much Not Wanted On Voyage, so I'm off for a little spin and probably a pub lunch somewhere. I see you're on two wheels yourself today.'

Ted explained about Trev's need for the car over the

weekend to take his mother to Wales. She immediately looked contrite.

'Oh, I'm sorry, I should have asked about your mother.'

'No worries. She's recovering well, physically. The downside for me is that's it scared her so much that she's decided to move back to Wales, permanently. It's not just a visit there.

'There's good news on the case, though. Océane found some footage of the assault on social media so Uniform should hopefully be able to make an arrest, probably today with any luck.'

'We need to deal with this most robustly. We can't have this type of thing going on in this division. And what about these happy slappers? Is there any progress on that case?'

'I've had Jezza's proposal. It's meticulous, as you would expect, and I think any risks in her intended course of action are manageable, with care. I'm proposing putting her on it for a trial period initially, to see where it leads us. It will mean I need to get to the dojo on Wednesday evenings for as long as she needs to complete the operation, so we can have a scheduled meeting without raising the suspicions of anyone who might be watching her.

'I'll forward the proposal to you for approval. But why don't you go and enjoy some free time first? And thanks for coming to my rescue. I appreciated it very much, although I'm not sure Mr Marston did.'

'Make sure you get away at a decent time, too. If this is your last evening with your mother for some time, go and make the most of it. Heaven knows, we get little enough time for family life in this job.'

After she'd left, Ted went down to the front desk to talk to the sergeant on duty.

'I hope I did the right thing there, sir? Only the Super always likes to be kept informed of incoming aliens on her territory, and the Chief Super didn't look entirely sweetness and light when he asked for you.'

'You did absolutely the right thing, Sergeant Wheeler. It's the Super's station. Her rules. I just wanted to thank you, and to ask what was happening about the racially aggravated assault? You know the victim was my mother, I'm sure.'

'Yes, sir, and we were all sorry to hear about it. The attacker is known to us; we were able to identify him from the mobile phone footage your CFI sent through. There's an area car on its way now to find him and bring him in. With the form he's got, we should be able to send him on a nice little holiday, keep him off the streets and make them a bit safer.'

'Excellent. I'll be in all day. Please can you let me know when he's been brought in?'

The sergeant hesitated.

'Er, sir, you do know I can't let you anywhere near him, don't you? Only I know how I'd feel about anyone who did that to my mum, and I'd hate for any of us to have to try to arrest you.'

'I promise to behave, sergeant. Just let me watch him on camera when he's being interviewed, please. That's all I ask. And do you know if there's any news about the black VW, the one that ran me off the road on Dan Bank?'

'Nothing as yet, sir, but all units are keeping an eye out. Can I ask, is this something to do with this latest case? Are you being targeted in connection with that?'

Ted shook his head.

'I doubt it. The first incident happened before I appeared at the press conference and I wasn't high profile enough before that for anyone to know I'm involved. I think it's from something older; maybe the Sabden House case.'

'Well, you mind how you go, sir. You're always polite to us mere mortals in uniform, and so are all your team. It's not always like that, not in every nick, between CID and Uniform.'

Ted was already getting texts from Trev not long after lunch, urging him to be sure to get home on time to eat with his mother. Ted wanted to catch up with his team before he could think of leaving. He'd thrown Marston a crumb of a lead but he wanted something much more substantial.

Rob and Sal were back first from Wilmslow, but Ted hung on until Virgil and Maurice got in, to save having to go over everything twice. Both of them had good contacts on their patch, although Ted knew Maurice's would often involve visiting all the pubs and bars in town. Since his serious injury, Maurice was at least limiting his alcohol intake.

'Any signs of the murder weapon yet?' Ted asked.

'Nothing, boss, although Uniform are still searching. My best guess is that it went with the attacker in the car. I talked to the latest witness, the one who saw the car drive off. Nothing much to go on. Single male occupant in the vehicle; they couldn't give much of a description. I tried, without leading them, but the best I got was young adult, perhaps twenties, dark hair, smartly dressed, suit and tie.'

'Trying to look the part of a presentable copper who wouldn't spook Mrs Ashworth, no doubt. Any chance of them doing a likeness that we could circulate?'

'Wilmslow are working on that with the witness, but it's likely to be only a vague one at best.'

'Any further sightings of the car?'

'Not yet, boss. At some point it drops out of sight, so it's probable that the driver took it somewhere to change the plates.'

'And that would most likely involve an accomplice, since the bogus officer could hardly turn up to meet Mrs Ashworth with a set of dodgy number plates tucked under one arm. Virgil, Maurice, do any of your contacts know anything to help us? Anyone who could be supplying fake ID of that kind of quality?'

Both of them shook their heads. They were interrupted by a desk phone. Maurice was nearest to answer it.

'Front desk, boss. They said to let you know your man's

just been brought in.'

'Right, I'll be downstairs, if anyone needs me. This is the charmer who put my mother in hospital, so I wanted to see him get booked.'

Ted got another stern warning from Sergeant Wheeler that he was to behave himself and simply to watch the interview on camera without going anywhere near the suspect. Ted had no intention of doing anything which would give the man the slightest chance of avoiding going down for what he had done to his mother.

The suspected attacker looked bigger and bulkier in the flesh than on the footage Ted had seen. He must have dwarfed his mother. His name was Owen Davies. The ultimate irony. A Welsh name for someone accusing a Welsh speaker of talking Polish. He already had a record, mostly for petty theft and taking vehicles without consent, but also assault charges, one arising from a pub brawl.

Ted was sickened watching him being questioned. He didn't deny his actions. He sought only to justify them by insisting the person he had pushed, as he put it, was speaking Polish in public and should not have been doing so. Ted stayed just long enough to see him charged then headed home to tell his mother the good news.

Trev tried hard to keep the evening light and memorable but Ted couldn't escape his feelings of guilt. He felt as if he was losing his mother for the second time in his life, as if he somehow could, and should, have been able to do more for her. The same feelings of failure he'd had to deal with over his father.

'Sergeant Darling? I'm sorry to bother you at work. It's Julia, your dad's case worker. Have you got a minute?'

'It's fine, I was just going on a break. Is everything okay? Is Dad all right?'

'It's not an emergency or anything. But I don't think he is

all right, really. Do you?'

Ted went quiet for a moment. She was right. He knew it. He'd been telling himself for some time he should do something. Take his father to the doctor. Get him some more help. Do something about his drinking, which was getting steadily worse.

'Are you still there? I've just been for one of my routine visits. I'm concerned by how much weight he's lost since I saw him last. Is he not eating properly?'

'I try to get him to eat properly but he's got very difficult about what he will eat. I leave sandwiches for him when I go out to work, and the carers are supposed to make him something but he doesn't seem to have much appetite.'

'And the drinking? Is that getting worse? I noticed he had a bottle of Scotch on the go. Do you buy alcohol for him?'

'No! No, of course not.' Ted was aware he sounded defensive but he couldn't help himself. 'The carers know they mustn't get him any either, although I think he bribes some of them. And he can still get himself out and round to the offy. I've tried asking them not to serve him but of course he's a good customer, they don't want to lose the trade. I've also tried getting him to go to AA. He just went the once and said it wasn't for him.'

'Have you tried going with him?'

There was no trace of reproach in her voice but it filled Ted with guilt. He knew he should be doing more to help his father, the person who'd been there for him and supported him when he was a child. He was a coward, he knew. Refusing to face the reality of what was happening.

'I will try. Honestly, I'll see what I can do to help him a bit more.'

'And the incontinence problem? That seems to be much worse than when I saw him last. Is there nothing that can be done to help him? It would improve his dignity no end.'

'He's had a lot of trouble with his waterworks, since the

accident, and it's been getting worse. Especially with the drinking. He refuses to have an in-dwelling catheter. We have tried, but he can be a stubborn old bugger. He's got single use ones and he is perfectly capable of using them. Trouble is, when he's had a few, his hands shake too much and he just gives up.'

It sounded like excuses. It was. Ted should be doing more and he knew it. The guilt was eating him up, driving him in his turn to drink more and more. Just one more snakebite with the lads. Anything to delay going home to find his father once more on the floor in his own mess.

'What about incontinence wear?'

Ted gave a short laugh, devoid of humour.

'I'm a policeman. I shoot people for a living. But I'm not brave enough to tell my dad he needs to start wearing nappies.'

'Would it help if I fixed up a review meeting? With your dad present, of course. And someone from the home carers. To discuss how we can meet his needs better. If I arrange it, would you be free to attend?'

'It's never easy, with work. My job's not predictable. I'm never sure when I'm going to be free.'

'We need to do something for him, Sergeant Darling, as a matter of some urgency now. It's not good at all that he's living like this. Not good for him and, I imagine, difficult for you, too. Leave it with me and I'll see what I can set up, as soon as possible.'

Chapter Eleven

Ted was anxious to get out of the office at lunchtime on Monday. He wanted to call at the nearest estate agents' office to at least test the water for putting his mother's house on the market, as she'd asked him to.

They'd said an emotional goodbye the previous morning. Ted had woken both her and Trev early with a cup of tea. Trev had about nine hours' driving in front of him, doing the Amman Valley and back in the same day, so he'd asked Ted to make sure he was up in good time.

Ted was consumed with guilt that it wasn't him taking his mother, or at least going with them to share the driving. But with Marston on his back and the case going nowhere, he didn't dare take the risk of absenting himself. There would be hell to pay if the Chief Super called a snap briefing and Ted was nearly five hours' drive away.

He grabbed a sandwich at his desk before deciding to walk round to the nearest agent. It would help him clear his head and organise his thoughts. He really didn't want to be doing anything as drastic as putting the house up for sale yet. He still clung to the faint hope that his mother would decide not to stay in Wales, once she'd recovered from her ordeal. He realised he was being selfish but he wasn't looking forward to losing her again so soon after she'd come back into his life.

The agent was helpful, upbeat. She mentioned a possible asking price which seemed reasonable and Ted promised to let her know as soon as he had chance to discuss it with his mother. They'd need to sort out what to do with her things before letting the agent show anyone round.

The number calling Ted's mobile, as he set off to walk back to the station, was masked so he answered with a guarded, 'Hello?'

'Seriously slack, Gayboy. There's not just me on your tail and you've not noticed either of us.'

Ted recognised the voice immediately. And there was only one person who would ever dare use that nickname to him. He carried on walking, just slowing his pace slightly. The hairs on the back of his neck were bristling.

'Understood,' he said neutrally. 'And do you have a suggestion of how to deal with the situation?'

'I've got your back. He's a rank amateur. He has no idea I'm there. Just lead us somewhere nice and quiet and we'll sort it.'

'Minimum force,' Ted said, more in hope than anticipation, as the call ended.

The man on the phone was Marty Green. His martial arts mentor. The man who had taught him everything he knew about self-defence and survival, plus a few skills Ted fervently hoped he would never have to use.

Green was a hard man. Ex-Paras, ex-SAS, ex-mercenary. Although Ted was never sure if the ex still held true in the last case. He'd met him in his own days as an SFO, a Specialist Firearms Officer, when Green had taught him Krav Maga. Depending on how big a threat was posed by whoever else was following him, he knew he was in safe hands with Green as his rearguard. He just had no idea if he could control him sufficiently to stop things passing beyond the bounds of legitimate defence.

There was a ginnel coming up not far in front of him. A passageway between buildings, high red brick walls making it a gloomy place, even in daylight. It wasn't much frequented. It would fit the bill nicely.

Ted ducked into it, walking along far enough to check there was no one around. Then he stopped and spun round lightly on the balls of his feet to face whatever threat was heading his way.

His action clearly startled the man following him. Ted could see straight away what Green had meant about an amateur. Nothing about the way he held himself suggested much of a threat. Not even when a knife appeared in his hand and he flicked open the blade.

He looked to be in his twenties. Skinny, acne marks on his cheeks, lank hair that looked in need of a wash poking out from under a knitted hat. Even with his weapon out, there was nothing particularly intimidating about him. Ted could have happily dealt with him himself, although he was more wary of tackling anyone with a knife since his serious injury from one.

'Can I help you?' Ted asked pleasantly, watching Green manoeuvre closer in total silence.

Ted had no idea what concealed weaponry Green might be carrying. Whatever it was he knew he would have no need of any of it. He could easily deal with a would-be attacker of this calibre with his bare hands, which knew so many ways to kill. Ted was almost feeling sorry for his stalker.

Green moved with the silent, stealthy menace of a panther. The man with the knife still had no clue as to the serious threat behind him. He lifted his knife arm and began to make wild, stabbing gestures towards Ted, which were clearly meant to be intimidating. Ted could see now that the hat was in fact a folded balaclava. His would-be attacker had obviously intended to pull it down before his prey saw him.

The speed and efficiency with which Green moved was such that Ted could barely follow the movements. In short order, the knife clattered to the floor as the man's arm was jerked up and out, the wrist bending back at such an angle that there was a loud, sickening crack as at least one carpal bone was fractured.

With a gesture almost of contempt, Green flung the man against the wall, moving in close to block his entire body with his own, his forearm across the failed assailant's throat. His face was barely an inch from the other man's as he spoke.

'Listen carefully, sonny. I don't like having to repeat myself.'

His voice was quiet, almost conversational. The menace in it was such that even Ted felt an involuntary shudder.

'This man is a friend of mine, and I don't have many. You're annoying him, with your silly little games. So why don't you piss off back to whoever sent you and tell them next time they need to send a man to do a proper job.'

'I don't know who he was!' the younger man gabbled, his face panic-stricken. 'Some bloke come up to me in a pub and gave me some money. Told me to follow that bloke and scare him a bit. That's all. I swear to God. Don't hurt me!'

'What did he look like, this man in the pub?' Ted asked him.

'I don't know, honest. Just some bloke. Talked posh, like. Built like a rugby player.' He threw a pleading look at Ted as he said, 'Please don't let him hurt me! I was just meant to follow you, scare you a bit. The knife was just for show, I swear.'

'Was it you in the car? You ran me off the road on Dan Bank.'

'I didn't mean to hurt you, honest. The bloke just told me to put the frighteners on you. Please just let me go. I won't come near you again. Promise. Don't let him hurt me. He's a fucking nutter.'

Green moved his own feet further apart and sneered as the front of the other man's trousers darkened and a thin trickle of urine snaked its way towards his scuffed military-issue DMS boots.

'You dirty little bastard. Think yourself lucky I don't make you lick my boots clean. It's about all you're fit for. Now piss off, you little piss-weasel. And if I hear you've been anywhere near my friend again, I will find you, and I will eat you.'

Green's voice went up in volume at the end of what he was saying, so that the cowering man let out an involuntary sound like a whimper. Then he stepped back to let the other run for it, taking a threatening swing at him as he did. Ted would have bet money that the final threat would have made him lose more than bladder control.

'Piss-weasel?' he asked mildly. 'Now suppose you tell me what you're doing here and why you're following me around?'

But Green was looking anxiously around him, unusually on edge, as he retrieved the knife from the ground, folding the blade away and putting it in his pocket. Ted had never seen him jumpy like that before. Things must be serious.

'We've been in one place for too long. We need to go somewhere to talk, in private.'

'I was on my way back to the nick. There's a pub just near it.'

'The Grapes. I know. Or The Grapes of Wrath, according to the modification to the sign.'

Ted's eyebrows went up.

'How long have you been watching me?'

'Long enough to know if I could risk making contact. It's not a good idea for us to be seen together anywhere public.'

'There's a back room at the pub. The landlord lets me use it sometimes. We could go there.'

'You go on your own. I'll make my own way there. I'll only come in if the coast is clear. If it's not, I'll bell you again.'

'As serious as that?'

'More so,' Green replied as he disappeared.

Ted walked briskly back towards the station, calling Jo's number on his mobile.

'Jo? I need to be somewhere for a while. I'm not sure how long. Call me if you need me, but cover for me if you possibly can. I won't be far away. There's just someone I need to see.'

'No worries, boss. We've got plenty to be getting on with. I'll only disturb you if it's absolutely essential. See you later.'

Something else Ted was grateful to the Ice Queen for – DI Jo Rodriguez. He was more than worth his weight in gold in freeing Ted up when necessary. He owed it to Green to find out what the problem was. It must be bad if he'd come to Ted for help. He was usually more than capable of taking care of himself.

Ted got the drinks in at the bar then asked the landlord, Dave, if he could use the back room for a short meeting with someone. Ted and his team were good customers. Dave was happy to help.

His mobile rang again as he was sitting down with his drink. An unknown number.

'Yes?'

'This room you're in. Is there a back way in?'

'Not officially, but I'll open it for you. Go round to the back yard.'

'I'm there now.'

Ted went through to open the back door for him. He knew Dave wouldn't ask questions. Close to, Green smelt of stale sweat and musty clothes. He clearly hadn't washed properly in a while and his grey stubble amounted almost to a full-face beard. There was dirt deeply ingrained in the skin of his hands and under his fingernails and Ted could see that he'd lost weight. He'd clearly been living rough for some time.

'I got you a bottle of Becks. Is that all right?'

Green sat down with his back to the wall, on a stool from which he had clear line of sight to both doors in the room, as well as the frosted glass window. He had a holdall with him which he'd not been carrying before. He carefully put it down on a second stool right next to him. Ted could imagine what it contained.

Almost half the bottle went down on the first few swallows. Ted knew Green would never drink more than the one bottle before switching to soft drinks. He was someone who could never afford to let his guard down, to be caught the worse for wear. He looked like a man who'd needed a drink, and could do with a good meal even more.

'Do you want to eat?'

Green shook his head.

'I need to eat, but not here. It's too public for me to stay long enough. I need your help, Ted, and you know I wouldn't ask you if I wasn't desperate. I need somewhere to lie low, just for a day or three. Somewhere safe and quiet where I can get some rest, eat a bit, get cleaned up. I wondered if you might be able to help.'

'I can't take you to my place,' Ted said, instantly wary, his immediate instinct wanting to protect Trev and the sanctuary of his home from whatever danger was clearly badly rattling Green.

'I wouldn't go there. It's the first place they'd look, and I know you've already had Spooks there in the past.'

'Just who are you on the run from?' Ted asked him, curious in spite of himself.

'The less you know, the better it is for you,' was all Green would say.

'As it happens, my mother's just gone away and I have the keys to her house. You could go there, for a few days. I could take you there now.'

'Far too risky. You mentioned your spotty friend running you off the road, so he knows your car. I don't want anything or anyone attracting attention to me. Give me the address and I'll make my own way there.'

'The neighbours might get curious enough to call the police, if they spot you arriving.'

Green threw him a scornful look.

'Nobody is going to know I'm there because I won't be

walking round with my head up my arse like you were doing earlier. You've clearly forgotten every bit of training I kicked into you.'

'Help yourself to anything you can find. I was going up to clear out the fridge later today anyway. My mother's gone away for a bit. Is there anything you need me to get you?'

Green reached into his pocket for a crumpled piece of paper.

'I made you a list. Other than that, I've got everything I need here.'

He patted the holdall with a gesture almost of affection. It confirmed Ted's initial thoughts about its contents.

'And for God's sake buck up a bit, Gayboy. Make sure you lose any tail before you come anywhere near the place. What about this man in the pub who's trying to get you scared off something? You'll need to get that sorted, and soon. And be very careful about how you let yourself into your mother's place while I'm there. You need your wits about you so you don't get any nasty surprises.'

'From the description, I'm pretty certain I know who's behind it. I recently arrested his daughter and had her charged on five counts of murder. She's currently remanded in secure custody. She's sixteen.'

Green got up to leave, completely unmoved by the news. He'd known worse. Far worse. Ted gave him the keys and the address and let him out the back way, promising to get up to the house, with his shopping, as soon as he could. First, he had somewhere to be, now he knew who was behind the recent scare tactics.

Ted went to find Jo as soon as he got back to the station. Maurice Brown was at his desk as Ted went through the main office so he stopped to have a word with him.

'Maurice, I'm going to need you shortly for something that's not quite, shall we say, exactly by the book. Someone I can trust to keep quiet about it.'

'Sounds right up my street then, boss. Just say when and where.'

'Jo, I need to disappear again for a bit and take Maurice with me this time,' Ted told his DI when he went into his office. 'Is there anything I should know about before I do?'

Jo looked up at him enquiringly.

'Nothing here, boss. But you're being very mysterious. Is there anything I should know about?'

'It's nothing of any significance, really. We won't be long. It's just something I need to nip in the bud before it gets completely out of hand. Something I need a witness for, hence Maurice.'

'You're the boss, boss. If you say so. I presume you know what you're doing.'

Ted wasn't sure he shared his confidence but he had to do something. He filled Maurice in briefly on the details as they walked across the car park together to Ted's official car. He handed Maurice the keys.

'So Edwards is not likely to be thrilled at getting a visit from you, alive and kicking, boss? I assume he might be tempted to shut the door in our faces, which is where someone of my build comes in handy.'

Maurice was right. They found Clive Edwards at home, as Ted had hoped they would. He knew he worked from home. He had no idea if he was still able to work since Ted had arrested his young daughter for a series of horrendous crimes. As soon as Edwards saw who was on his doorstep ringing the bell, he tried to shut the door. Maurice took a step forward, making it impossible.

Ted's would-be attacker had been spot-on in his description. With his thick neck and broad shoulders, Edwards looked as if he would have made a useful addition to any local club in a rugby scrum and his accent could well appear posh to some.

'Mr Edwards,' Ted said, pleasantly enough, 'we just need to come in and have a quick word with you, please.'

It was a difficult interview. Although it was not particularly cold, Edwards was wearing a shapeless fleece which Ted recognised. He had seen it on the man's daughter, Morgane, the first time he'd clapped eyes on her. There was something unsettling about seeing her father wearing it now. There was still a lingering trace of her scent on it.

As they talked to him, the man went from blustering angrily through hurling abuse and threats at Ted, to sobbing uncontrollably. He was still refusing to accept that his daughter could possibly be capable of any of the charges she was facing

Ted's voice stayed quiet and calm, but he did need to mark Edwards' card for him.

'Mr Edwards, it's important that you understand that even if something were to happen to me, Morgane's trial would still go ahead. Even if I wanted to halt it, it's not in my power to do so. Which means that you're wasting your time with this campaign against me.

'I got a good description of you from the man you paid to try to scare me off. Enough for me to know it was you and to come round here. Enough for me to have you charged with a serious offence. But I don't want to have to do that. I think you're probably suffering enough. I also think that what happened with Morgane has caused you to lose your judgement and behave inappropriately.

'But I'm here to tell you, Mr Edwards, that this stops. Now. You're not helping anyone by your actions. Certainly not Morgane. I can promise you that she will have a fair trial, but that's all I can promise you. I can't guarantee the outcome. I can tell you that if you persist in this behaviour, the next time anyone knocks on your door, it will be to arrest you, not just to ask you politely to stop. And you're going to be of absolutely no use in supporting your daughter if you are yourself locked up. Do you understand what I'm telling you, Mr Edwards?'

Chapter Twelve

Ted had kept his phone on silent while he was talking to Edwards. He checked it as they went back to the car and saw there were several missed calls from Marston. He decided he'd wait until he got back to the office in the optimistic hope that Jo would have some news of a breakthrough for him, which he could then pass on.

Jo was the only one in when they got back. Ted had, that morning, authorised Jezza to go off and start working on her own on the happy slappers. Ted's was one of the few phone numbers she had saved to the phone she would be using, along with Virgil's. He was also adept at looking nothing like a copper when the need arose.

'The Big Chief's been looking for you, boss,' Jo told him, as soon as Ted went into his office. 'I explained that you were briefing the team on new developments and you'd call him back as soon as you'd finished.'

'Have I got new developments to brief them on?' Ted asked hopefully.

'Nothing to get wildly excited about, but there have been some calls about the likeness Magnus's officers have been putting up around Wilmslow, and even a name or two suggested. I sent Rob and Sal over there to help with checking them out.'

Marston sounded almost disappointed when Ted phoned to apologise for the delay and to explain that they were chasing up leads on a possible ID of the killer. He was clearly more interested in seeing Ted fail than bringing a criminal to justice.

'Well, keep me up to date at all times. I want a full written report at the end of each day. I expect to see some progress, and soon.'

He ended the call abruptly. Ted headed for the kettle and the comfort of a mug of green tea. He wanted to get back up to see Green and take him the things he'd asked for, as soon as possible. He also needed to get home to collect the spare keys to his mother's house before Trev got back from work. He was quite likely to take them to go and clear out whatever his mother had left in the fridge and check that everywhere was secure, thinking he was helping. The last thing Ted wanted to happen was for Trev to come face to face with the new lodger. Green was highly trained, enough to distinguish a real threat from an innocent civilian wandering into his line of fire. But as hyped up and wary as he currently was, anything could happen.

Ted caught up with all his messages and emails then went back to see Jo.

'Have we cross-checked the names being suggested from the likeness against known associates of Kateb?'

'On it now, boss. Nothing up to now. I don't want to make assumptions but I'm getting the feeling there's no substance to our info so far. But I've also contacted Fraud for a wider list, associates of associates, if they have such a thing. See if that throws anything up.'

'Excellent, thank you. The Chief Super wants a daily written update from me, and I'll be back to do that as soon as I can, if you can forward anything you've got. But I do need to disappear again for a short while. I'm sorry to keep asking you to cover for me, and I wouldn't if it wasn't essential but ...'

'Like I said, you're the boss, and you've never given me any reason not to trust you – yet. I have to warn you, though. I know full well the team would kill me if I didn't make sure you weren't putting yourself in any danger. I've no idea how, you with your martial arts and me being a lover, not a fighter. But I would try, boss.'

Ted grinned, in spite of himself.

'Thanks, Jo. I appreciate your loyalty. And loyalty is what this is all about. I'm having to help out a friend in need and it's … complicated. It always is, where this particular person is concerned.'

Ted left his car a street away from his mother's house and made the rest of the journey on foot, carrying Green's shopping in two carrier bags, held in one hand. Before he went through the garden gate, he put the bags down to make a show of searching his pockets for the keys, taking the opportunity to check all around that there was no sign of anyone watching him. None of the nearby parked cars had any occupants in. If he was being observed, it was from some distance away, through binoculars or the lens of a high-powered camera, but he could see no indication of it.

He let himself in and shut the door before he spoke. Any of the neighbours who happened to be passing would think it strange, him calling out, knowing that the house should have been empty. He spoke quietly.

'It's me. I come in peace. Take me to your leader.'

There was no sign or sound of anyone. From the kitchen came the delicious wafted smells of frying bacon. Still keeping the bags in one hand, so he was free to put up at least some sort of a defence should it be required, Ted headed that way, down the narrow hall.

The kitchen was empty. The heat had been turned off under the frying pan but the bacon was still crackling and spitting in the hot fat, so it had been recently done. The table was set for one. Everywhere was immaculately tidy. Green, like many soldiers, always kept his personal space perfectly organised so there was nothing to encumber him if he needed to move fast.

Ted was just about to turn round and start searching the house when once again he felt the hairs on the back of his neck start to stand up. He dropped the bags and pivoted on the balls of his feet in one fluid movement, his right arm instinctively going up to protect himself from any possible knife attack.

Instead he found himself staring at the unwavering, unblinking eye of a Glock, held in Green's rock-steady hand.

Green had a pleasant smile on his face as he said quietly, 'Boo!'

'Shit!'

Ted's hand went automatically to his chest where his heart was suddenly dancing a jig, as adrenalin flooded his body

'You did a bit better this time, Gayboy. At least you weren't being tailed to the door. I was just making myself some bacon banjoes. Your mother has good taste in bacon.'

He'd clearly had a long soak and a clean-up. He was wearing track suit bottoms and an ancient, washed-out rugby shirt with the Springboks' emblem. Ted knew he had connections to Africa, which probably explained the way he massacred some of his vowel sounds. He'd seen from the time he had spent with him in the past that Green had a springbok tattooed on his chest, as well as regimental badges of the Paras and the SAS on his upper arms.

The washing machine was already turning. Green had shaved off his beard, leaving just a full moustache. It showed hollow cheeks, emphasising how much weight he'd lost since Ted had seen him last, on a punishing training march in the Brecon Beacons.

Green padded silently across the kitchen in bare feet, heading for his food. Ted noticed a mug with the strings of at least three teabags showing. He couldn't help wondering if his mother's china would ever recover from the onslaught.

'I got what you wanted,' he told him, putting the bags down next to the table.

'I'll have to owe you, until it's safe for me to go out to the bank.'

Ted knew Green was well paid for the work he did. The

man had also told him once, in a rare moment of talking about himself, that he had a wife and four grown-up children, to whom he regularly sent money. He hadn't seen them in years.

'That's no problem. I trust you. So, are you going to tell me a bit about what's going on?'

Ted went to make himself a cup of tea while Green sat down and attacked the first of his sandwiches like a starving man. He spoke between mouthfuls, eating methodically and systematically. Although he'd complimented the bacon, he was as much refuelling his body of necessity as eating for the sheer pleasure of it.

'Like I said, you're better off not knowing too much. But you're helping me, and I appreciate it, so I'll give you the bare bones. I'm sometimes asked to do jobs for various agencies. Special jobs, which could compromise them if they used one of their own operatives and it all went tits up. I'm expendable. If I get caught, the trail back to them would be extremely hard to follow. I'd just be passed off as a psychopathic lone wolf suffering from PTSD.

'Unfortunately, because it's all done on the hush-hush, other agencies often don't know that the operation was sanctioned from high up and may decide to come after me. None of them have succeeded – yet. I usually just drop out of sight until things calm down. And that's all you need to know for now.

'But tell me what's got you so distracted you're wandering around in a daze. Your boyfriend playing away while you're busy playing cops and robbers?'

Ted wouldn't have taken that from anyone else. From Green, it was just a matter-of-fact question, with no hidden agenda.

'Tricky case, bastard of a new boss who hates me and thinks I'm a crap copper. And with so little progress made to date, I'm not sure I can entirely blame him for that opinion.'

Ted finished making himself a brew whilst he was

speaking. His mother's brand of tea was stronger than he preferred, so he barely dunked the teabag in the boiling water. Because he couldn't resist the smell, he cut a slice off the loaf of bread Green had started on, dipped it in the hot bacon fat and started to devour it, realising that the earlier sandwich was but a distant memory. It was still edible, although the bread was no longer fresh. Green was right about the bacon. It tasted excellent.

Green paused in his eating to take a large swallow of the tea. Seeing how stained the inside of the mug was looking already, Ted wondered idly what all that tannin was doing to his insides.

'Tell me about the case. It's possible I might be able to help while I'm holed up here kicking my heels. I have good contacts.'

Ted knew that Green had the highest level of security clearance, so there was no problem over sharing confidential information with him. Just as he knew that, because of the type of agencies he worked for, Green would almost certainly have authorisation to carry the Glock at all times.

He gave him the broad outlines of the case then added, 'I'm not asking you to take anyone out, though. Just so we're clear on that.'

Green scoffed, then took another swallow of his tea.

'You couldn't afford me, not on a copper's budget, for sure.

He finished eating, wiped his mouth and fingers fastidiously on paper kitchen towels, then took his plate to the sink and washed it up, firing suggestions at Ted as he did so.

'You've checked the forger, of course? Tried to trace the one supplying the phony police badges? I know some people who supply stuff of that quality so I can ask around. I can probably find out much more in half an hour on the mobile than you lot could do in a few hours of legwork. Although that side should be easy enough, I might be better leaving that to you and looking at other stuff which I can probably access more easily than you can.'

He sat back at the table with his cup of tea before continuing.

'I've found, from bitter experience, that when a usually successful MO goes as badly wrong as this one did, it's often down to nepotism. I had a young officer foisted on me for a very difficult operation once. A completely useless arse-wipe, but the son of a colonel. He was assigned to my troop, and he risked getting us all killed. I had a little word with him.'

Ted could just imagine what the 'little word' had consisted of. He'd been on the receiving end of more than a few himself, in his time, when being trained by Green.

'If I were you, I'd look at someone who might have been brought in because of who they were related to, not any skills they could bring to the party. Does your man Kateb have kids, for instance?'

Ted shook his head.

'We don't know much about his personal life. Intelligence so far suggests he's not married, and he would be too young to have fathered children old enough to do this type of work in any event. We're trying to look at anyone outside the usual gang circle.'

'Has he got a bit on the side? Another woman who might have older kids? Someone who might pester him to take their sprog along? A kid not experienced enough to hold it together when things got difficult?'

'He's been under observation for some time and there's nothing in the notes that I've seen to indicate that he might have a mistress.'

Another snort of contempt.

'Observation? What, the same incompetent tossers who decided to concentrate on him rather than the mark and lost him? A decision which may just possibly have cost a woman her life?

'It's going to depend on the dynamics of this gang, but it must have been someone with some clout to have let in anyone that inexperienced to handle such a delicate and important part of the operation. If you've not found a body yet – although you may never find it of course – that suggests even more to me that this is a case of keeping it in the family. If they've not taken them out, they're keeping them under wraps until they can move them somewhere safe. So you need to be looking for a son, a nephew, a brother of someone high up. Someone who decided to let them have a go when they weren't up to it.'

Ted was interrupted by his mobile phone before he could answer. Trev calling him. He answered with his work voice, so he would know he was not alone.

'Hey, you, I was just going up to Annie's to clear out the fridge and have a check that everything is all right, but I can't find the spare keys.'

'Yes, sorry, I picked them up by mistake, forgetting I had mine. Senior moment, probably. I'm just about to go there now, as it goes, so don't worry about it. I'll have to go back into the office so I'm not sure what time I'll be back. Eat when you're hungry, don't wait for me.'

Trev laughed.

'What are you like? You're going senile. I'll see you when I see you. Love you.'

'You too,' Ted told him, feeling embarrassed with Green in the room.

'The boyfriend?'

'The partner,' Ted corrected him. 'I took both sets of keys, so he couldn't drop in on you.'

'It would be in his best interests if you didn't tell him I was here,' Green told him warningly.

Ted left, wondering if he was doing the right thing in sheltering him. His suggestions were helpful, though. It had given him another new direction in which to look. He'd submit it in his report to Marston before he left for the evening. He never liked taking credit for someone else's ideas, but he was not about to mention Green's presence to anyone.

As he walked back to his car, he phoned ahead to see if Sal was still in the station and to ask him to wait for him if he was. He had a feeling Marston was the sort to grab all the glory for himself and Ted wanted to make sure it was known that the latest idea was not the Chief Super's own. He'd heard plenty of rumours which suggested that was how Marston's promotions had been so rapid. He let someone else do the legwork then he took all the credit.

'Sal, I know you still have good contacts in Fraud so I want you to pass on an idea I got through talking to someone. I'll be sending my report through to the Chief Super later on, but just to give them an early heads up,' he told him when he got back to the station.

'A friend was telling me about something they'd encountered in the forces. It's just a possibility that whoever was brought in to do the pick-up was related to someone either high up in the gang, or connected to someone who is. If nothing shows up on the contacts we have so far, we need to check carefully if Kateb or anyone else in the upper echelons has a mistress who's not yet on the radar. Someone who might have a son, perhaps, who wanted the job.

'Has anyone heard anything from Jezza today? I know she's not likely to be in touch yet, but I just wondered. Virgil?'

'Nothing, boss. We left it that she'd only contact me in an emergency, but otherwise she'd see you on Wednesday at the dojo to report in.'

'And everything's going to be all right with Tommy, Maurice?'

'Should be fine, boss. Me and Steve are staying at the flat. Once he and Steve get playing on the computer, he barely notices whether Jezza is at home or not. Plus she'll phone him when she can.'

It was getting late by the time Ted had done his report and sent it through, as well as sorting out his paperwork in case of another unscheduled visit from Marston.

Trev was in the kitchen when he got home. He'd clearly eaten, his crockery and cutlery sided to the work surface but, as usual, not having made it as far as the dishwasher. He had his TEFL paperwork all over the table, a couple of the cats sitting on some of it and watching him in fascination as he worked. He was humming totally tunelessly to himself as he did so.

'Hey. Do you want food? I just need to heat it up.'

Ted bent to kiss him then sank into the next chair.

'I am hungry, if it's not too much trouble.'

'Did you empty Annie's fridge? Where are the contents? Did you forget and leave them in the car? Another senior moment?'

'Ah,' Ted said, cursing himself inwardly that he hadn't prepared a cover story. Trev had been right. He was rubbish at lying, so much so that he hadn't even thought of something to say.

'Ted, you're behaving very strangely. What's going on? Why didn't you let me go to Annie's?'

'I don't want you going there just at the moment. Can you just accept that, without asking too many questions?'

Trev sat back down and looked at him, his face concerned.

'No, I can't, and you worry me when you say stuff like that. I want to know what's going on. Are you in some kind of trouble? Why won't you tell me? I thought we'd sorted out the trust issues.'

'It's sometimes better if you don't know stuff.'

'Now you've got me really worried. You can't leave it like that. What's going on?'

Ted sighed and took hold of one of Trev's hands. He told him the edited highlights of his encounter with the same young man who'd run him off the road. He said only that someone he knew had come to his aid and that, as they currently had nowhere to stay, he was letting them doss at his mother's house. He explained it was someone who valued their privacy so he would prefer Trev not to go there for the time being. He didn't believe half of what he was saying himself. He hoped it didn't sound quite as lame to Trev.

'But Edwards tried to kill you and you're doing nothing about it? Ted, you can't let him get away with it. You say you've warned him off, but what if he takes no notice? What if he gets someone more up to the job and they come after you and do you serious harm? You have to bring him in.'

'It'll be fine, really. Trust me. The man's broken. Think of what he's been going through, and he still has the ordeal of the trial, and the verdict, to get through. It's only natural he blames it all on me. He'll let it drop now. I'm sure he will. Don't worry.'

Chapter Thirteen

Ted was not at all surprised to get an early morning summons to a briefing at Central Park. This time it was in the form of a circular text to all involved, which arrived while he was in the shower. It was followed shortly by a call from the Ice Queen saying she would pick him up in her official car in twenty minutes.

He was washed and dressed in time, but only managed to gulp half a mug of green tea and swallow a round of toast before he heard the car pull up outside. He scribbled a hasty note to Trev to say that once again, he had no idea what time he would be back.

'New developments, I understand,' the Super said by way of greeting, as her driver turned the car round at the end of the cul-de-sac in which Ted lived.

'We had a bit of a breakthrough last night, with an idea or two, which I sent through to Mr Marston.'

'Which he will no doubt be about to claim as all his own work.'

She surprised him by her comment. Even more so by her acerbic tone. She clearly had Marston's number but he was shocked she had voiced her feelings in front of him, let alone in front of her driver. No doubt he was carefully selected and vetted to make the Three Wise Monkeys seem like gossips, but it was still a departure for her.

'He wasn't the only one we passed it on to, so he might not get the chance.'

She surprised him again with a smile of amusement. He seldom saw her smile, in the work setting.

'I never had you down as a game player, Ted.'

They arrived in time to get a drink and a limp Danish from the long table down the side of the conference room before Marston marched in and called the briefing to order. The liquid refreshment was no better than on the previous occasion. Tepid, unidentifiable.

'Right, everyone, in light of new information I've received, we're widening the scope of our investigation into the gang members.'

Ted noticed he gave no credit for where the idea had come from. It didn't bother him, as he'd never expected him to.

Marston laid out for those assembled the sort of information they were now looking for. He looked surprised and irritated when a member of the Major Fraud Team stood up to interrupt him.

'Sorry, sir, but we're a bit ahead of you there, although we haven't had time to update you until now. We got the same intelligence late yesterday and made a start on it. We have some updated information now, if you'd like me to present it at this point?'

Marston flapped an irritable hand and told him to get on with it.

'Samir Kateb has a cousin, Damon Bacha, who's in France. As far as we know at present, he's not involved in Kateb's scam operation. He has a business sending Moroccan goods to the UK. Ceramics, rugs, leather goods, that type of thing. It seems to be decent stuff, not tourist tat.'

'Is there a point to all this, Inspector Smith?' Marston asked testily. 'I doubt if any of us are planning on buying the merchandise.

'Sorry, sir, yes, just getting there. Bacha has a son, Dorian, twenty-two. We're not sure, from our enquiries to date, where he is at the moment. We've only just got started on this line of enquiry following a suggestion to look at wider family. We've just begun checking flights into Manchester from anywhere in France with a Dorian Bacha on board, but of course, we don't know if, let alone when, he may have arrived in the country. He could even have travelled with one of the vehicles his father uses for his export business.'

'This is all very tentative. Have we nothing at all more concrete than that to go on? What about the names suggested in Wilmslow? Have they all been checked yet, and have they thrown anything up? Any mysterious sightings of Moroccans?'

'French, sir,' the inspector from Fraud corrected him. 'Bacha junior is a French national. And his father, and Kateb's family, are naturalised French, of Algerian origin.'

'Thank you, we're all capable of reading the notes. I was using the term figuratively. Chief Inspector Darling, what is the latest from Wilmslow?'

'Sir, none of the sightings or names suggested has led us anywhere useful for now. All the names provided have been checked out and have solid alibis for the time in question. Following on from what Inspector Smith just said, may I ask him a further question and then perhaps make a suggestion?'

In an open meeting, there was little Marston could reasonably do except to tell Ted to go ahead. He looked across the room at Neil Smith, from Fraud, and asked, 'Neil, is there any suspicion of anything else coming in with Bacha's merchandise? Any hash in the handbags or anything like that.'

Smith threw him a grateful look as he replied, 'I was just coming to that, sir. Nothing definite, no arrests or anything. I've been talking to the French police and they've had the operation under observation for some time now, with that in mind. They had a tip-off which might, of course, just be rival dealers trying to stitch Bacha up, but there was suggestion of drugs and possibly arms being shipped along with the other, legit, merchandise.'

Seeing that Marston was about to interrupt again, Ted put

in quickly, 'Sir, if there is any suggestion of arms coming in this way, is it worth contacting Counter Terrorism Units to see if any of them are involved in monitoring the company, and if they may have more intelligence than we do at the present?'

'How have we gone from rugs and bags to terrorism? I'm surprised at you, of all people, Darling, making the judgemental leap. Not everyone from a Muslim country is a terrorist.'

'Sir, I think France is actually a secular country,' Ted said smoothly, 'and just because the family are originally from Algeria, we don't yet know what religion, if any, they follow. I just made the suggestion because, as you know, Counter Terrorism have a way of finding out information more quickly than we do, in many cases. Would you like me to make some enquiries? I have one or two contacts still who may be of use.'

Again, there was nothing Marston could do in public other than to agree, but not with any good grace. And once more, Ted was sure he saw his own Super lower her head to hide a smile.

Detective Superintendent Jim Baker erupted into the main office, flinging the door open then slamming it shut, using one of his crutches, with such ferocity that the hinges creaked in protest. It had clearly cost him some effort to stump up the stairs, with his leg still in a plaster cast.

There weren't many team members in. Those who were looked up in alarm. The DSU was a big man. At the moment he had the look of a grizzly bear which someone had foolishly poked awake with a sharp stick, long before hibernation was over. It didn't help the overall impression that he was clearly in a lot of pain, which his medication was not keeping under control.

His angry eyes glanced round the room, falling on Rob O'Connell, the most senior present, as a DS. Rob half rose to his feet, hesitantly, not quite sure what was going on but certain it didn't bode well for someone.

'Who's in?' the Big Boss barked.

'Just us four, sir, and the boss, in his office.'

'You three,' he jerked his chin at Rob, Maurice and Steve. 'Piss off out and do policeman stuff. Come back in half an hour.'

Then he looked across at the CFI, working away on her hi-tech computer at things he wouldn't profess to fully understand.

'You. Ocean, isn't it? Go and get a cup of tea. Same to you. Back in half an hour. No sooner.'

He didn't quite get her name right but Océane wisely deduced it was not the best moment to pull him up on his pronunciation.

Steve was already hurrying out of the door, Rob not far behind him. Only Maurice Brown stubbornly stood his ground, looking defiantly at the Big Boss.

'What part of piss off did you not understand, DC Brown? Don't try to cover for him. Not this time. You're better off keeping out of it.'

Ted had been on the phone in his office when he'd heard the door crash. He'd wound up the conversation as soon as he could and had come out of his door into the main office to see what was going on. He opened his mouth to greet the Big Boss in their usual joking fashion.

The Big Boss's voice was a snarl as he bellowed, 'You! Back inside. DC Brown, if you know what's good for you, do one. Now.'

Ted backed meekly into his office and headed instinctively for his kettle. He was clearly in line for a monumental bollocking but he couldn't for the life of him think what for. At least, he couldn't think of anything Jim might know about which would warrant one.

The two of them may have been good friends outside work but they were both policemen, first and foremost, and good coppers. Jim was his boss, more than capable of handing down discipline when necessary. And because Ted respected Jim as much as he liked him, he would take it. He just couldn't figure out what Jim knew about, or how he'd come by the intelligence.

The door to Ted's office suffered the same fate as the outer door, making the whole partition wall shake as it crashed closed. Ted was just about to make Jim a coffee when the Big Boss pulled him up short.

'This is not a social call. I want to know since when do you think you have the right to decide what bloody laws we uphold and which we ignore?'

'Ah,' Ted said quietly. It was what he always said when he knew he had to measure his words carefully before giving a response.

Jim was showing no signs of sitting down. He was standing, propped up on his crutches, a light sheen of sweat on his face at the physical effort the stairs had cost him, looking fit to explode. Ted didn't sit either. He stood behind his chair, his hands resting on the back of it, and tried to formulate his words carefully. It would help if he knew what the Big Boss knew.

'Someone tried to kill you. Twice. And all you've done about it is go round and ask him nicely to stop. Is that about the long and the short of it?'

'How did ...?'

'Never mind about how I bloody know. I just bloody do. You're a police officer, Ted, for god's sake. It's your job to uphold the law, not to pick and choose which bits of it. You know perfectly well all this not wanting to press charges shite only happens in crime fiction. So, someone ran you off the road and you did nothing.'

'I didn't really have anything to go on.' Ted was aware as he said it how weak it sounded. 'It could just have been bad driving, and I didn't get a number. I reported it, though, as a damage only.'

'That was bloody big of you! It's your job, Ted, dammit, I shouldn't have to remind you of that. Did you check CCTV? No! Basic bloody errors. So now tell me about the man with the knife.'

'Ah,' Ted said again.

'Never mind bloody ah!' Jim's voice went up a few more decibels. 'Someone made an armed assault on a police officer and it seems all you've done about it is go round and have a cosy chat with the person behind it. Because you know full well who it is and you've chosen to do nothing about it. Isn't that the case?

'Please tell me you didn't go there on your own? That you have an independent witness of what was said? Who went with you?'

'I'd rather not say, boss,' Ted said, looking mutinous. He would always defend his team, against all odds. 'It was my error of judgement; it's not right that anyone else gets the blame for my actions.'

'Bloody Maurice Brown, then. I knew it from the way he was behaving just now. And he's just about stupid enough to let you get yourself into a mess like this. If this Edwards bloke has a contract out on you, you should have brought him in and had him interviewed under caution, at the very least. What happens if he ignores you and next time he's successful?'

'Boss, I put his teenage daughter away. She's likely to get life with a recommendation she's never released. He's a broken man. A father. He didn't want me killed, just scared off. Imagine the publicity if I arrested him as well as the daughter.'

'You arrested a psychopathic serial killer. Which is your job. It's what you get paid for. You do not get to choose which laws you uphold. You're a senior serving officer. You should know better. You'd better start talking and it better be good because I tell you this, Ted. I am a whisker away from taking your badge and sending you home.'

'It's … complicated. I was with someone. When the knife

attack happened. Between us, we dealt with it with no trouble. But it's someone I can't involve in this. Which is why I let it drop and just went round to have a word with Edwards. It should be over now.'

'And who is this mysterious other person?' Then, seeing Ted open his mouth, he cut across him, 'And don't even think of saying bloody ah again.'

Despite the situation, Ted couldn't hide a grin. Jim knew him so well.

'I think we perhaps both need to go and talk to Debs about this whole thing.'

That took Baker by surprise. He was amazed at Ted voluntarily involving his other boss, Superintendent Caldwell, in all of this. He'd happily take a kick up the backside from Jim, but the Ice Queen was a stickler for formality. She'd be far more likely to make it official. Ted could find himself in the situation of having a less than favourable report on his otherwise excellent record, at the least.

'Are you sure that's what you want to do?'

'Oh, I'm sure. She knows who the other person is, and she'll no doubt be in agreement with me that we need to protect his identity at all costs.'

Jim was intrigued now, though still angry. He turned and led the way, slowly, awkwardly and painfully, down to the Ice Queen's office. She looked up in surprise as the two men trooped in, after the briefest of knocks. She glanced from one to the other shrewdly then stood up and went to the coffee machine.

'Gentlemen,' she said by way of greeting. 'I'm sensing this is not a social call. I'm also getting the feeling that coffee may be of help to us all. Please sit down.'

Ted talked, while she prepared the drinks, placing them on the desk then sitting down. She said nothing, allowing Ted to finish.

'The other man was Marty Green. He's up here because he

needs somewhere to hole up for a while, so he has to keep a low profile. Debs and I can both probably hazard a guess as to why.'

'Well, I bloody can't,' Jim Baker grumbled. 'Who is this Green and why are you both shielding him? Is he's some sort of criminal?'

Ted looked at the Ice Queen and nodded to her to speak.

'Ted and I have both met Green in our Firearms days. He's used by the police and other services for teaching special skills, including martial arts and personal survival. He's,' she hesitated, then continued, 'unorthodox. He's sometimes hired by certain services to carry out tasks which, let's say, may not be suitable for them to risk using their usual operatives on.'

Jim looked at her in astonishment over the rim of his coffee cup.

'Are you telling me he's a Spook?'

'He's someone it's not really possible to categorise. Let's just say that it would be best if minions at our level were to leave him well alone when he says he needs to stay under the radar.'

She looked at Ted again as she asked, 'Is he still on our patch?'

'I've sorted him with a safe house for now. Not an official one. He just needs somewhere to lick his wounds for a few days then he'll be out of our hair. It's also best that neither of you knows where he is. That way you're not compromised.'

Jim was shaking his head in disbelief.

'This is all going way over my head,' he grumbled. 'If Debs says that's the way it needs to be, then I'll accept it. But we can't just let the Edwards matter drop, even if we have to leave this man Green out of it.'

'Jim, I'm sorry, you're right, of course,' Ted said contritely. 'I'll get the DI to bring him in and interview him under caution. We haven't enough to charge him, and he probably realises it, but at least that makes it official, puts it on the record. I should have put you in the picture earlier and I apologise for not doing so.'

It was a weary Ted who finally got home, later than usual. Trev was in the kitchen, looking anxious. Ted went over to kiss him on the cheek then sank down in the nearest chair, reaching out a hand to stroke the procession of cats which appeared to greet him.

'Tough day?' Trev asked, sitting down next to him and taking hold of his other hand.

'Jim chewed me up good and proper. What you see before you are the mangled remains he spat out when he'd finished.'

'I'm sorry. Are you all right?'

Ted abandoned the cats to take Trev's hand in both of his as he smiled gently.

'It's all right. Everything's all right now. I know it was you who told Jim. He didn't tell me, of course. But I know it had to be you. And I understand you did it because you were worried about me, because you care about me. So it's fine. We're fine. Everything's going to be fine. I'm past the stage of wanting to eat, so why don't we just have an early night?'

Chapter Fourteen

It was even less of a surprise for Ted to get a call from Marston again first thing the following morning, sounding tetchier than usual. He was at his mother's house when the call came through, catching up with Green and asking his advice about making good use of Counter Terrorism.

'What the fuck was all that shit about terrorists and arms dealers yesterday? Were you trying to make me look a total twat, bringing something like that up in public without discussing it with me first?'

As soon as he began speaking, or rather, shouting, down the phone, Ted held it slightly away from his ear so Green could get the gist of the conversation.

'Sorry, sir, that was certainly not my intention. It was just something which came to me, so I thought I'd mention it.'

Green grinned at him and made a coarse gesture with his hand, expressing his opinion of the unknown, to him, caller.

'We all know you like playing cowboys, waving a big weapon about. But this is my operation, and I'm the one who decides which direction it goes in. I'll say if and when I decide to bring in any other units. Is that perfectly clear?'

'Yes, sir, completely clear.'

Marston rang off without another word as Green laughed aloud and asked, 'Why do you take that kind of shit, Gayboy?'

'Rank structure. You know how it is. I'm stuck with him on this case, whether I like it or not. And he's always careful how he speaks to me in public. He'll get his comeuppance. My team are good. We'll get him his killer, and he's welcome to take the glory. We'll just get on with doing the job.'

'I'll make a few phone calls, find out if anyone knows anything about this lot you're investigating. Might as well do something while I'm around. One thing I do need to do is a good training workout. Is there a dojo you can get me into?'

'I'm going to my own this evening, as it happens, but that wouldn't do. I need to take you to the Krav Maga club I use occasionally, on the other side of the Pennines. That's suitably discreet and better for your needs. I'll see what I can fix up. Getting away will be the problem for me. I can get you in there, it's just the transport. You've not got a vehicle with you?'

Green gave him one of his knowing looks.

'I always have a vehicle at my disposal, wherever I am. But you need seriously sorting out as well. I can't believe how sloppy you've got again. It would be a good idea for you to come, too.'

'Leave it with me. I'll see what I can arrange.'

It was a day for early morning encounters. Ted was surprised when the Ice Queen came up to his office, before even his team members were in for morning briefing. She, like him, was often an early bird. He wondered what had brought her this time.

'If your kettle is hot, I would quite like some green tea,' she began, sitting down in the spare chair opposite him.

'Do I sense I'm not going to like what you have to say?'

'Almost certainly not. But I am nevertheless obliged to say it. Or at least to ask it. I know you get asked this question every year, and that every year you refuse, sometimes slightly more forcefully than others. So I do hope you will remember that I am merely the messenger.'

Ted banged the mugs down on the desk so that the liquid in them sloshed about dangerously.

'This is about Pride? The Chief Constable wants to know if I have any views on a recruitment drive to attract more gay people to join the force? Tell him that I'll give an opinion on that once he can assure me that every officer of my rank in the force is consulted on every recruitment drive for an event which is not LGBT orientated.'

Ted took a large swallow of his tea. It was too hot and made him wince. Then he grinned apologetically.

'Sorry, I didn't mean to shoot the messenger. I just wish he could understand how it comes across when he singles me out for something like this.'

The Super was sipping daintily and more cautiously at her tea, not making the same mistake. Ted took another gulp, smaller this time, before he continued.

'On reflection, though, I think I may have been a little hasty in my reaction. Tell him that this time, since you asked me so nicely, I'd be more than happy to have a look at what was planned and give him my input. As a serving police officer of rank who is in a same sex relationship. You'd better just warn him that using the phrase "openly gay" in my presence is always guaranteed to make the red mist descend, since nobody ever says "openly straight".'

She was studying him suspiciously.

'Now you have me worried. As I said before, I've never considered you to be a game player yet you're showing distinct signs of it lately. You've always refused point blank, every year, and now you're meekly acquiescing. I'm wondering what the hidden agenda might be?'

This time Ted's smile was guilty.

'With Marston in charge of Croesus, it might be an opportune moment for me to make sure I still have friends in high places.'

'Well, while you're feeling amenable, I'll mention the second thing which brings me up here. The Chief Constable has been following the progress of the Mini Police project in

Durham and Merseyside. He's very keen to trial the initiative, and has decided that we, in Stockport, would be ideal guinea pigs to roll it out.

'It will, of course, come under Inspector Turner's remit. But because of the excellent work you do with young people in your self-defence club, the Chief Constable was wondering if you would consider assisting him in some way?'

Ted looked at her in disbelief. Had it been anyone other than the straight-laced Superintendent, he would have suspected a practical joke, to see how far he could be provoked before losing it. He could just imagine how Kevin Turner felt about it, with staffing levels at an all-time low. He hoped it wouldn't aggravate his stomach ulcers.

The idea of the scheme was to have children aged from nine to eleven volunteering to tackle local issues through community engagement events. Even if he had time for it, it was not the type of thing with which Ted would normally willingly get involved. He could see the surprise on the Ice Queen's face as he replied.

'Yes, absolutely, no problem. I'll talk to Kevin and see what I can do to help. I'll give the Chief Constable a call about Pride, too, as soon as I get a moment.'

She gave him a guarded thanks, still eyeing him in clear disbelief.

'Just one thing you can perhaps do to help me in exchange, Debs. I have to be at the dojo tonight, come what may, to meet Jezza to see what she's uncovered, if anything. Perhaps you can cover for me, if Mr Marston calls another of his snap briefings?'

'So, for the time being, Samir Kateb is being left in the wind and kept under observation. The Chief Super has done a risk assessment and it's considered unlikely that Kateb will allow anyone other than tried and trusted gang members to go near any scam targets in the future. So there should, hopefully, be no further violence. Kateb is still in the area, still operational, but clearly being extremely cautious. Leaving him for now risks more scams but it may be the only way to bring the whole gang in, including the killer, and to close down the operation when the time is right.

'At the moment, our interest centres on this man, Dorian Bacha. So far, we've had nothing to show him as being in the country, or being in contact with his uncle, Kateb. Or whatever relation a person's father's cousin is to him. We merely have intelligence to indicate that he may well be the person involved.'

He put up some still shots on the white board as he was speaking. It felt good finally to have something to show for their enquiries, the face of a suspect, at last.

'Dorian Bacha, twenty-two. We don't have anything on him yet in the way of a criminal record, and these shots aren't brilliant. The surveillance teams watching his father's export business snapped him going in and out a few times, but he's of no real interest to them as he's not directly concerned in the export business.'

'Boss, I can do better than that. I found him on Facebook,' Océane told him. 'It's an unusual name, so I was able to pin him down. There are some much better photos there. I'll print them off. Not all his posts are public and he posts a lot in French, but luckily, with a French mother, that presents no problem for me. He hasn't posted anything public in the last couple of months.'

'Great, Océane, thank you. I know it's not in your remit, but if we needed to speak to the French police and couldn't immediately find an English speaker available at their end it would really help no end if you could interpret for us.'

'No problem at all, boss. It's my second language, so it's nearly fluent.'

'He doesn't look much like an Arab,' Maurice Brown, politically incorrect as ever, mused aloud.

'His mother's French, father is Algerian,' Ted corrected him. 'Dorian Bacha was born and educated in France, to a reasonable level, speaks fluent English, according to the information we have to date. From that point of view, well up to the job his uncle gave him. What we don't know at this stage, if indeed he is the one who was involved, is why he lost it and knifed Mrs Ashworth.

'Apparently he sometimes helps out in his father's company, presumably because of his skills in English, and has no record, as far as we are aware. He's studying law. It's quite likely he's visited England before, for the business, and of course, as a French citizen, he can travel freely with few checks on his comings and goings.

'The question is, if it was him, where is he now? As he's close family, it's less likely that he will simply have been disposed of. More possibly, he will find himself packed off back to France in disgrace, as soon as they can get him safely out of the country. He may already have left, of course. But if not, we need to find him.'

'So to sum up, boss, we're looking for a suspect where we don't even know if he's in the country. He's not got a record, so we don't have his prints or DNA. That means nothing at all to link him to the crime scene if we do find him. We've no eyewitnesses to the crime and the only description we have matches him only because it's a bloke. Sounds like a doddle to me,' Maurice Brown said dryly.

'It will be, Maurice. You're a good team. You can do it. I'm counting on you.

'Just one more thing. Our friend Clive Edwards. Morgane's father. I think he may have been behind a couple of attempts to scare or intimidate me lately. Not personally, but using someone he paid. Running my car off the road last week, then, on Monday, a man with a knife, in a ginnel.

'A passer-by came to help me with that one. I had to let the assailant go, because of the risk to a member of the public, so

I've nothing at all by way of evidence. But I want him brought in and questioned under caution. Jo, that's one for you, please. Just make sure he knows we're on to him.'

The team looked surprised, except for Maurice, who wisely kept quiet. They knew the boss was well up to handling a lone assailant with a knife so they couldn't immediately understand why he'd let him go. Ted hated lying to them. He disliked being dishonest to anyone, but he was between a rock and a hard place on this one.

His mobile was ringing. Green calling, identified now Ted had confirmed the number. He headed for his office to take the call.

'Why is there some young girl sniffing round the house and knocking on the door?' Green asked abruptly, without any form of greeting.

'Young girl? I have no idea. What like?'

'Mousy. Nosy.'

'Did she see you?'

'Of course she didn't bloody see me. Unlike you, I stay alert. She's gone. But I need to know who she was and if she might come back.'

'Leave it with me. I'll be in touch.'

'Sort it, Gayboy. Or I will.'

Ted leaned back in his chair and sighed. He'd barely been in a couple of hours and things seemed already to be piling up to be dealt with, none of them advancing him far in his latest enquiry. He desperately wanted to phone Bill to see how he was, and to phone Jim to make his peace with him. But first he put through a call to the Chief Constable's secretary to say he needed to talk to him.

A text alert on Ted's mobile showed him Marston had called another early briefing for the following morning at Central Park. At least that might mean he could probably get to the dojo that evening without being summoned. Ted relayed the information to the secretary and suggested he could see the

Chief Constable after the briefing, if that was convenient.

'Could you just hold one moment please, Chief Inspector?'

The line went silent while the secretary presumably checked with her boss about his availability, then came back on the line.

'Sir? The Chief says he'll drop in at the briefing then talk to you afterwards, if that suits you?'

Ted couldn't resist a silent air punch as he thanked her, then rang off. The sight of the Chief Constable in person turning up just to speak to Ted would certainly ruffle Marston's feathers. Especially as Marston clearly liked to be called Chief himself. That wasn't going to happen, not with the real Big Chief in attendance.

Ted found he was looking forward to the next day's briefing. He'd need to tell his Super he'd take his own car, so he didn't delay her, not knowing how long his meeting with the Chief Constable was likely to last.

He picked up the first of his paperwork but had barely begun before his desk phone rang with a call being put through.

'Chief Inspector? It's Penny.'

Hearing his slight hesitation, she said, 'Penny Hunter. From the paper? I wondered if you had any time when I could talk to you? Just for ten minutes? Today, perhaps?'

'I've got a pretty full day, Penny. You might be better talking to the Press Office, if it's urgent?'

'It's you I really need to talk to.'

Realisation hit him. The young woman at his mother's house. Mousy and nosy. It must have been the reporter. He needed to deal with this, and soon. And preferably not in the nick.

'The coffee shop, round the corner, in ten minutes? Is that any good to you?'

Jo had already left in search of Clive Edwards, taking Virgil with him. Mike Hallam was holding the fort. Ted told him he'd be gone a quarter of an hour or so, but didn't tell him where he was going or why. The DS looked at him quizzically. It wasn't like the boss to be secretive, but Mike decided it might be wiser to say nothing.

Ted bumped into the journalist outside the coffee shop, each approaching from a different direction. He stood aside to allow her to go in first. He'd been properly brought up by his father, the old-fashioned way, and old habits died hard.

'Thank you for agreeing to talk to me. Let me get you a coffee.'

Ted shook his head and got his wallet out.

'If I accept a drink off you, I have to fill in forms to declare it. It's much simpler if I just buy the drink. What would you like?'

He went up to the counter to order and pay for the herbal tea she requested. He was just about to ask for a cappuccino when he decided it was a day for Maurice Brown's cure-all – a hot chocolate.

He put the drinks on the table in front of them then sat down opposite her.

'So, what can I do for you? I should warn you at the outset, I never say anything to the press without clearing it at higher level first. But if there's something I can help you with, I'll try to find out the information for you.'

'It's about the assault in Marple last Thursday. I'm trying to get in touch with the victim, a Mrs Angharad Jones. I've been led to believe by a neighbour that she's your mother. I wondered if you could tell me where she is at the moment? I've been to the house but I didn't find her at home and the same neighbour told me she thinks she's gone away.'

The use of his mother's full name sounded odd to Ted. She'd only ever been Annie, all the time he'd known her. That meant the reporter had got her information from an official source. He took a drink of his chocolate, trying to gather his thoughts before he replied.

'I'm afraid I have no comment at all to make on that. I would certainly not disclose any information relating to the victim of a crime. You must appreciate that. What makes you think I'm related to this Mrs Jones?'

'The neighbour was very helpful. She told me Mrs Jones has a son who is a high-ranking police officer. She didn't know his name, she said, but she told me he was short and always polite. Although I don't know you well, the description reminded me of you.'

She'd done a good job of digging, he conceded to himself. Now he felt himself backed into a corner, a position he always hated. He couldn't deny outright any connection to the victim but the last thing he needed was her going back to the house while Green was there. He measured his words carefully before he spoke.

'Mrs Jones is my mother. She has currently gone to stay with a friend while she recovers from the attack. I'm not prepared to give you her contact details. I can appreciate that you may want to talk to her about the assault, but I would just ask you, please, to give her some space for the time being.

'I can tell you, although I suspect you already know, that a man has been arrested and charged in connection with the offence. The best I can do is to promise to let you know as soon as I hear when his first court date will be. I'm sorry I can't do more for you.'

'Could you at least ask your mother, when you speak to her, if she would be willing to talk to me? I really would like to get her story of what happened to her. It's a terrible sign of the times, when things like this happen. Our readers would be interested. And she will, I presume, be coming back for the court hearing? Depending on whether the attacker pleads guilty or not guilty? She'll be called as a witness, of course.'

Ted still hadn't explained to his mother that she would have to testify, if the defendant pleaded not guilty. She would be called as a prosecution witness, and might not know until the day of the hearing what his plea would be. Ted should have talked her through it all, before she left, but it was yet another thing he'd been too busy to do. He'd call her, as soon as he could, to explain the situation to her in full. Perhaps they could Skype, now Trev had set it up for her. He just had to find the time.

Chapter Fifteen

'Is it sorted?'

'It's sorted,' Ted told Green when he called him back later in the day. 'She'll not be coming round bothering you again.'

'She'd better not. So in exchange, I have something for you. Your lad Bacha is in the UK. Has been for about a month now. He flew in from Marseilles to Manchester. The intelligence is reliable, but what I can't tell you is why. I've got feelers out, though, and I'm owed a few favours. That should buy you a bit of R&R time from your delightful prick-in-chief, so sort me out at this club of yours. And you need to come too. You're even more in need of a training session than I am.'

He gave Ted the flight details before he rang off. Ted knew the information would be accurate. He didn't know who Green's sources were, and was probably better off not knowing, but it would certainly be safe enough to follow up and to pass on to Marston.

He went out to the main office and handed it on to Steve, who was the only one in, other than Océane. It was a reliable lead but a cold one. Their chances of finding anything on CCTV from the airport for a month ago were not great, but better than nothing. He asked him to check to see if he could trace Bacha returning to France on any flights in the days following the killing, then the intervening dates from there.

Jo was back in his office and Ted was anxious to know how his formal interview with Clive Edwards had gone.

'He denies everything and blames it all on you, boss,

basically,' Jo told him. 'Wasn't him, he had nothing to do with it, but whoever is trying to do you harm has his blessing and he'd like to buy them a pint or two. You're just another crooked copper trying to fit up his poor innocent daughter, and so on and so forth. Like a broken record.

'I can't guarantee we've exactly warned him off. It could go either way, I reckon. He might stop, or he might just up his game and bring in someone more professional. I think you need to watch your back very carefully, boss.'

Not just from Edwards, Ted thought to himself, as he sat down to email his latest lead through to Marston. He'd made a bad enemy in him, too, although he didn't regret for a minute having stood up to him in the past. If he hadn't done so, Marston's arrogance and ignorance could have got some of Ted's team killed.

His mobile showed him an incoming call from Rob O'Connell who was over at Wilmslow with Sal, still trying to find any reliable eyewitnesses.

'A glimmer, at least, boss. I talked to the person who saw Mrs Ashworth's car pulling out of the car park, the one who'd given a vague description of the driver. I had someone show him a few photos, all reasonably similar. The only one he picked out was our suspect, Bacha. He was hesitant, but he didn't reckon any of the others.'

'Excellent, Rob. Good news, and good work.'

'There's a bit more, too, boss. Inspector Pierson's officers have been checking traffic cameras for any more sightings of a dark blue Peugeot. We've got one on the A538 heading for the M56. The timing is right for it being Mrs Ashworth's car, and there's enough time for the number plates to have been switched somewhere. And they have been, by that point. It's on cloned plates, same make and model, but from a different car. Single male occupant. That's all we have.'

'It's a lot more than we did have, so that's a good thing. Right, we'll need to search anywhere between the incident and where the vehicle was clocked to see if there is any trace of where the plates might have been changed. Ask Inspector Pierson what officers he can make available and if you need more, ask Inspector Turner if he can spare any, since it's partly coming under our remit.

He'll complain and say he hasn't got enough to go round so I'll go and have a quick word with him now, just to prepare the ground.

'Excellent work, Rob, you and Sal both. We need a break now, a witness who saw plates being changed or anything suspicious like that. Of course, on the telly, we'd find a stray screw with the killer's DNA on it. We also need to find out somehow who the other person was, who helped with changing the plates, and find out whether it was them or Bacha who drove off in the Peugeot to deliver it wherever it was going.'

'Boss, we also need to know at what point the rest of the gang found out that Mrs Ashworth had been killed. Because if Bacha handed her Peugeot over and took the second vehicle, the one whoever had the false plates for him was presumably driving, he could be anywhere by now and we don't even know what car he drove off in.'

'Spare officers for a search? I've got bloody dozens of them, Ted. All aged under eleven. So you can have them for a half-hour slot between when they finish school and before they start their homework.'

Inspector Kevin Turner went into rant mode as soon as Ted went downstairs to ask him.

'Honestly, bloody Mini Police? It's great PR, a good community initiative. But what I need is grown-ups, to do proper policing. But they cost money, which is being cut back all the time. I don't have enough officers to send to even the most serious crimes, half the time. And we get plenty of that. We've just had a shout, as it goes. I'm passing it over to your lot. Suspicious death. And get this, initial reports at the scene say it was a couple rowing over assembling flat-pack furniture. Looks like she's lost it, grabbed the screwdriver and stuck it in his neck. Are you going to take it yourself?'

Ted shook his head.

'More than enough on just now. I'll call one of the team to pick it up. Give me the address, though, and if I get chance, I'll swing by. I've got to get to the dojo this evening. I've got Jezza out looking for happy slappers and that's our meet-up place.'

Ted knew that DC Jezza Vine was an expert at blending in and looking nothing like a copper. Even so, he was impressed when he saw her at the dojo. If he hadn't known she was a police officer in her twenties, he would easily have taken her for a teenager, and a stroppy one at that.

Her spiky hair was once again bright pink, and several of her piercings were back in place, just as when he'd first encountered her, the worse for drink and spoiling for a fight, shortly before she joined the team.

Ted had sworn Trev to secrecy and told him not to show any recognition for Jezza, whom he'd met at the annual Christmas drinks. He just hoped he could trust him to keep a straight face. Trev was notorious for collapsing in mirth at inappropriate moments.

Ted and Trev had already changed into their judogis and were starting stretching exercises as the young members of their self-defence club began arriving. Seeing Jezza, Trev turned away to do hamstring stretches, clearly worried about keeping it serious at the sight of her. She was playing the part to perfection.

Jezza looked around her, her expression arrogant, her gaze falling on Ted as if seeing him for the first time. Clearly senior in years, he was still shorter than some of the teenagers present.

'Who's in charge?'

'Trev and I run the club. I'm Ted. And you are?'

'Jas,' she told him, her accent different to her usual one.

'Jas Vaughan. I want to learn this stuff.'

The simplest cover was always closest to the truth. Jezza Vine, Jas Vaughan. Easy to remember, and with the same initials.

'There are some forms we need to fill in first before I can let you start. And I'm afraid you'll have to take your piercings out before you go on the mat.'

Some of the others were watching the newcomer with interest. Many of them had appeared as aggressive as she did when they first started at the club. The bravado was to hide the fear many of them had known in being bullied. Jezza's cover couldn't have been more perfect.

'I don't take them out, ever,' she told him defiantly, totally in the role.

'Shall we go and sit down and fill the forms in, then I can explain to you why it's necessary? And why I can't let you take part unless you do? Trev, if you could start the warm-up, please?'

He guided her to a low bench, further down the gym, out of earshot, pausing to collect the clipboard and forms he kept for signing up new members. They sat down side by side, talking quietly. The other members were too busy with Trev to take any notice.

'You have me convinced,' Ted told her. 'We'll need to fill these in for form's sake, excuse the pun, and you will have to take the piercings out, but you know that. So, anything useful so far?'

Jezza slowly started to take out her piercings as she spoke, making it look reluctant, automatically putting them into the soft exercise shoes she had on and had removed for the purpose. Ted knew she would have proper kickboxing gear because it was her sport, but she'd opted for a close-fitting T-shirt and leggings. She would have stood out too much in expensive, proper clothing.

'I've been hanging around areas where the little charmers

L. M. KRIER

seem to congregate. I'm glad I know how to protect myself, otherwise I would have lost my mobile, even though it's a cheap one, and possibly a few teeth.'

'Don't put yourself in any danger. Risk assessment, remember. At the first sign of things getting out of hand, you get yourself out of there.'

'It's fine, honestly. They're like a pack of feral animals. As long as you show no weakness, they're not brave enough to do anything. They're after soft targets, which I'm not. Especially once you've shown me some nifty self-defence moves.'

'First rule is always not to put yourself into a situation where you need them. Flight is always better than fight.'

'Yeah, just remind me how you got that scar on your left hand,' she told him with a cheeky grin.

'I mean it. Your role is purely to try to identify the members of the gang, not to finish up as a victim yourself. Is there anyone who stands out so far?'

'There's a girl called Tara. She's a right gobby mare, who seems to be a ringleader. A lot of the others are scared of her. We had a bit of a square-up, early on, but nothing more. As soon as I get any more on who she is or where she's from, I'll make contact. Other than that, I'll just see you here next week.'

'Remember what I said. You don't put yourself at risk, at any time. Right, we better get this form filled in. It's starting to look suspicious, us just sitting here. It shouldn't take me that long to persuade you to take your piercings out.'

It felt strange to Ted, having one of his team witnessing a side of him he normally kept private. As he expected, Jezza was a quick learner and her existing skills meant she was good at what he was teaching her. She also stayed faithfully in character, quick to fly off the handle if anyone got too close or even looked at her in the wrong way.

Before the juniors finished and the seniors started arriving for their judo session, which Ted and Trev always joined in,

148

the young members always wanted the two of them to demonstrate some fast work together, using their judo and karate skills, with Ted throwing in some of his Krav Maga moves. For some of them, it was the highlight of the evening. Ted felt a strange reticence, in front of Jezza, but he couldn't disappoint the youngsters and any change from the normal pattern would look suspicious.

When they'd finished and Ted had picked up his towel to wipe the sweat from his face, which the exertion had produced, Jezza sauntered casually past him to collect her shoes and her piercings.

'I hope we'll see you again next week, Jas?'

'I wouldn't miss it for the world, Ted,' she replied, then, in a much lower voice which only he could hear, 'Morning briefing will never be the same after witnessing that.'

'That was amazing,' Trev said on the short drive home after their judo training. He'd walked down earlier but Ted, running late as usual, had driven straight to the dojo, after phoning Trev to ask him to take his kit bag there for him.

In the work setting, Ted was obsessively punctual and a stickler for the same from officers under his command. With his personal life, he was always playing catch-up, sometimes to Trev's annoyance, although he was used to it by now. Especially as he hadn't been able to resist dropping in on the latest murder scene on his way to the dojo, although Jo and Megan Jennings were there and had everything under control. Bizzie Nelson, the senior Home Office pathologist, was in charge as it was a possible murder enquiry, and she took time to exchange a few words with him.

'This shouldn't tax your team too much, Edwin.'

She lapsed into first name terms as they were out of earshot of anyone else.

'It all looks straightforward, from my point of view. A single stab wound to the neck with a screwdriver, which is obligingly still in place, and which hit the carotid artery. I believe the girlfriend has admitted it, so I think it should be simple for both of us.'

'I didn't dare look at Jezza. I would have giggled and given the game away,' Trev continued. 'I would be rubbish working as any kind of undercover operative. But she's incredible. She really did look exactly like any of the others, when they first joined.

'By the way, don't forget I've got karate club tomorrow, then I'm going to do my first volunteer stint teaching English on Friday evening, so you'll have to fend for yourself. I'll make you something to leave ready. Just make sure you eat. And make sure you phone Annie when we get home. Or Skype her. She was hinting how much she'd like to hear from you.'

Ted knew Trev phoned Annie every day, for reports of how she was doing. He felt guilty that he hadn't made the time himself. He'd managed a quick call to both Bill and Jim before he'd even called his own mother. Work always got the better of him, somehow.

When they got back, Trev forcibly sat him down in front of the laptop, called Annie, had a brief exchange with her in Welsh, which he was clearly picking up rapidly, blew kisses at the screen, then went to make them both something to eat while Ted talked to her.

He felt awkward, sitting there, staring at her on the screen. He would have preferred to use the mobile. Looking at her, seeing the fading bruises on her face, the sight of her wrist still in plaster, made him feel guilty again, as if he should have been able to prevent it from happening.

He asked inane questions – how was she feeling and did it still hurt – then mentally rebuked himself for the empty words.

'He's been arrested and charged now. The thing is, mam, you'll have to come back for the court case. You'll be called as a witness, in case he pleads not guilty, and I'm afraid you have to attend. You don't have the choice.'

Seeing her worried face, he went on hurriedly, 'But don't worry, one of us will come and collect you and you can stay here. You don't want to be on your own at the house. And I'll do my level best to get time off to come to court with you. It'll be all right, mam. I promise.'

The bottle of Scotch on the table was still half full and the wheelchair was upright but his father was on the floor yet again when Ted got home. It was slightly later than he'd planned. He'd stopped for just a quick one with the rest of the team after work, which had somehow turned into two. Or perhaps even three, he couldn't be sure. To be on the safe side, he'd left the car in Openshaw again and come home by bus and on foot.

'Sorry I'm a bit later than I intended, dad. Let's get you up and sorted then I'll do something about some food. Do you fancy fish and chips, for a change?'

No reply.

'Dad? Or a Chinese, maybe? Dad?'

He knew, before even he crouched down next to him. A copper's instinct. Knew before he took hold of the outstretched hand that it would be as cold as marble to the touch and as unyielding.

Mechanically, he felt for a pulse at the throat, although he knew he was wasting his time. When had his father's neck got to be so skinny, so scrawny?

Ted stood back up and took the bottle from the table. Then he sank slowly to the ground so he was sitting next to his father. He stretched his legs out in front of him, unscrewed the bottle and put it to his lips. He didn't like Scotch. It tasted as bad as he anticipated.

'I'm so sorry, dad. I'm sorry I was a rubbish son to you. You were a brilliant dad. You were always there for me, when I was a kid. After mam left. Even with all your own problems.

You never let me down. I should have done better for you.'

He took another, longer, pull at the bottle, grimacing at the taste.

'I wanted to tell you that I've met someone. At the dojo. Just recently. Well, not met, exactly. I've just seen him. I've no idea if it will ever come to anything. He's way out of my league. I think you'd have liked him. He talks posh, but he's interested in everything. You could have talked about literature and politics together. He's much younger. I've not been out with him, just drinks with the others from the club. He doesn't even know how I feel about him. Not yet, anyway. But I'm going to try, to see if I stand a chance. I've finished with Philip, just in case. I don't want to two-time anyone. I just wish you could have met him.'

The whisky didn't taste quite so bad now. He was getting used to it. It helped him. It felt right, sitting here, talking to his dad. He wished he'd spent more time doing it, especially of late.

The insistent trilling of his mobile phone finally dragged Ted out of a profound sleep. He opened bleary eyes, found himself lying on the carpet, looking into the sightless eyes of his father, less than two feet away from him.

Cautiously he rolled onto his back to take the phone out. His boss calling. He couldn't make out the time displayed on the screen. His vision was not yet fully cooperating. His tongue was thick, making it hard to articulate even the simple, 'Hello?' with which he finally answered the call.

'Where the bloody hell are you? You missed briefing.'

Ted tried to sit up. Decided it was a bad idea, then turned to his other side, hoping to make speaking easier. At least it meant he wasn't having to look at his father.

'Sorry, boss, I was just going to call you. My dad died.'

There was a pause. Ted could sense the suspicion behind the silence from his cynical boss.

'Are you pissed, sergeant?'

'A bit, sir. But my dad is dead.'

'Right, take the rest of the day off. Sort out what you need to. And for god's sake, sort yourself out. Getting pissed is getting to be too much of a habit. This is your last warning. Any more of it, and you're off the team. Whatever the reason.'

'Sir.'

'And sergeant? I'm sorry for your loss.'

For some reason his words made Ted well up. He struggled to his knees then got unsteadily to his feet. He only just made it to the kitchen sink before the vomiting started. Great gut-wrenching heaves which had as much to do with self-loathing as the alcohol. Once the retching stopped, he drank a glass of water, which promptly came back. It took several attempts before he could successfully get much-needed liquid into his dehydrated system.

He went back into the living room to retrieve the now empty whisky bottle, then took it and hurled it into the ceramic sink with all his force, so that it shattered into pieces which flew up all around him.

Then he took out his mobile phone and called the doctor.

Chapter Sixteen

Chief Constable Jon Woodrow was Ted's kind of copper. He'd been fast-tracked, largely because of his outstanding management skills, but he'd still been a front-line policeman, and a good one. He sported an impressive scar down one side of his face, a legacy from arresting a villain with a history of violence who was wielding a broken bottle.

There was no side to him, no airs and graces. He was medium height and, as Ted's dad would have said, there was more meat on a budgie's lips. He played squash, like a demon, whenever he got the opportunity, and he was good at it. Ted had played him once at his invitation and been soundly thrashed, although he was fit and no slouch at it.

Woodrow liked Ted. He knew he hadn't had it easy through his career. He deplored discrimination of any type in the force but he was not naïve enough to believe that it had yet been completely stamped out.

Ted admired Woodrow. He knew he was more than just a political animal, the likes of Marston, and had got where he was on merit. He respected him, too, even when he'd been on the wrong end of his wrath a time or two. He took that from him, because he knew Woodrow had been an outstanding copper, not just a pen-pusher going through the motions.

Ted had just finished updating all present on the latest developments from Wilmslow at the morning briefing at Central Park. He mentioned the number plate change and his hope to find out more if they could identify where it had taken place and get a lead on the second vehicle.

'So with resources already stretched, you want to waste officer hours on scrabbling about in lay-bys looking for … what, precisely, Darling? Inspiration?'

Marston's tone was openly scornful. It was unfortunate for him that he spoke at the precise moment the door opened quietly and the Chief Constable walked in. Every officer present immediately made to rise, but Woodrow waved them down and walked across to Marston.

'Good morning, Mr Marston, ladies and gentlemen. Please don't let me disturb you. I needed a word with DCI Darling, so I thought I'd just gatecrash your briefing to see what the latest developments are with Operation Croesus.'

'DCI Darling was just outlining the switched number plates, sir ...'

'Yes, I heard what was said,' Woodrow cut in smoothly as Marston shifted uncomfortably on his feet. 'Please continue, DCI Darling.'

'Sir, it is a long shot, and it will probably take a lot of personnel hours, but we clearly need to trace the second vehicle. It's potentially a valuable lead. It could, of course, be anything – car, van, motorbike. There must have been an accomplice somewhere as Bacha, if it was him, couldn't have turned up to meet Mrs Ashworth with a pair of plates under his arm. And somebody must have dropped him off to meet her. I doubt he went there on the bus.'

'This is probably a stupid question, but why has Bacha not been on the radar before? If Kateb has been under surveillance, there must have been contact between them.'

There was a brief, awkward silence, in which Marston glared around the room, willing someone to come to his rescue with a suitable answer. Inspector Neil Smith from Fraud risked putting his head above the parapet first.

'Sir, from the enquiries so far, we think that Kateb knew he was being watched. That might well be why he brought in

Bacha, if he did, and why he kept him at a distance. It's possible they only spoke by phone, and if Kateb had a pay as you go, we wouldn't have known. We had a trace on the numbers we knew about, but that's all.'

'Let me just say, at this stage, that although this case, to date, has not represented the GMP's finest hour, we do not operate a blame culture within this force,' Woodrow told them all. 'Mistakes have been made. Serious ones, tragically resulting in the death of an innocent woman. Measures will be taken to make sure they are never repeated. But we are moving forward, not dwelling on the past. There may very well be disciplinary procedures following the conclusion of the operation, but they are with a view to preventing any such errors being repeated. There will be no witch-hunt.

'So what is the plan, going forward, to trace Bacha? Chief Superintendent?'

Ted didn't know if Marston played any type of racket and ball games. He doubted it, from the size of his girth. He certainly knew how to bat a hot potato of a question right out of his court to land squarely in Ted's.

'DCI Darling?'

'Sir, I think the key to this might possibly be family. We know that when Kateb moved to France, it was with extended family. So there's a chance that some of them moved to the UK as well as him. Bacha could just be staying in a hotel somewhere; he may even have gone back to France already. We haven't found him listed anywhere as an airline passenger on a return flight, yet, but we're still looking. He could, of course, just have hitched a ride with one of his father's lorries.

'But it would be worth looking more closely into the family tree, to see if there's someone on the fringes we're not yet aware of. It seems as if they are a close family network. I would suggest that's a line worth exploring, at least.'

'It sounds to me as if the enquiry is now going in the right direction, Mr Marston. Talk to me about the personnel budget whenever you need to. I'll leave you to get on, ladies and gentlemen. DCI Darling, come and find me in my office when you're done here. The coffee up there is considerably better than what's on offer down here.'

Ted wished he dared get his phone out to snap the furious expression on Marston's face as the Big Chief went out of the room, once again motioning to those present not to bother standing. Marston remained tight-lipped for the rest of the briefing, which passed off without incident. Ted thankfully made a speedy escape, sprinting up the stairs to Woodrow's office.

The Chief Constable's secretary tapped on his door to let him know Ted was there. She ushered him in as instructed, then went to make the coffees the Chief asked for and bring them in.

'Come in, Ted, sit down,' Woodrow was informal now it was just the two of them. 'How are you getting on with Marston? And it's just you and me now, so I want the true version, not the spin.'

'I don't think he's my number one fan, sir, but it's workable.'

Woodrow was looking searchingly at him, while Ted held his gaze.

'Seriously, Ted, if there is a problem, I would appreciate you telling me. If it needs to go no further, it won't. But after so many years of refusing to give any input for Pride, you can't blame me for being suspicious at your sudden change of heart. That's not to say I'm not grateful. I really am. But the motives behind your about-turn intrigue me.'

'And if I said it was because Superintendent Caldwell had asked me so persuasively, sir?'

'I would say that's complete bollocks, but I respect your desire to drop the subject. Please remember, though, that my door is always open to you and any conversations are in confidence. So now let's talk about how we can make the force more inclusive, shall we?'

Mike Hallam was holding the fort when Ted got back to Stockport after the briefing. He told Ted that Jo and Megan were downstairs talking to the girlfriend about the fatal screwdriver stabbing from the day before.

'She was completely off her face when she was brought in, boss, so we had to wait to question her. She's got the duty solicitor now and seems to be fit to interview. So far she's admitted everything, but no doubt her brief will urge caution until he's had more time to talk to her.'

'Anything else new I should know about?'

'Boss, I've been speaking to the police in Marseilles about Bacha. A really helpful officer from their criminal division, who speaks reasonable English. He said he'd be happy to talk to you. Do you want me to set up a conference call? I could help to interpret, if there was anything he didn't know the English for, if that would help?'

'That sounds excellent, Océane, thank you. As soon as you can, please. I'll be in my office, drowning under paperwork, no doubt.'

It wasn't long before Océane buzzed him to say that she had the French police officer online ready to talk to him. Steve was out, so Ted pulled his chair across and sat down next to Océane, in front of her screen.

'Boss, this is Commandant Olivier Moreau.'

'Thank you for agreeing to talk to me, Commandant. I apologise for not speaking any French at all, but Océane tells me your English is good.'

'I enjoy to practise my English, *inspecteur,*' the other man replied. His accent had a mid-Atlantic twang to it.

'Please call me Ted. Now, can you tell me anything about this man, Dorian Bacha?'

'We have no real interest in him. He has not yet a rap sheet. Is that right? I like to watch American crime on the *télé.*'

Ted smiled. It showed, in his choice of words.

'We usually say record rather than rap sheet, but that's fine. But I think you have his father under observation?'

'*Stups* are interested in him and are watching him.'

'*Stups*?' Ted queried, looking at Océane.

'Drug Squad, boss.'

'But the son, no, not so much. We know about him. He has some bad friends. They are always in trouble. But his *papa* keeps him clean. He has plenty of *fric*.'

'Cash, boss,' Océane told Ted when he looked at her questioningly.

'He protects the boy because he wants to be a liar. And that will be helpful to him.'

Seeing Ted's puzzled face, Océane helpfully corrected the mispronunciation of lawyer, then fired off a rapid stream of French, which made Moreau laugh out loud.

'Excuse me, I am very stupid. But it's a good joke, *non*? Many lawyers are also liars.'

'Do you think Bacha is capable of killing someone? A woman?'

Moreau spread his hands.

'Who knows? He may already have killed and *papa* has just hidden the facts so we do not yet know. I think he is not very brave. Perhaps if things go wrong, he panics? We know already that he does a lot of sheet.'

'Dope, boss. Hash. The French call it shit.'

'His father does not approve. He is happy to sell it to others, but he does not like that his number one son does drugs. *Cocaïne*, also. It might explain the violence, *non*?'

'And as far as you know, he's not in France at the moment?'

'We have not seen him for some time. If we do, I will be happy to contact Océane to tell you.'

From the way he smiled as he said it, Ted was relieved that Steve was not in the office. He and Océane were something of an item and Ted didn't want any jealousy getting in the way of work. It seemed as if the French officer was openly flirting with Océane. And she didn't seem to be objecting.

'God, sir, you're on fire! I don't know who your informant is but you're coming up with better stuff than we are, that's for sure.'

It was Neil Smith, calling Ted's mobile, later the same afternoon.

'You know the rules, Neil. If I tell you my sources, I'll have to kill you. So, what have you got?'

'We've only gone and got some second or third or whatever Bacha cousin we didn't even know about, living in Manchester. Stretford, to be precise. So we're betting there's a reasonable possibility young Dorian, if he's still in the country, could be staying there.'

'I've been speaking to the French police about him. I'll circulate the information I have from them as soon as I get time to write it up.'

Smith laughed.

'Too busy hobnobbing on the Eleventh Floor, eh, sir, leaving us mere mortals to do the dirty work?'

Although HQ had moved long ago from the old Chester House building, the term "Eleventh Floor" was still used by longer-serving officers to allude to the hallowed ground where the top brass had dwelt when they were not descending to walk among the mere mortals.

'I don't need to tell you this is going to need careful handling. The French police say Dorian Bacha has no known record of violence, but he is a known drug user. His father has the money to have covered up anything he's done at home. And if it is him, now he's killed once, he's going to be dangerous. It's going to require careful surveillance this time, then quite possibly Armed Response to make an arrest. Have you told Mr Marston yet?'

'Same as you, I just need to find the time to file my report, sir. So stand by for one of his snap briefings. Knowing him, it could be in the middle of the night. I suppose if we're bringing the shooters in, you'll want a piece of the action, for old time's sake?'

'Well, I'm in charge of the murder enquiry, and he might be my killer, even if he isn't holed up on my patch, so I might well claim rights over him.'

Both men were laughing as they ended the call, but Ted was worried about history repeating itself. With Marston in overall charge of Croesus, he might want to take command of any arrest operation. With the combination of his arrogance and his refusal to listen to officers with the right experience, it could be a disaster waiting to happen. And the presence of his old enemy, Ted, could be like a red rag to a bull.

Trev was sprawling on the sofa, buried under cats, watching a French news channel when Ted got home late. He sank gratefully down next to him, picked up his hand and kissed it.

'I saw you hadn't been home yet. I've not eaten, either. I thought we could eat together, if you weren't too late back. Like a proper old married couple.'

Even without understanding the language on the television, Ted could see that the news was the same as everywhere. Terrorism, fear of a far right resurgence, homelessness and poverty.

Trev smelt of shower gel and shampoo and was wearing sweat pants with a vest top which showed off the muscles in his arms and shoulders. He muted the sound on the TV with the remote.

'How was karate?' Ted asked him. 'I'm sorry I couldn't get there. I could really do with a good workout, but it's finding the time. I might try for some Krav Maga this weekend if I can get away.'

'Excellent. Billirant, in fact.'

They still made a joke of Trev's drunken typo in a text home from his recent trip to France.

'There's a tournament coming up and they want me for the team.'

'I should think so too. You're excellent; the best they have.'

'You taught me well.'

'Perhaps. But the pupil is better than the *sensei* these days. Where is the tournament? I'd love to watch you thrash the opposition. But you do understand I can't promise to be there, not with the way work is at the moment?'

'It's in London, and that's fine, I understand. In fact, I assumed you wouldn't be able to come, so I was planning on making a weekend of it. I thought I'd go down on the coach with the rest of the club, but then stay over for the night with Laurence and get the train back. You do remember who Laurence is, don't you?'

Ted grinned ruefully.

'I'm never going to be allowed to forget making such a prat of myself, am I? It's fine, I'm glad one of us will be having some fun.'

'Good, because while you're in a generous mood, there's something else I want from you. Willow and Rupe are having a big bash on Saturday week and we're invited, of course. I won't tell you where it's being held because you'll only complain and say it's too posh, but it is black tie.'

Ted groaned. He disliked dressing in a suit for work, never mind the idea of parading himself like a penguin for a social occasion.

'It's a bit short notice, isn't it?'

'You'll understand why when you see where it's being held. The waiting list is months and months, literally, and they got a cancellation, somehow. I think they probably had to kill to get it.

'A lot of their friends couldn't get to the wedding reception because of work commitments, and of course, we both missed most of it, so I really want to go. They'll certainly all drop everything for this, though. It's going to be fantastic. An all-night do. Carriages at six, that kind of thing. There'll be dancing, and a karaoke.'

'Karaoke? Isn't that a bit nineties?'

'Ted, you're hopeless when it comes to trends. It's so *passé* it's now back in fashion. Retro chic. Anyway, here's the thing. When I went to France with them, I discovered Willow is a massive country fan, like you. Can you believe it? She also sings really well, too. So I said you'd do a duet with her. You know, a bit of Kenny and Dolly.'

Ted turned and gaped at him in horror.

'Hello, have we met? You think I'd get up in public and make a complete idiot of myself singing? When you know I can't even get pissed to have the nerve to.'

'I could always get you stoned.'

'Don't you dare! Seriously, though, I don't even know if I'll be able to go, what with this case ...'

'I know that. But it's always the same. Last time it was that case, now it's this case, next time it will be another case. You keep saying you'll make it up to me so please just do this one thing for me. And don't drop out on some lame excuse. Just if you get another body.'

Ted let out a long sigh.

'*We've Got Tonight*?'

'I said you'd do that one. Willow's already practising. I said you'd do *Islands in the Stream* together as well.'

'Two?' Then, seeing Trev's look, he nodded. 'All right, both of them. But I'm not growing a beard. And no rhinestones.'

Chapter Seventeen

'Right, so we now have a house in Stretford under twenty-four hour obs, with reason to believe that if Dorian Bacha is anywhere in the country, he may well be there. As we think he's already killed, and we don't know what weapons he has at his disposal, it's likely to involve an Armed Response team to arrest him. But – and at the moment it is a very big but – before we can do anything, we first need to establish if he's there. And then if we have any evidence at all against him to warrant such an operation.

'So, Rob, anything yet from Wilmslow on a second vehicle?' Ted asked.

Rob and Sal were doing good work at Wilmslow, handling things well. Magnus Pierson had phoned Ted to say he was impressed with them and glad of their help, having such a complex case as his first murder enquiry.

'We've identified and searched a few places so far, boss, but nothing as yet. There are still plenty of places to look. It's going to take a lot of hours, though.'

'You just do what it takes and leave me and the Super to worry about the budget. No point pinning down where Bacha is if we have no evidence at all to move against him. We need to know how he left the scene and where he went. Did he change to the second vehicle or did he drive Mrs Ashworth's Peugeot to its destination?'

'Boss, if Kateb or any of the others had heard early reports on the news about a fatal incident in Wilmslow, it must surely have crossed their minds that it could have been Bacha, especially if this was their first time of using him,' Mike Hallam suggested. 'I can't imagine they would be waiting to welcome him with open arms if they'd got wind of how badly their operation had gone wrong.'

'What I don't get, boss, is why he's still hanging round here, if it was him,' Maurice Brown put in. 'Why didn't he just leg it and jump on the first flight back home to France?'

'Can I say something, boss?' Océane looked up from her computer. She had a knack of getting on with her own work, seemingly ignoring what was being said around her, but still aware of it and ready to jump in if she had a useful contribution.

'Of course, Océane. You know that any input is always welcome.'

'From what Commandant Moreau was saying yesterday, it sounds as if there's friction between Dorian and his father, certainly over his drug use. Perhaps he was sent over here to keep him out of whatever trouble he was already in there, and now he's afraid to go back and face the music after what he's done here.'

'So we think he definitely still made the meet-up for the car?' Maurice again.

'Keep up, Maurice. The plates were changed at some point so it's likely he did,' Megan told him, gently teasing. Then she asked reasonably, thinking from a parent's perspective, 'If he was already in trouble, would his father send him over to work with someone running scams and fraud?'

Océane gave a very Gallic shrug.

'White collar crime. It's not quite the same thing. *Papa* might have thought it was preferable to whatever Dorian had been getting up to over there.'

'Sir, would he have had much blood on him after the stabbing?' Steve asked. 'That would take some explaining, turning up at the meeting place with the car and the rest of the stuff, but covered in blood.'

'Good point, Steve. I should have thought of that myself. I would imagine so, but I'll check with Professor Nelson, to be sure.'

'So we could be looking for blood traces, too, at the meet-up site, when we find it? Is it too late to think of getting dog teams in, boss?' Rob asked.

'We got lucky that way with the last big case, but we did, at least, have a rough idea of where to look. It's a good point, but at this stage it would be real needle in a haystack work. If we could at least pin down roughly where to start looking, it might still be worth a shot.

'Today's priority needs to be to find something solid, anything, to put Bacha somewhere near the scene of crime, or the house in Stretford. And to trace who the second person was, whoever helped him change plates. Rob, go back to that witness again and probe a bit more.'

'Will do, boss. We're also working with Inspector Pierson's team to check all the CCTV on the route to see if we can spot another vehicle hanging around, or even in convoy with the Peugeot at some point after the plates were changed.'

'Anything else? Virgil, have you heard anything from Jezza?'

'Nothing, boss. Maurice, have you spoken to her when she phones Tommy?'

'Not a great deal to report, boss. She just mentioned this girl Tara. She's ok though.'

'And the DIY stabbing, Jo?'

'All over bar the shouting, boss. Girlfriend has admitted everything. We have her full statement. There are also witness statements from neighbours saying that loud and sometimes violent arguments were commonplace there, and not just over flat-pack assembly. She has previous for thumping the partner, too, and him for hitting her. Just the paperwork to sort now and the job's a good 'un.'

'I know I don't need to tell you, but let's be sure that's all sewn up tight. Get us a nice solid result, while we're waiting for positive news on Croesus.'

Ted called Bizzie Nelson as soon as he'd wound up the briefing.

'It wasn't a spurting, arterial bleed, Edwin, but there was considerable blood loss. From the depth of penetration of the blade, unless it was a knife with an extremely long handle, I would expect the perpetrator to have had blood on their knife-hand at least. As they withdrew the blade, it's quite probable that there would also have been drops on their clothing.

'But I stress this is speculation, and you know how it goes against my scientific grain to rely on that. On balance, I would have to say that it is more likely than not that whoever stabbed Mrs Ashworth would have had blood on their person and their clothing.'

Professor Nelson was nothing if not guarded when dealing with anything which was not a simple matter of provable fact. It was helpful, though. It made Ted think it was less likely that Bacha would have delivered the car himself to Kateb, if he was in a state like that. He would know he couldn't hide for ever, but he could at least delay the inevitable if he had time to clean himself up and compose himself.

Ted's next port of call was to Kevin Turner. He wanted to know how the case against his mother's attacker was progressing. In particular, he wanted to know the likelihood of a guilty plea. He was hoping his mother could be spared the ordeal of having to travel back up from Wales to give evidence in court.

'He admitting to pushing your mam but is denying intent to cause her any harm.'

'Have you got any photographic evidence from the eyewitnesses? She said there were plenty there filming what was happening but not doing anything to help. And what about the two lads who did come to her help? What are they saying?'

'Ted,' Kevin told him patiently, 'we may only be humble Woodentops, not clever detectives like you lot, but we do know our job. I know it's worse because it's your mam, but we will nail the bastard. Don't worry about that. You know well enough he could go down for up to five years on an ABH, especially as he has form.'

'Actual Bodily Harm? You're not pressing for Racially Aggravated Assault, then? You know he could go down for longer on that.'

Kevin shook his head in mock despair.

'Ted, Ted, the reason you and I mostly get along is that you're not usually a patronising bugger, like some of your type. I've spoken to CPS at length. They're happier with a strong chance of conviction on ABH than taking a punt on Racially Aggravated and it not sticking.'

Ted grinned ruefully.

'Sorry. I should know better. You know what you're doing. It's just, you know ...'

'It's your mam. Of course I know, you daft bastard. I'd be the same if anything happened to any of my family. You worry about Croesus, I'll see your mam right.'

While he was downstairs, Ted decided to put his head round the Ice Queen's door for a catch-up. There was always the prospect of good coffee if he visited her.

'Come in, Ted, I was just about to call you,' she said, as she looked up from her paperwork.

It sounded ominous. Or maybe he was still wary after the run-in with Jim. He had phoned him to put things right, but he'd still had to accept a further tirade before the Big Boss calmed down enough for things to be back to normal. Ted had a suspicion his painkillers weren't strong enough.

'Mr Marston has called another briefing for this afternoon. Much smaller, this time. He's planning the arrest of Dorian Bacha so he wants input from you and me, from Armed

Response and from the surveillance team.'

'He's jumping the gun, there, pardon the pun. We're a long way from being ready to move. We still have only the shakiest of evidence against him, and we really are doing all we can.'

She'd stood up to produce the coffee. She was always the soul of discretion, but Ted detected a note of something like irritation in her voice as she replied.

'You and I both know that but mounting armed operations is not his speciality. I just hope that between us, we can make sure the operation is not rushed and badly managed. I suggest we go in my car, then we can discuss strategy in more detail on the way there.'

'This is probably going to be impossible, but I desperately need to get away for about four hours, possibly tomorrow. Green is still on our patch and wanting somewhere to train. As he's got the drop on me, twice, he's insisting I should go too. It would mean going to my club over near Sheffield, so I'm an hour or so away if the Chief Super calls yet another briefing. Or if he decides to go ahead with the arrest with indecent haste, before we're ready.'

'We need every member of the team on peak form for this operation, with whatever update training is necessary for their specialist skills. Leave it with me.'

It was a much smaller team which sat around a table in a briefing room, rather than using the large conference room. Marston had taken his position at the head, flanked by a Firearms inspector, Alex Porter, whom Ted knew well, and Neil Smith from Fraud, whose team members were involved in keeping the house in Stretford under surveillance. Marston invited Smith to speak first.

'Sir, we still have no definite sightings of Bacha at the house. What my team have noticed is that there's one room at the front of the house where the curtains have stayed closed the whole time it's been under observation.'

'Who lives at the house, sir?' Porter asked.

Marston was passing round a folder with all the available intelligence to date.

'Mother, father, three daughters and now, we think, Dorian Bacha.'

'And what weapons do we think are in there, sir?'

'We believe he has used a knife and may still have it. We have no information to suggest firearms are involved.'

'Sir, with all due respect, we do have information which could suggest there might be. Bacha's father's firm is under surveillance in France in connection with suspected drug smuggling and gun running.'

Once again, Ted found himself in the position of having to confront the Chief Super. At least this time he was with two other officers with firearms experience, who were nodding their heads in agreement at what he was saying.

'Suspected, suggest, might be. It's all a bit tenuous, Darling.'

'Sir, with respect from me also, this is my team I'm sending in. I need as much information as possible to make the risk assessments and plan the best way to proceed. All of that takes time and careful planning. Sir.'

The hesitation was pointed, the most Inspector Porter dared do to make his objections clear.

'For instance, do we have plans of the interior of the house yet, sir? It's vital that I know which way the stairs go, for one thing. If Bacha is in the room at the front of the house and the stairs rise towards the back, that makes it all the more tricky for my officers to approach without alerting him. And is this going to be a Fahrenheit op, sir, or is our brief to bring him in alive for questioning?'

Fahrenheit was the shoot to kill code, normally only used if the suspect was thought to represent a real and present danger, as in the case of a suspected terrorist. It would be highly unusual for such an operation to be coded as Fahrenheit. Ted hoped even Marston would not be stupid enough to do it for a suspect on whom they had so little information.

'Not at this stage, Inspector.'

Marston was beginning to sound irritated. He hated to be challenged. But if this operation was to go smoothly, with minimal risk of loss of life, especially to civilians, he needed to be made to listen to the firearms experts present.

'Chief Superintendent, if I may, since I, too, have firearms experience,' the Ice Queen began, her tone measured but her message clear. 'I agree wholeheartedly with DCI Darling and Inspector Porter. This is an operation with the potential to go badly wrong.

'Bacha is a French national, but the family is of Algerian origin. We must, of course, do all we can to bring in a murder suspect. But if we go in mob-handed and unprepared, we run the risk of accusations based on ethnicity. When were you planning for, sir?'

'Sunday morning, bright and early, when everyone is still tucked up in bed.'

The four other officers exchanged looks of barely concealed horror.

'Sir, we don't even have enough for a warrant yet ...' Ted began, but got no further.

'Then get me something,' Marston barked. 'You've had nearly two weeks and nothing to show for it. Shake your team up a bit. There must be something. Find it.'

'Sir, I'm going to need much more intelligence to go on ...'

Porter got no further than Ted had.

'There's too much negativity here. Stop telling me what you can't do and tell me what you can and how you're going to do it.'

'Sir, I say again that we need to exercise the utmost caution with this operation.'

When Superintendent Debra Caldwell used that tone, everyone sat up and listened. Even, to Ted's surprise, Marston.

He looked at her with barely concealed annoyance while he considered. But he was at least listening and seemed to be weighing up her input.

'All right, I am prepared to modify my plans to the extent of saying that the expectation is to go ahead on Sunday. That will be subject to full risk assessments being carried out after further intelligence gathering, all of which are to be signed off by me then countersigned by the ACC (Crime).

'I'll leave you now to come up with a workable plan before any of you think of leaving. I suggest at some point you send out for food; ask the front desk to organise it for you. Prepare yourselves for a late one. And make sure I have your full proposals before you leave here. Good day.'

Once he'd left the room, the Ice Queen looked at her companions with a wry smile.

'Well, gentlemen, this is the first time in my life that I have been kept in after school.'

Ted always said that a difficult case was like playing dominoes. Once the first tile fell, others quickly followed. Between the four of them, they had a lot of experience to bring to the table and they were making the best use of it.

It was the first time that Ted had worked side by side with his Superintendent in the planning of a big operation and he was impressed. He also suspected she was enjoying herself. It was a far call from her usual largely administrative role.

Ted had phoned through to Steve to get him to find out what he could about the house and its interior and he had come up trumps in short order. The house was in a road of semi-detached properties. Their target was a right hand one. He'd found a similar one in the road for sale and sent the link through so they could look at it from the inside and out while he was tracking down detailed architectural plans to work from.

'They may not all be identical, of course, but this confirms what I was most worried about. To get to that front room, my team have got to go upstairs then double back along the landing. It looks like there's no room to swing a cat, so protective covering is going to be difficult.'

Porter had voiced the first thing that Ted and the Ice Queen thought, looking at the pictures.

'With luck, you'll have the element of surprise,' Ted reminded him. 'We definitely need to know more about the occupants, and most importantly, if Bacha is there or not. We don't want to go storming in on a perfectly innocent family.'

Smith's team had been tasked with finding that information. He read from the messages he'd received.

'The father works in the accounts department of a firm in town, usually Monday to Friday. The wife doesn't work. There are three daughters, sixteen, fourteen and eleven, all living at home. Let's hope they're like my kids and don't stir early at the weekend. At least if they're tucked up in their rooms, we may be able to keep them safe, even if we do scare them a bit.'

'If it's a three-bedroomed house and Bacha is there, does that mean all three girls are squashed into one bedroom? I'd be happier if we knew for sure the likely location of the occupants.'

'That's the logical conclusion, ma'am, unless perhaps one of them is sleeping downstairs while Bacha has their bedroom,' Smith suggested. 'I'd be happier, too, if we knew more. And if we had more time to prepare.'

Even Ted's stickler of a boss let the implied criticism of the Chief Super pass without comment. She was probably feeling as frustrated as they all were, with the pressure they were under. She surprised them all further by paying for the Chinese takeaway they sent out for as the evening wore on, which they ate companionably, still working away at the table.

It was her idea, too, of a possible way to get more information, and a feeling for whether or not Bacha was at the house. With her suggestion, and Ted's input, they arranged for

DC Megan Jennings to visit the road the following day, with a set of suitably impressive papers, to do some door-to-door canvassing, supposedly a poll about traffic calming measures. Ted would be nearby at all times in case of problems.

They were enjoying their food when Rob O'Connell phoned Ted's mobile with just the breakthrough they were needing.

'Boss, sorry to disturb you, but we're finally getting somewhere with CCTV. We've got a silver Vauxhall Astra tailing the blue Peugeot closely on the M56, then heading for the M60. Going in the direction of Stretford. Same thing again, cloned plates.'

'I'll give that to my team and get them to start looking for it,' Smith said when Ted relayed the information.

'Observe, but not approach, at this stage, I would say, Neil. If the Chief Super does want this to go ahead on Sunday, we don't want to do anything to spook Bacha into running, if he's there.'

'We could maybe get it clamped? Wouldn't look too suspicious and at least it would stop him driving off in it before we can collar him.'

It was nearly eleven o'clock before Ted got home. Trev was watching a news channel, buried under cats, looking extremely pleased with himself. Ted planted a kiss on his cheek as he sat down next to him.

'How did the teaching go?'

'Fantastic. I really enjoyed it. I should have done it ages ago. I'm going to do a lot more of it. Have you eaten? Do you want me to make you something?'

Ted shook his head, then kissed him again.

'I'm very proud of you, you know that? It's a really good thing you're doing. And I have eaten, thanks. We had a late-running briefing and the Ice Queen bought us all a Chinese.'

'How tired are you, on a scale of one to ten? Because I'm

feeling wide awake and pinging like Tigger, after having so much fun, so I have plans for you.'

Ted smiled as he rose to his feet, pulling his partner up by the arm.

'Suddenly not tired at all. Tell me about these plans.'

Chapter Eighteen

Trev was still spark out, dead to the world, when Ted got up early for work the next day. Ted had expected objections when he'd told him he had to work most of the weekend. Instead, to his surprise, Trev told him he was taking Bizzie Nelson shopping.

'She's going on a hot date. With my cardiac consultant, Douglas Campbell, can you believe it? They've known each other forever. They just drifted apart at Cambridge when she had that disastrous affair. He married someone else but is now a widower so thought he'd try again. And she's been off the dating scene for so long, she asked me for help in what to wear.'

Ted smiled to himself at the thought as he drove towards the station. He was pleased his partner would be having fun. Trev adored shopping. Ted only went under sufferance. He was also glad there was the prospect of someone nice for Bizzie, if only for the occasional meal out. He knew she had been especially lonely since her elderly dog had died.

Working this weekend meant he would need a solid excuse to bail out next Saturday and he wanted more than anything to escape the ordeal of singing in public. In case it proved impossible, he put *We've Got Tonight* on as he drove to the station and sang along with it to practise.

It didn't sound too dreadful within the confines of his Renault but just thinking about doing it in public made him squirm. He played it a couple of times, then, as he parked his car and finished the last note, he let his head fall forward on to his steering wheel and groaned aloud. The things he did to keep his partner happy.

There was a tap on his side window and Megan's voice asked him anxiously, 'Are you all right, boss?'

Guiltily, Ted sat up straight and smiled at her in what he hoped was a reassuring way, undoing his seatbelt and getting out of the car.

'Yes, fine, thanks, Megan. I was just summoning my thoughts. I'll nip in to the office to check if there's anything new, before we go. Perhaps you could get my car, and I'll be out again in a minute. Don't forget your vest.'

Ted had insisted she wear a stab vest, hidden under a bulky outer coat, in case she came face to face with Dorian Bacha. He wished he knew more about the likelihood of firearms at the house. But risk assessments had been prepared and would be signed off by both Marston and the ACC (Crime) one today's intelligence had been gathered. It was scant consolation to Ted to know that if something happened to one of his officers, the blame would not rest solely with him.

He got Megan to park the black Ford well back from the target house, but where he would be close enough to keep an eye on her as she went from door to door. He'd clocked a surveillance car with two officers in plain clothes sitting inside it. He also knew that there was a team in the house directly opposite, a camera trained on the target property, hoping for any sightings of Bacha.

Ted and Megan had decided between them that she would do the houses on the same side of the road as the target, then report back to the car and see if it was worth continuing. The team in the surveillance house had already got quite a bit of information on the family from the owner of the property they were in. They described her as an older woman with time on her hands, who loved standing in the downstairs bay window, watching the comings and goings of her neighbours. They weren't surprised to hear that she was an active and enthusiastic member of the local Neighbourhood Watch. She wasn't aware of a visiting relative or any young male at the house, although she did confirm that it was unusual for the curtains in the small upstairs room to remain closed all the time.

Megan was perfect for the role she was in. She had an open, honest face which inspired confidence. Jezza had once rather unkindly referred to her as 'mumsy', but in a way it was true. She was so convincing as a concerned young mother wanting something done to make the road safer for children that she was constantly having to turn down invitations to 'come in and have a cuppa'.

She got to the target house and rang the bell. She had to ring it a second time before the door was opened, but only as far as the safety chain would allow. A teenage girl, long, dark hair loose around her face, peered suspiciously through the crack as Megan showed her clipboard with the petition on it, and her specially prepared photo ID.

'Hello, sorry to bother you. Is your mum or dad in?'

'They're busy at the moment,' the girl told her.

'It won't take long. I'm just talking to parents of children about road safety issues in the area. Could one of them spare me five minutes, perhaps?'

A woman's voice called out from the back of the house in a language Megan didn't recognise. The girl replied with a rapid stream of incomprehensible words then turned back to the door.

'Not today, thank you,' she said politely enough, before shutting the door firmly in Megan's face.

Megan carried on to do the rest of the houses on the same side, to avoid looking suspicious, and in the hopes of picking up more information. Then she walked on round the corner at the end of the road and waited for the boss to drive round to pick her up.

'Very cagey response at the target house, boss. I don't know if you could see from where you were parked? A teenage girl, one of the older daughters I would think, although it's impossible to tell age these days, opened the door, but only as far as the chain. There was an exchange, in Arabic, I imagine, I didn't know the language, but that was as far as I got.

'The neighbours know them but don't know a lot about them. They say they're a quiet, close family who keep to themselves. No one knew anything about a visitor. It's still not a lot to go on, is it, boss?'

'And there's no sign of a silver Astra in this road, or a dark blue Peugeot.'

'I did think of something else, although I'm sure you're ahead of me there. If Bacha is a regular drug user and has been holed up there for a couple of weeks without his regular supplies, he's going to be even more dangerous, isn't he?'

'Good point, Megan. Can you include that in your report? Get it written up and mailed to me as soon as we get back, please. Are you on a day off tomorrow? Got anything planned?'

'Felix wants to go on a picnic, boss. He's obsessed with them. Maurice has the twins, so we thought we'd make an afternoon of it and take them and Tommy too. They usually get along well together, although, of course, Tom can be unpredictable. What about you? Any chance of a break for you before tomorrow?'

'I have a hard training session with my martial arts instructor this afternoon. The idea is that it will help me to be on top form tomorrow. Knowing him, I'll be lucky if I can still walk.'

Ted's suggestion that he should swing by his mother's house to pick up Green had met with biting scorn.

'Did you sleep through all of the training sessions I gave you, Gayboy? Or were you too busy playing with yourself to concentrate? Text me a time to meet up and I'll tell you where. And try not to get followed, or run off the road.'

Ted took it from him because he was the best there was and he knew he was right. It was a sloppy suggestion. He shouldn't have made it. He had paid attention through training. Green knew perfectly well that he had passed with the highest overall mark on one of his courses. But it was his job to keep him on his toes. Ted knew he was in for a rough time as soon as they got to the dojo. It would do him good, but he just hoped he would be in a fit state to return to work afterwards.

Unsurprisingly, Marston wanted a briefing before the following day's operation, which he was still determined should go ahead. He'd called one for the afternoon but the Ice Queen had come to Ted's rescue. She had explained that she had personally sent him on a training course for the afternoon to ensure he was on peak form. As SIO on the murder enquiry, and the one with the SFO training, he was an essential presence at the briefing, so it had been put back to early evening.

The club he was taking Green to was one he used infrequently. It was rough and there were no rules. Ted usually emerged black and blue but feeling better for it. The members were hard cases. It was only Ted's technical skills and speed that got him out in one piece. Tough as they were, they had never seen anything like Green.

He was the highest graded Krav Maga instructor in the country, and held black belts at high level in other martial arts. Travelling light as he was, he didn't have his kit with him so the other members had no idea what they were about to confront when they saw the medium-sized older man in his tracky bottoms and washed-out Springbok rugger.

They soon started to realise what they were up against once he began tossing even the biggest and best of them around the mat. After a taster, most of them were quite happy to back away and leave him to concentrate his efforts on Ted. In all the time they'd known one another and trained together, Ted had only had Green down twice and the second time had been through sheer desperation.

Because of the sort of club it was, Green was not being particularly careful about whether or not any blows landed. Ted was now going to have to turn up to the briefing sporting the beginnings of a black eye from getting careless. He could just imagine what Marston would make of that. But the hard, intense workout was just what he need to focus and he felt better for it.

As they started the return journey over the Pennines, Green unzipped his kit bag and pulled out a brown paper envelope, which he stuffed into the glove compartment of Ted's car.

'That's the money I owe you, and the keys to your mother's house. You can drop me anywhere here. It's time I moved on.'

Ted had long since learnt not to expect any fond farewells from Green. He wanted to thank him for his help but knew it would not be well received. It had been quid pro quo for putting him up, no more than that. He pulled over to the side and watched as Green went on his way, his kit bag slung over his shoulder, with the familiar loose-kneed rolling gait of someone used to yomping for miles under a heavy pack.

In a strange way, he would miss having him around. He had contact details for him in dire emergencies but it was a messaging service, not a direct line, with no guarantee Green would return his call. He didn't expect the mobile phone number he'd used recently to still be in service after Green left. But right now, Ted urgently needed a shower, a clean shirt and something to eat before the briefing.

They went up in the Ice Queen's car, with her driving. Cutbacks meant no drivers available for non-essential weekend trips, and as they had no idea how long they would be, it seemed a waste of resources to have a driver sitting waiting for them.

'I see Mr Green was on form,' she remarked at the sight of the red swelling on Ted's right cheekbone, already causing his eye to puff up underneath. She had also experienced some of his training methods during her time in firearms. 'I hope he's left you in a fit state for tomorrow. Is he still around?'

'Moved on, once he'd finished knocking the stuffing out of me. The bits that aren't bruised are still functioning, though. And I still say we're moving too fast, without proper intelligence.'

'I agree, up to a point. But we can't just leave Bacha sitting there indefinitely. And as soon as we have him safely in custody, we can get forensics on to the Astra, once it's found, looking for traces of the victim's blood, and we'll have his clothing for testing.

'With Bacha out of the way, it allows us to go after Kateb and the rest of the gang and hopefully wrap up Croesus with some positive results. For which, of course, Mr Marston will take all the credit whilst you and I just go back to our day jobs.'

Ted smiled to himself. They were gradually becoming easier in each other's company. She was starting to let her guard down more often than before.

Marston was clearly itching to make a sarcastic comment about Ted's face when they arrived at the briefing. His style was cramped by the presence of the ACC, there to sign off on the relevant orders for the operation to go ahead, so he contented himself with saying, 'I hope you're fully operationally fit for tomorrow?'

'Perfectly, sir,' Ted assured him.

The ACC was more relaxed about it. He knew about Ted's SFO training and martial arts skills.

'Looks painful, Ted. Is the other bloke worse?'

'Not this time, sir, but it was a useful training session. I'm ready for action.'

'Right, you all have the final reports,' Marston cut in, his tone impatient, pushing things along, despite the presence of a senior officer. 'I think we need to take this time to go over every last detail, to make sure there is no margin for error. I've got forensics on stand-by for the car and the house search, and the warrants have been issued. Once Bacha is arrested, he can be taken to Stockport, and you organise from there who's to interview him, Darling. We need to get him to start talking and naming names as soon as possible, then we can look at rounding up the rest of them.'

The briefing dragged on. Ted suspected Marston was making a show of covering all bases, in front of the ACC. There would be a command post vehicle close to the scene of the raid, with Ted, the Firearms inspector, Alex Porter and Marston in it. The ACC would be on call but not attending, with Superintendent Caldwell and Neil Smith from Fraud monitoring from the control room. It was unusual for an officer of Marston's rank to attend the scene. It confirmed the suspicions he was determined to grab any glory going, especially if any press cameras turned up.

'I'm sensing you still have reservations?' the Super asked Ted as they drove back together.

'You can't tell me you don't have any yourself, with your own background and training? It bothers me that we don't know for sure about possible firearms in the house.'

'Unfortunately, we won't know that definitely until tomorrow. I'll see you then. Let's hope it all goes well and there are no nasty surprises in store for us.'

'How was the shopping trip?' Ted asked, as he went into the kitchen, where Trev had his TEFL papers strewn everywhere.

Trev looked up, then frowned as he saw his partner's face.

'Ouch. That looks sore. Is the rest of you all right?'

He stood up to plant the gentlest of kisses on the developing bruise.

'I'll live,' Ted smiled. 'Is there any food? I'm quite hungry now. Tell me about your day.'

'Bizzie's great company. We shopped until we dropped and she bought me lunch. I hope her date goes well. I've got some supper on a low light for us. I haven't eaten yet, I was too full after the lovely lunch. Let me just clear the table. I'm doing lesson plans for my next teaching sessions.'

'You're a great teacher. Look how well you've managed getting me, of all people, to ride horses. I'm sorry I'm working this weekend. I'm quite looking forward to taking old Walter out for a gentle jog sometime soon – words I never thought I'd hear myself say.'

'This job tomorrow. Is it going to be dangerous?'

Trev looked at him directly as he asked, wanting to see whether Ted was telling him the truth when he replied.

'For me? No. I'll be tucked up in the command post, out of harm's way, trying not to punch Marston's lights out if he gets above himself. It could get dodgy for the Firearms team going in, though, so try not to worry if you see anything about it on the news.'

'Phone your mother.'

'It's getting a bit late for that. She'll probably be getting ready for bed.'

'Phone your mother,' Trev said, more firmly. 'If anything did happen to you and I hadn't made you call her, she'd never forgive me.'

'Nothing's going to happen to me. Apart from a possible disciplinary for thumping a senior officer. All right, all right,' he went on, seeing Trev's face. 'I'll phone her.'

'Then eat your supper and take me to bed. I'll be gentle with you, because of the bruises.'

Chapter Nineteen

Early Sunday morning on the quiet Stretford side streets. Barely a soul was stirring. Curtains stayed resolutely closed, putting off confrontation with the outer world on a weekend day.

Last minute intelligence had been gathered from all available sources. The Vauxhall Astra, with the false plates, had been found a few streets away. It had been clamped and immobilised and was under observation. If it was the car Bacha had used, there was no way he could drive off in a hurry in it, if he should somehow manage to slip through the closing net of Authorised Firearms Officers surrounding the property.

The surveillance team opposite the house had reported no signs of life. All the curtains were currently closed and there were no sightings of Bacha.

'I'm still not happy we have sufficient intelligence to proceed, sir,' Inspector Porter told Marston.

'Objection duly noted, Inspector, but the risk assessments have been signed off. All appears to be quiet and you tell me your teams are experienced. So let's do this.'

Porter had deployed two squads of four AFOs, each headed by a sergeant. His most experienced officer, Sergeant Julie Hawkins, would lead her squad in through the front door, once it had been broken open for them. The second squad would go round the side of the house to cover the rear in case Bacha decided to make a break for it through a back window.

'Bravo Zero One, we have visual on the AFOs now, just

moving into position outside the target property. All is quiet.'

It was the call sign of one of the surveillance team members in the house opposite. Then the same voice continued, with a note of tension this time.

'Cancel previous. The curtains in the small upstairs room just twitched. There is a possibility the AFOs have been clocked.'

'Alpha Zero Two to all units, stand by,' Porter ordered.

Marston glared at him as he barked, 'If we delay now, we blow the operation.' Then, into the radio, 'Alpha Zero One, on my authority, go, go, go.'

Porter slammed his hand down on the table top and said a resounding, 'Shit.'

Ted agreed with him, but decided it was wiser to keep his counsel. Marston had just ordered the squad to go in, not knowing what fire-power they were facing, and with the suspect now possibly on alert for their arrival. It was potentially their death warrant.

'Charlie Zero One, confirmed. Going in.'

Julie Hawkins' voice was calm and measured as she prepared to do the job she and her team were trained for.

'Bravo Zero One, AFOs approaching the front of the property. Enforcer deployed. Door is open. Team going in.'

The Firearms team had radios on for contact with the command post. Ted, Marston and Porter could hear the familiar shouts of, 'Armed Police,' as the four officers burst into the house and started to make their way up the stairs.

Ted's heart was in his mouth and he knew Porter's would be, too, thinking of the difficulties of going up those stairs with their target above and behind them, before they could make the turn on to the landing at the top. Both knew, from operational experience, how difficult that would be to cover.

Then they heard an unidentified male voice screaming in evident panic, 'Keep away! Keep away or I'll kill her. Get back!'

There was momentary confusion; so much noise and so many voices all at once.

'Armed police! Drop your weapon!'

'Get back! I'll kill her, I swear.'

'Daddy, daddy, help me! Please! Mummy! Someone help me!'

'Armed police! Put the knife down and let the girl go.'

Julie Hawkins' voice, trying to alert the listeners to the situation and the weaponry involved.

Then a man's voice, muffled, roaring in a foreign language, and more screaming, female voices.

'Alpha Zero Two. Sitrep, someone, for fuck's sake. What's going on?'

In his concern for his officers, Porter abandoned all radio protocol in demanding answers.

'Charlie Zero Two. Boss, suspect has a young girl in his room and is using her as a human shield. Charlie Zero One can't get near. He's armed with a knife. That's all we can see.'

'Jesus H. Christ. What's he doing with a girl in his bedroom? Filthy bloody pervert,' Marston spat.

'That's the least of our worries right now,' Porter told him angrily. 'We need to get her and the other civilians out of there alive.'

'Can they not get a shot off?' Marston asked him.

Ted was already on the radio to the Ice Queen asking for a trained negotiator as a matter of urgency. Porter didn't bother dignifying Marston's question with a response. He was too busy talking to his officers.

'Charlie Zero One from Alpha Zero Two. Back away if you can, Julie, just keep him in view. The rest of you, take control of the other civilians. The last thing we need now is any heroics from the father to make things any worse.'

'Charlie Zero One. Boss, there isn't room for anyone to get past me to the bedroom where the parents are. I've told them to stay there, and so far they are doing. But the father is doing his nut, understandably. We can get the other girls out to safety. Their room is directly opposite the stairs. But we need a negotiator in here urgently, boss. He looks off his face and appears unstable.'

Ted got to his feet and took his suit jacket off. He put his Kevlar vest on, then hung his photo ID round his neck. He didn't want to be fishing in a pocket for his warrant card.

'Where the hell do you think you're going, Darling?' Marston demanded.

'Anything could happen while we wait for the negotiator. I'm not trained for that, but look at me. How much of a threat do I look? An unarmed short bloke in shirtsleeves? Let me go over there and see if I can at least assess the situation at first hand. I am SFO trained, don't forget, so if I can get near enough, and get the girl out of harm's way, there's a chance I can disarm him. If you don't want to take responsibility for the decision, sir, ask my Super. Or the ACC. I'm sure they'd both agree.'

Marston was hesitating and there was no time to. Ted fixed his radio to his vest and switched it on. He was going, whatever the Chief Super said.

'Thanks, Ted,' Porter told him gratefully.

'Do it,' Marston spat.

'Get the road sealed off from both ends and don't let anyone near to spook him. I'll let you know the situation from inside as soon as I can.'

'What about gas?' Marston had one last try at managing the operation himself.

Ted ignored him and left the vehicle, jogging up the road to the target house. One of Sergeant Hawkins' team was ushering two frightened teenagers down the stairs and into the front room on the ground floor, where they would stay with them to prevent them trying to rush to the aid of the rest of the family. A wise decision had been made by the AFOs on the scene that any move to evacuate the family into the road risked distracting

Bacha and making him even more dangerous.

The staircase went up towards a wall, then made a right-angle turn with a wider step, then up two more stairs to the landing. One of the team was standing at the top of the stairs and pressed back against the wall to allow Ted to pass. The sergeant was at the end of the landing. There was a closed door to her left and an open one straight in front of her, through which Ted could see the suspect, holding a knife to the throat of a clearly terrified young girl wearing pyjamas.

'Dorian? My name's Ted. I'm a police officer, but I'm here to see if I can help you. To calm the situation down a bit. It's bad, but if we all just calm down and take a breath, we might be able to stop it from getting any worse. I'd like that and I'm sure you probably would, too.'

A man's voice was shouting continuously from behind the closed door. A foreign language, the tone alternating between evident menace and entreaty. A woman was clearly arguing and pleading with him. Ted hoped the man would have the sense to stay where he was and not escalate the situation any further.

Sergeant Hawkins still had her sights trained on Bacha, looking for the slightest opening to get a shot off when she received authority. She never moved her head but she just had Ted in her peripheral vision. She'd been informed by radio that he was coming, but nothing more about him. If she'd been hoping for the cavalry, she seemed disappointed in this short, slight man with the quiet voice and no visible firearm.

'Sergeant, could you take half a step back, please. To allow me to come a little closer? Dorian, is that all right, if I just come a bit nearer? You can see that I'm not carrying any weapons, and I'll keep my hands up where you can see them.'

'If you come nearer, I'll kill her.'

'Yes, you said. But I don't think you want to do that. Not really. Not a little girl. A cousin, is she? You don't want to kill a family member.'

He looked directly at the girl and smiled reassuringly.

'Hello. I'm Ted. What's your name?'

She was trembling like a leaf and he could see that her pyjama bottoms were wet where she'd panicked and lost control.

'Y-Yasmine.'

'Yasmine. That's a pretty name. How old are you, Yasmine?'

She stammered again. 'Eleven. Please, I'm frightened. I want my mum.'

'Dorian? Do you hear that? She's a frightened little girl and she wants her mum. Why don't you let Yasmine go? Then you and I can talk.'

'As soon as I let her go, you'll shoot me.'

'We won't shoot you. We are here to arrest you, I won't lie to you about that. But we won't shoot you, unless you force us to. Don't make this any worse than it is. Let Yasmine go to her mother. If you want a hostage, you can have me instead. Like I said, I'm not armed. You don't want to kill Yasmine. Let her go.'

'She'll shoot me as soon as I do.'

His wide, terrified eyes swung to the armed officer nearest to him, then back to Ted.

'What if I get her to lower her gun? And what if I stood in front of you, like a human shield. Then will you let Yasmine go?'

He could see Sergeant Hawkins' eyes widen. He just hoped she would trust him enough to obey his orders.

'You see, Dorian, the problem is this. If you harm Yasmine in any way, then the sergeant will immediately shoot you, on my order. This way, we can at least get you out of here alive. And I can promise you, all the officers here today are highly trained and ethical. You will be treated properly. Just let Yasmine go. I'll get the sergeant to lower her firearm, then I'll come in and we can talk. If she takes a shot, it will hit me, and not you. This vest will stop the worst of it but I'll still be seriously injured and she knows that.'

He wished he had a way to let Sergeant Hawkins know he was an ex-SFO, but he couldn't risk anything which might give the game away to Bacha.

'How do I know I can trust you?'

'I'll show you. Sergeant, can you please lower your weapon?'

Inspector Porter was listening to the entire exchange, holding his breath. He spoke softly into the radio, his voice barely discernible.

'Do it, Julie.'

Slowly, reluctantly, she let the muzzle dip down so it was no longer trained on Bacha.

'Now, what about letting Yasmine go?'

'I could walk out of here now with her in front of me. You won't be able to shoot me because of her. You'd risk hitting her instead.'

The man's voice had gone up in pitch and was sounding panicky, irrational.

'Yasmine, look at me. Don't be afraid. We're going to get you out of here safely and back to your mum and dad very shortly. Dorian, that's not true, I'm afraid. We've clamped your car, for one thing, so you can't get away. Secondly, there's not just the sergeant here. There are seven more highly trained firearms officers, any of whom is capable of shooting you without causing any harm to Yasmine. But none of us wants that. So let's find an easier way.

'Let me come in and take Yasmine's place. Just let her go to her mum and dad. You must see she's terrified. Don't put her through any more of this, Dorian. Look, you can see I'm not carrying a firearm, and I'm happy to keep my hands up. What harm can I do to you? Let's just talk about this sensibly. Can I come in, and will you let Yasmine go?'

Bacha was looking wild-eyed. It was starting to dawn on

him that he was caught like a rat in a trap with no way out, unless he allowed himself to be arrested. He appeared to be looking for something, anything, to delay the inevitable.

'Take off your vest thing. Your protection,' he ordered. 'I can't see what you might have hidden underneath it.'

'All right, if that's what you want.'

Ted lowered his arms slowly and carefully then started to remove the stab vest.

'Sir, you can't do that ...' the sergeant began.

'What the hell is he doing?' Marston asked of no one in particular in the command vehicle.

'He's doing his job,' Porter told him. 'He's getting a kiddy out of there unhurt.'

Moving slowly, Ted slipped out of the vest and lowered it cautiously to the floor by his feet, then once again held his hands up where Bacha could see them both clearly. He turned round slowly on the spot, so Bacha could see the front and back of him.

'There you are. You can see now. No hidden weapons. Just a clean shirt. Now, will you let me come in and stand in front to protect you while you let Yasmine go?'

'Sir, you're putting yourself at risk ...' the sergeant tried again.

Ted ignored her as he asked, 'What about it, Dorian? Can we do an exchange? Me for Yasmine?'

He again looked directly at the girl and smiled as encouragingly as he could.

'Don't worry, Yasmine. We're going to get you out of here. As soon as Dorian lets go of you, you run straight into your parents' room and you stay there, and tell them to stay there, too. You're doing very well. Good girl.'

Time seemed to have slowed to a crawl, with everything happening in slow motion, while Bacha tried to weigh up his options and decide what to do next. Ted began to step cautiously into the room, his body effectively blocking any chance of a shot from the sergeant's gun from reaching the target.

It was a small room, more box-room than bedroom. It seemed to take an eternity for him to cover the short distance. As soon as he was within grabbing range, Bacha took his knife from the girl's throat, shoved her forwards, away from him, then reached out to take hold of Ted, pulling him closer.

Freed from the paralysis of terror, the girl fled out of the room and burst through the door of the bedroom next door to find sanctuary in the arms of her parents.

When Sergeant Hawkins came to write her report later on, she found she had no real idea at all of what had happened next. Everything suddenly seemed to go so fast. She was fully expecting the knife to be plunged into the DCI's now unprotected body. Instead she saw him make a series of lightning-quick but economical movements with arms and legs. Before she knew it, the knife had flown from Bacha's hand and he was face down, eating carpet, and with both hands immobilised behind his back.

'Could you lend me your handcuffs, please, sergeant? I don't want to let go to get at mine.'

'Bloody hell, sir,' she said in awe, producing her cuffs and handing them to him so he could secure his prisoner, as he cautioned him.

'Please can you confirm to the command vehicle that the prisoner is now secure. Then perhaps you'd like to get him taken away and stand your teams down.'

'Bloody hell,' she said again. 'Sorry sir, but I've never seen anything like that before.'

Ted grinned at her conspiratorially as he pulled Bacha to his feet.

'Sorry about that. I'm an ex-SFO, but clearly I couldn't tell you that because I didn't want to alert the suspect. People tend to look at me and dismiss me because I don't look threatening. It comes in very handy sometimes.'

Two members of the squad had come upstairs now their sergeant had given the all clear. They escorted Bacha downstairs and out of the house to the awaiting transport. Marston had issued instructions from the command post that he should be taken directly to the Stockport station. Ted was SIO on the murder enquiry; his team would deal with questioning the prime suspect.

The car with Ted's own boss and Inspector Neil Smith had appeared and parked near the command vehicle which had also now moved closer. Ted saw to his horror that there were already press vehicles at the scene, down by the tapes cordoning the road off.

Ted knew he needed to go and report in as soon as possible for a debrief. But first he found himself confronted by Yasmine's father, appearing from the bedroom, eyes brimming with tears of relief at the safe release of his daughter.

He was still in his pyjamas, hair wildly ruffled. He seized Ted's hand in a strong grip, pumping it up and down as he expressed his thanks. Through the now open door, Ted could see the girl folded protectively in the arms of her mother who was rocking her gently, talking constantly to her in a foreign language.

'Thank you, sir, thank you so much for saving my little girl. I wanted to try to myself, but my wife kept telling me I would only make things worse. But what could be worse than knowing your daughter is being held by someone with a knife and to hear her screaming in terror for her daddy.

'I have been weak and stupid in letting my cousin's son into our house and bringing the police to our door, then not having the courage to protect my girls and my wife.'

'Sir, you did absolutely the right thing in staying in your room with armed officers in the house. Please don't worry about that. We're going to need to get statements from all of you about Dorian and his time here. We are also going to have to search your house, so we'll have to arrange to move you out somewhere while that's done.'

The AFOs were still in front of the property when Ted came out, putting his vest back on, not because he anticipated further danger but because he was feeling cold now after the earlier exertion. They formed a loose guard of honour as he walked past, each of them giving him a 'Nice one, sir,' or similar as he did so, appreciative of a senior officer with the balls to be in the front line, and without his protective vest.

Ted stopped to have another couple of words with Sergeant Hawkins before he left and to thank her for her work, and that of the teams. She'd not met him before, but she had heard he was a different sort of senior officer.

'That was pretty awesome in there, sir,' she told him. 'It took some bottle to go up against a nutter with a knife, without your vest on. Even with SFO training.'

Ted looked down to the end of the road where he could see the tall and imposing figure of the Ice Queen standing outside the command vehicle, looking hard in his direction.

'I have a feeling not everyone is going to be all that pleased with how I handled it.'

Chapter Twenty

Ted wasn't surprised to see Marston hurrying down the road towards the waiting press pack, probably intent on claiming the credit for a successful arrest. Ted didn't care. As far as he was concerned it was job done, move on with the next part of the enquiry. He took his mobile out of his trouser pocket to call Rob O'Connell. He wanted him and Sal to start questioning Bacha as soon as he arrived at the Stockport station and had been processed.

Inspectors Alex Porter and Neil Smith were coming up the road to debrief their teams. They paused to thump Ted on the back in recognition and have a few words with him.

'Bloody good job that, Ted,' Porter told him. 'Still got the moves, eh? It could have got messy in there, all thanks to that prick not listening to people who know.'

'I don't know your Super, sir, but from the look on her face when we passed her just now, I'd say she's not standing there to welcome you with open arms. Who's been a naughty boy, then, sir? Still, just as well you ripped up the rule book and got stuck in.'

'Meanwhile that useless piece of piss is down there parading himself in front of the cameras playing Man of the Match, while it was you and my teams in there doing the dangerous stuff. Probably telling them he single-handedly shinned up the drainpipe with a dagger between his teeth to overpower a heavily armed assailant.'

The three men laughed, united in their dislike of the senior officer who had been foisted on them and who had nearly let the operation go badly wrong through not listening to those who knew what they were doing. The other two went on their way, leaving Ted to go and face the music.

As he got nearer, he could see what Neil Smith had meant about the Ice Queen. She could be cold at the best of times. Right now, she looked positively glacial.

'Am I to assume, Chief Inspector, that you are not familiar with the latest regulations and directives on the wearing of body armour for officers in this force?'

'I am, ma'am.' Ted decided to be formal and to try to sound as contrite as he could manage. 'I had to make a rapid reappraisal of the situation and I took the view that the risk was justifiable in the circumstances.'

'I see,' she said levelly, then her expression softened. 'You didn't hear this from me, and I will deny saying it, but very well done, Ted. I'm a mother and I can't begin to imagine what that young girl's parents were going through. Not to mention the fear she was in herself.

'You do know there will now have to be endless debriefings and enquiries. But for what it's worth, I'm prepared to accept that you had to make a judgement call in extremely difficult circumstances and that, although your actions were unorthodox, they may well have prevented loss of life. Also that, given your particular skills, it was a calculated risk to take.'

'Thank you, ma'am,' Ted replied cautiously, still half expecting a sting in the tail of her compliments.

'While Mr Marston is busy with the press, why don't you and I go in search of some decent coffee and something to eat before we make our way to Central Park? I don't know about you, but the tepid liquid they produce for us there is not my idea of what we need after a morning like this. Certainly not much of a Central Perk.'

It was the first time Ted had heard her make anything close

to a joke. She was clearly in a good mood.

They arrived at Central Park for the debrief, pleasantly replete with cappuccino, and bacon rolls. The Super had wanted to pay but Ted insisted it was his turn, after she'd bought the Chinese at the pre-op briefing. It had been a surprisingly relaxed and informal time between them. No shop talk, just two work colleagues chatting about nothing of any consequence. There would be time for the inquests into what had happened when they drove home together at whatever time the debriefing with Marston ended.

At the Super's suggestion, they each took a quiet moment to call their nearest and dearest, checking in after a difficult operation, full of reassurances, not yet knowing what, if anything, had appeared on the local news channels.

'Oh my God, it was you, wasn't it? The unidentified plain clothes officer who disarmed a raving nutter with a knife? What were you thinking of, taking risks like that?' Trev sounded horrified, rather than reassured, when Ted called him. 'I caught it on the local news just now.'

'It was nothing like as dramatic as that, honestly,' Ted hastily reassured him. 'Really. I had armed officers backing me up and there was no real danger.'

'Ted Darling, as soon as you start saying honestly, I know you're telling porkies. I want to know all the details, as soon as you get back. But I imagine you'll be ages yet, with debriefs and so on?'

'I honestly have no idea what time I'll get away. But if it's at a decent time, do you fancy going out for a meal somewhere? Save you having to cook, and just a little celebration that this part of the operation, at least, is pretty much wrapped up now.'

'That sounds good. I'm actually taking Bizzie out for a spin on the bike and a pub lunch today. She's probably even worse at appropriate small talk than you are, so I'm going to coach her for this hot date. I have a feeling that Douglas is more interested in a different aspect of the human heart to the medical one.

'So I'm going to need to find a way to burn off a lot of calories, if I make a pig of myself with two meals out in the same day.'

'Oh, I think we can probably think of something which would fit that particular bill.'

The ACC (Crime) was attending the debriefing, as overall head of the operation. He was the one who would have to justify every action of all the officers present. He was clearly going to need some answers as to what had gone on. In particular, he would want to know what had led to Ted going in against an armed suspect without wearing the regulation body armour.

'Mr Marston, perhaps we could begin with your report, please?' the ACC asked him, to start the ball rolling. 'In particular, tell me why you took the decision to go ahead with the operation, despite the warning from the surveillance team.'

Everything which was said was being recorded and would be transcribed. Then it would be gone through, painstakingly, at executive level, to see what lessons could be learnt and what actions needed to be taken.

'Sir, a great many hours and a great deal of expense had already gone into this operation. The arrest of Bacha was viewed as the critical pivot, without which we might not have sufficient information to bring in the rest of the gang. There was no evidence of firearms present in the target house, just a suggestion that there might be. On balance, I took the view that we had enough trained officers to go ahead and enter the property.'

'So it was largely a financial decision?'

'No, sir, not at all. I felt the arrest of Bacha was an achievable objective so I gave the order to go.'

'Inspector Porter, from what I heard, you were not entirely

happy with that decision?'

'Sir, I would have preferred more intelligence before deploying, it's true.'

Porter was being economical with his words, knowing Marston's reputation for revenge.

'I see. And Mr Marston, when the situation developed into a hostage one, you authorised Chief Inspector Darling's presence at the house?'

'I did, sir. But at no point did I authorise him to remove his body armour, which is in direct contravention of the regulations.'

'Sir, the decision to take my vest off was mine and mine alone.'

Much as Ted disliked Marston he didn't expect the Chief Super to carry the can for any decisions he had made.

'I see,' the ACC repeated. 'In which case, Chief Inspector, you and I need to talk further, in private. Mr Marston, I'll leave you to finish your debrief and I look forward to your report as soon as possible. Chief Inspector, come and find me in my office when you're done here. Are you independently mobile?'

'No, sir, I came up with my Superintendent.'

'Very well. I'll try not to keep you too long, in that case. And what of Bacha now? Where is he and what's happening with him? Time is of the essence, I imagine, with a limited time to hold him for questioning before you either charge him or will have to release him. It seems as if you haven't a great deal to go on yet.'

'He's been transported to Stockport, sir, and I've put DS O'Connell and DC Ahmed on to questioning him. Forensics are all over the car and the house and they know the deadline is tight so they're working on it flat out.'

'And are those two officers up to the task?'

'I believe so, sir, and I will go and oversee them, as soon as I'm finished here.'

'Then we'd better get on. Thank you, everyone, as you

were.'

All assembled, even Marston, had made to rise as the ACC got up to leave, but he waved them down as he left the room.

The last thing Ted wanted to do now was to spend hours going over what had happened, what didn't happen, what might have happened. He also found himself pondering anxiously what the ACC was going to say to him in private. He may have got a good result but he had broken all kinds of rules in doing so. He could possibly get the book thrown at him.

Marston wanted every I dotted and every T crossed before he ended the meeting. Ted got a surprisingly sympathetic look from his Super and a promise to wait for him while he went to his meeting with the ACC.

There was no secretary on duty on a Sunday so Ted knocked and waited to be told to enter. He got an idea of the serious trouble he was in when the ACC looked up and said, 'Remain standing, Chief Inspector.'

'Sir.'

'Tell me in your own words why you took the decision to ignore regulations and go into that room with a suspect armed with a knife, having removed your body armour, rather than waiting for the trained negotiator to arrive. A person you knew was on the way because they had been summoned at your request.

'Sir, I went to the house to attempt to get more detailed intelligence on the situation. I thought that, because of my appearance, I might seem less intimidating than AFOs in full gear and I might even be able to calm things down. I could see immediately that the situation was becoming critical and that the suspect was losing self-control, so there was a real and present danger to life.

'It was not my intention to remove my body armour, but the suspect insisted on that. I carried out a further risk assessment and decided that, being ex-SFO, I had the skills necessary to manage the situation and to have a realistic chance of success.'

'Precisely, Chief Inspector. Ex-SFO, with the emphasis on ex. When did you last do any update training connected to that role?'

Ted's hand went up to the side of his face in an involuntary gesture, touching the sore and inflamed area Green had inflicted on him the day before.

'Yesterday, sir. My Superintendent agreed to me doing a crash update course with a Special Forces trainer, to help me prepare for today, just in case.'

The ACC lowered his head to look down at his desk. Ted couldn't swear to it, but he thought he saw the ghost of a smile before his face was hidden. Then he looked up again, his expression serious once more.

'I could make a disciplinary out of this, you realise? But having listened to what you've said, I think there is a more appropriate way of dealing with this. Something I know you will dislike sufficiently for you to consider your actions carefully in the future, should anything similar arise.'

Whatever was coming next, Ted knew he wasn't going to like it.

'I'm minded to put you forward for a Chief Constable's commendation for bravery. I know others have tried before me, and failed. This time, you are going to accept. You are also going to attend the black tie reception to receive it. There's one scheduled for next month, so I'll get you added to the guest list, with your partner, as it's open to Other Halves. And you are going to pose, smiling nicely, for any publicity photographs required. That should give you pause for thought next time you decide to rip up the rule book and play heroics.

'Right, we're done here. Go and sort out this suspect, now you have him under lock and key.'

'Yes, sir. Thank you, sir.'

As soon as Ted left his office, the ACC put a call through to the Chief Constable. He was at home and on call, and had been waiting for news.

'Like a lamb to the slaughter, Chief,' the ACC told him. 'He thought he was accepting the commendation to avoid a disciplinary, so he was happy to accept. You'll finally get him at your black tie reception, and have some photos of him to show how inclusive the modern police force is.'

Both men were chuckling as they ended the call.

Seeing Ted's glum face as he slid into the car next to her, the Super asked, her tone solicitous, 'It didn't go well, then, with the ACC?'

'He's putting me forward for a Chief Constable's commendation and I have to accept it and go to the reception and everything.'

She paused the car before pulling out from the car park on to the road, so she could turn and look at him.

'You really are a very strange man, Ted. From the look on your face, I thought at the very least you'd been put on restricted duties pending an investigation. This is actually good news.'

'Is it?' Ted said glumly. 'I hate anything like that. Mind you, Trev will love a black tie do.'

'Speaking of Trevor, there was something I wanted to mention to you, if you wouldn't consider it impertinent. You'll almost certainly have thought of it yourself, but it was something which was going through my mind during your heroics today. So I thought I would raise it with you, if you would excuse the apparent intrusion into your private life.'

'Go on,' Ted said guardedly, intrigued, in spite of himself. The Ice Queen was not one to make any kind of intrusion, or at least, she never had, to date.

'I'm sure I wasn't alone when I say that there was a brief moment there, earlier on, when I was not sure if you were going to emerge from that house alive. So I thought it was worth mentioning to you that if you were to die in the line of duty and Trevor was your partner, not your husband, he wouldn't get any of your pension, nor a lump sum payout. I'm sure you must have considered that already, but I just thought I'd flag it up.'

He was quiet for so long she asked anxiously, 'I do hope I haven't crossed a line?'

'No, not at all, I appreciate your concern. I have asked him to marry me, several times. He just doesn't believe in it. Thinks we're fine as we are. And that's true, we're a lot more solid than a lot of married couples I know. But I do think about the financial thing. A lot. I'll talk to him again. Because you're right. He's entitled to have my pension, as my next of kin. We just need to make it formal, as things stand at the moment.'

Rob and Sal were doing a good job with Bacha. He was trying to stay tight-lipped, on his solicitor's advice, but would make occasional attempts to ask for some sort of a deal, if he provided names of all the gang members he knew, in exchange for a lighter sentence.

Jo was watching the interview on a monitor, noting down anything which needed more checking or could help them progress the enquiry.

'How did it go, boss? What happened in the end? We only got snatches from the radio, and from the two officers who delivered him. They said they'd heard the arresting officer was some high-kicking bloke in plain clothes, so I'm presuming that was you?'

'Something and nothing really,' Ted shrugged it off. 'With the hostage situation, the shooters couldn't do much so it needed someone with close combat skills. No biggy. Anyway, we have plenty from this morning to hold him on and forensics are working flat out on the car, the house and his clothing, so we might finally be getting somewhere.'

'What about the rest of the gang? When are they going to be rounded up?'

'That's up to Mr Marston and the ACC, but there's nothing to be gained by leaving them at large for any longer now we have Bacha in custody.

'I'm going to try to get away at a reasonable time today if I can. I don't seem to have seen much of Trev, certainly not this weekend, so I'd quite like to take him out for a meal tonight.'

'No worries at all, boss. I've got this, and knowing you, you'll keep your phone on so I can always contact you if necessary. You go, have a good time. Oh, and boss? You perhaps don't know it but I know Neil Smith well. We trained together. So I will find out how much of a biggy it was.'

'Right, you, tell me all about it, and don't leave any details out. I want to know what you were thinking of, putting yourself at risk like that. And remember, I can always tell if you're trying to lie.'

Trev had greeted him with a hug when he got home, one which effectively immobilised him, unless he used his skills to detach himself. It made it even harder for Ted to be economical with the truth, which is what he would have preferred.

'I don't know what they said on the radio but it was really nothing all that dramatic at all. A suspect with a knife holding a young girl hostage. I just went in and disarmed him.'

'Just like that?'

'Just like that. Now, I need a shower and a change of clothes if we're going out to eat but first I wanted to ask you something. I want us to get married.'

Trev released him from the hug and stepped back so he could study his face.

'Ted, we keep going over this. I don't want to do the whole marriage thing. You're just about accepted for having me as a partner. It would change everything, me being your husband. And what about Jim? You know he could never cope with that and he's your best friend.'

'But you know that if anything should ever happen to me

on an op like today's you wouldn't get a penny of my pension, unless we were married.'

'Honestly Ted, that is about the least romantic proposal I've ever heard. Do you really think I'm only interested in your pension?'

'You want romantic? I can do romantic. I'll do the full down on one knee thing, if that's what you want. I just don't want you to miss out, if ever anything did happen to me. The person I'm with is entitled to that pension, but the current rules say I have to be married to them. So would you at least think about it? Please?'

'So you want me to do the whole 'will you take this man, and his police pension, for your lawful wedded husband' thing? It makes it all seem so mercenary. I think what we've got is special. I don't want to change it. If we do get married, we might spoil it. Just like mentioning it, like this, has a bit spoilt my appetite for what I thought was going to be a nice evening out together.'

'I'm sorry, I didn't mean to. Look, let me just get showered and we'll go out. Forget I brought it up so clumsily and spoilt the mood. Please?'

He could tell Trev was thawing, so he threw in the clincher.

'And I'm going to be taking you to another black tie occasion soon. The ACC put me forward for a commendation and I've accepted.'

Trev looked at him suspiciously.

Well, you look like Ted, but who are you really? My Ted has never accepted a commendation in his life.'

'I was a bit backed into a corner. I didn't quite follow operational procedure, so this is my punishment.'

Trev was shaking his head in disbelief.

'I do honestly sometimes wonder what I see in you, thinking you're hard done by being forced to attend a formal reception and accept an honour that you deserve.'

'I know. I'm hopeless. But I do love you, you know that.

I'm sorry I screwed up my latest proposal, but let me take you out for a meal, and I'll try to make it up to you. I just need that shower first, then I'm all yours for the evening.'

'I could do with a shower, too. Why don't we share, to save on water? Then we'll see if I've worked off my big lunch and have enough of an appetite to go and be piggy again.'

Chapter Twenty-one

Bill was back on duty at the front desk when Ted signed himself in on Monday morning. Fire regulations meant a record had to be kept of who was on the premises at all times, and when they left, even in a relatively small station.

'Here he is, the hero of the hour,' Bill greeted him. He certainly looked a lot better than he had the last time Ted had visited him.

'Shut up,' Ted told him mildly. 'I was doing my job, nothing more. And how the heck do you know anything about it? How are you, anyway? You look better than you did. Sorry I couldn't get up to see you again, it's been manic.'

'Oh, I wasn't expecting any more visits from a highly commended senior officer,' Bill told him with a wink, although his own uniform sported a few medal ribbons, including one for bravery. 'And surely you know by now there are no secrets at all in the force. Everyone knows about your flagrant disregard for regulations yesterday.'

'I'm never going to be allowed to live this down, am I?' Ted asked, as he headed for the stairs.

He was in ahead of the team, as he often was, wanting a few quiet moments at his desk to catch up before they got together for the morning briefing. He kept an eye out for when they were all in, then went out into the main office to join them. As he did so, every team member present rose to their feet and began to applaud.

'Behave yourselves and sit down,' he told them, but he was

smiling as he said it. He hated fuss, but it meant more to him that his team applauded him than any award the Chief Constable could give him. Unless Trev stopped him, that would go straight up into the loft with his many shooting trophies from his Firearms days.

'I told you I knew Neil Smith well, boss,' Jo reminded him. 'I got the full, unabridged version from him of what you did and how you saved that young girl. We're all proud of you, and those of us who have kids of their own are especially grateful.

'Neil also told me enough about a certain amount of rule-bending which we may just have to remind you of in the future, when you're chasing any of us for procedural misconduct. And if we get chance after work today, we'd like to buy you a drink. If we all club together, we might just about be able to afford one of your ginger beers.'

'Thanks, everyone, I appreciate it, but don't count on it today. We've got a lot to get through. Rob, give us a quick update on Bacha, then you and Sal get back to him, if he's had his rest period. The Super has already said she'll give us a twelve-hour extension to hold him if we need it while we're waiting for something from forensics. We can certainly charge him from yesterday, but make sure it's clear to him and his solicitor that there are likely to be more charges to follow.

'Océane, any mobile devices, laptops or whatever coming from the scene will be your department and will take priority over anything else. We're looking, of course, for any links between Bacha and Kateb, or any other known associates. You have the list of names. I'm assuming some of his interactions, at least, will be in French, so that's definitely one for you, please.

'The knife that was taken from Bacha at the scene had been cleaned but forensics found blood traces on it. They're working on matching those to our victim, Mrs Ashworth's, blood.'

'You mean the knife you took off him, boss? After taking off your body armour?' Maurice asked innocently.

'All right, everyone, listen up. That subject is now closed and off limits, please. Unless anyone fancies being confined to their desk doing filing for the rest of the week?'

He looked round at the team as he spoke. They knew the boss was easy-going, but they also knew that when he spoke like that, he meant it. Ted was just glad Jezza wasn't in. She would no doubt have enjoyed teasing him about his heroics.

'No? Good. So let's get on. Time is pressing. I can't yet tell you when Mr Marston is planning to start rounding up the rest of the gang. No doubt he'll be calling a briefing at some point today, but that's probably dependent on what we get out of Bacha.

'Some of the rest of you may well be involved in other arrests. Virgil, you need to stay close to home again, just in case Jezza needs you in a hurry.

'I want to use my own team members to talk to the family in whose home Bacha was staying; all of them. Megan, in particular, I'd like you to interview the youngest daughter, please. I'm sure she'll find it much easier talking to someone like you. We'll need to arrange appropriate adults to be with the daughters. Clearly not their parents, in case of co-witnessing.'

'Boss, do we know why that piece of shit had the young lass in his bedroom?' Maurice asked, scowling. The father of twin girls, his mind was working overtime on the implications.

'All we know from the scene is that Yasmine, the youngest daughter, was sleeping in her parents' room, on a fold-up bed just inside the door, while Bacha had her room, next door. It seems Bacha was awake and alert and may have seen the AFOs moving into position, so he grabbed the girl as a human shield.'

'With the father in the bedroom? Why didn't he do something?'

'There's nothing to be gained by making judgements when we don't have all the facts. At this stage, that side of things is not relevant to our enquiries. As soon as I know, from Mr

Marston, who's doing what, I'll assign further tasks to you all.

'Maurice, I want you on this too, you're good at talking to people. Perhaps you can take the father, but don't be judgemental of him, please. He's to be treated with courtesy. He was in an impossible situation and will probably blame himself for the rest of his life. I doubt he could feel any worse than he does, so let's not add to what he's going through by insinuating he's somehow at fault.

'He speaks excellent English, but I'm not sure about the mother. I only heard her speaking something else. Would it be Arabic, Océane, if they're from Algeria originally?'

'Arabic or possibly Berber, boss. But it's quite likely she'll speak French as well, if not English, especially if they lived in France.'

'Are we treating him and his wife as accomplices, boss?' Mike Hallam asked him.

'Rob, anything from the interview so far to suggest that we should?'

'Nothing, boss. He's not said anything to implicate them. Far from it, he's just said he was staying with them and they knew nothing about the work he was doing for Kateb.'

'Right, well, get whatever you can from him as soon as you can, and keep me posted. In the meantime, I'll talk to CPS and see what they're happy for us to charge him with as holding charges, until we get all of the forensics in.'

A call from the Ice Queen interrupted him before he could phone the Crown Prosecution Service.

'Anything yet from the suspect?'

'He's not saying a great deal at the moment. Have you heard when the next briefing at Central Park is? Or what the plan is for further arrests?'

'Mr Marston is being unusually quiet at the moment, but I've no doubt we'll be summoned in due course. I suspect there are still meetings at executive level about yesterday's events.'

'I want to get the team on to interviewing the family, but I was waiting to hear if he had other ideas about how things should go from here.'

'I would suggest that as you are SIO on the murder enquiry, you proceed as you would on any other such case. If Mr Marston disagrees with how you think things should be handled, I'm happy to say I authorised you to continue.'

Ted's next phone call was from Jim Baker. Even on sick leave, he'd heard all about what had happened the previous day. Ted had to listen meekly while his other boss first tore him off a strip about how he'd proceeded, then finished up with, 'Bloody good work, though, Ted. And about bloody time you agreed to accept a commendation. Yes, I heard about that, too. The jungle drums are still working.'

His next phone call was the one he'd been hoping for. Doug, from the forensics lab.

'Morning, boss, how are the pussy cats?'

Doug was another cat-lover, who showed his British Shorthairs. Ted was itching to know the results of forensic testing so far but took the time to chat briefly. It was always a good idea to keep the forensics lot on side. They would go out of their way to help anyone who was polite and treated them like humans. It was still something of a rarity from some officers. Ted was happy to make feline small talk, especially when Doug said he'd missed a cat show the previous day to work on the bloods Ted was waiting for.

'Bacha's DNA is all over the exterior and interior of the Astra. The traces of blood remaining on the knife are a positive match for the victim, Vera Ashworth. So as you took the knife from him – and well done for that, boss – we have him handling the knife which was almost certainly used to kill the victim. We're still working, so you'll have more as the day goes on. I know you're coming up to your twenty-four hours of holding him, so I thought you'd like that to be going on with.'

'Thanks so much, Doug, I really appreciate your hard work. And I'm really sorry Cadfael missed his show.'

A damp Monday lunchtime in a park. A bunch of teenage girls, sitting around on benches, swigging from cans, smoking cigarettes, taking endless selfies. Waiting for something – anything – to break the monotony of the day. Some of them should have been in school. Others were meant to be actively seeking work, to appease parents and try to earn some money.

One of them, with pink hair and piercings, would probably have been interviewing witnesses to yesterday's hostage situation, had she not been hanging out with the others who had no clue at all as to her true identity.

They watched, like a pride of hungry lionesses, on the lookout for sufficiently vulnerable prey to come along. Even hunting in a pack, they ignored those who looked strong enough to put up a fight. Sometimes people would appear at the end of the path leading towards them, see them lying in wait, then suddenly remember an important appointment elsewhere and turn tail. There weren't many people about. The odds of any who were nearby being have-a-go heroes who would come to their aid were too slim to gamble with.

Jezza was sitting companionably close to the ringleader, Tara. She was slowly gaining her trust. She had earned it by showing no fear in the face of aggression. The others were afraid of her, she knew, as they'd seen early on that she could handle herself. She was gradually slipping into the role of lieutenant. She knew a lot about Tara and the individual members now, almost enough to go on. It was getting nearly time to wind up her undercover operation.

'Eh, Tara, look at this,' one of the girls said to attract her attention.

Tara and Jezza looked up. A young woman was walking along the path towards them, seemingly unconcerned. She had a camera on a strap around her neck. Even from a distance, Jezza recognised her immediately. The local reporter. Pocket Billiards' replacement, Penny Hunter. She knew there was no reason for Penny to know her by sight. Even if she'd glimpsed her before, she would never recognise her in her current get-up.

Tara sprang up off the back of the bench she was sitting on and stepped into the path of the oncoming reporter, who was continuing on her way, apparently unconcerned by the reception committee. Jezza got up to stand next to Tara, her mind already racing to find a way to get the journalist out of there unharmed. She must surely realise what a target she presented, carrying what was evidently an expensive camera.

Penny Hunter still seemed calm as she walked closer. She was either blissfully unaware of the danger, or she had some secret weapon to deploy at the last moment.

'Hi,' she said in greeting. 'I'm from the local paper. I wonder if I could talk to you? I want to do a piece about what there is for young people to do in Stockport. What their job prospects are like, what needs to be done to make things better for them.'

She was either fearless or naïve. Jezza didn't yet know which, but she was becoming worried about the situation getting out of her control. Tara was prowling round the reporter now, in menacing circles, eyeing up the camera.

'What is there for us to do? Fuck all. What are our job prospects? Fuck all.'

The rest of the girls laughed, but there was an edge of nervousness to it. They knew that something was about to kick off. The reporter still seemed oblivious to the menace in the air.

Tara's hand shot out and grabbed the camera by the strap, yanking the journalist towards her so that their faces were inches apart.

'But this? This would get us a few bob to buy a load more voddies and cranberry, then we wouldn't give a shit that there was nothing for us to do round here.'

Penny tried to pull away but the grip on the camera strap was too tight.

'The camera's not mine. It belongs to the paper. I just wanted to talk to you, to give you the chance to talk about how things are, growing up in Stockport. To put your point of view across.'

Tara jerked on the strap once more, then her spare hand went up to grab a fistful of the reporter's hair. Jezza saw her leg start to come up to smack her in the face as she lost her balance. She moved fast to get between the two of them.

'Wait! Don't mark her. This one's mine. You have the camera. I've got a mate who'd pay good money for her, but not if she's damaged. That part will come later.'

Tara hesitated as Jezza squared up to her. Jezza had no idea what would happen if the rest of the pack backed their leader and waded in. At the moment, none of them seemed to have much appetite for a fight. Even Tara was hesitating.

'We want a share of the money.'

'Yeah, no worries. You just have to trust me. Let me take her to my friend then I'll come back with the cash. If I don't, you know where I live.'

As part of establishing her cover, Jezza had had Tara and a couple of others round to the miserable one-bedroom flat she was using. It had seemed to convince them that she was one of them. That and her drama skills.

'Give us your phone,' Tara told the reporter, dragging the camera roughly from round her neck.

Penny had obviously decided by now that if she was to get out of there unscathed, the line of least resistance was the best one to follow. She fished in her coat pocket and pulled out an expensive-looking smartphone, which she handed over reluctantly.

Jezza took the opportunity to grab her roughly by the arm, pulling her away from Tara and ordering, 'Move it, bitch.'

She was sure the others would follow them but she needed to put distance between them so she could get her own phone out and call Virgil. Penny started to say something so Jezza quickened her pace, making a show of grabbing her by the neck and pulling her head closer.

'Shut up and keep walking. I'm going to get us both out of here, hopefully, but I need to make this look convincing. So scream.'

When the reporter didn't immediately react she squeezed her neck tightly, which made her call out. It was not so much a scream as a monotone shouting of 'ow-ow-ow' as they walked. Jezza hoped it would sound realistic enough.

As soon as she could, she pulled her mobile out and called Virgil.

'Virgil! Urgent pick-up required, now. Hollywood Park, Hardman Street steps. And for God's sake don't worry about speed limits. I need a pimp.'

They'd arranged between them that in case of emergency, that would be their cover. Virgil, in his black BMW, with his body-builder's figure and wearing his mirrored shades, was another one who looked nothing like most people's idea of a policeman.

If Virgil was free to leave immediately and got his foot down, he could be with them in minutes. Jezza risked a look over her shoulder. The others weren't far behind but were walking slowly, keeping them in sight but not making any attempt to catch them up. Yet.

'Who are you and where are you taking me?' the reporter asked, trying to wriggle free of Jezza's secure grip.

'I'm taking you to safety, so I can't tell you any more until our lift gets here. You'll just have to trust me.'

Virgil must have broken every speed limit and possibly jumped some lights on the way because it was a mercifully short time before his big black Beamer came squealing up the road towards them. He got out himself so anyone watching could see him, an imposing figure, standing at the top of the steps Jezza and Penny had jogged up, his arms folded across his powerful chest.

Jezza wrenched open a rear door of the BMW and shoved Penny inside, shouting loudly, 'Get in, bitch.' She wanted to make sure that Tara and the others, who were lurking at the bottom of the steps, could hear what she said.

Then she slid into the front passenger seat. Virgil paused a moment longer, looking down at the pack of girls who had stopped in their tracks at the sight of him. As he got back in, Jezza told him, 'Drive. Fast.'

'Who are you and where are you taking me?'

'We're police officers and I've probably just blown my cover getting you out of there. Have you got a death wish, going in there and talking to that lot on your own?'

She had her mobile out and was calling the station to get Uniformed officers mobile and on their way to the park as soon as possible to round up the teenagers.

'We'll need to take you back to the station to get a statement from you. I'm sorry about your camera and phone. With any luck, they'll be recovered when they're arrested.'

'She didn't check my other pockets and I've got a voice recorder in another one so I've got it all recorded for you.'

Jezza rolled her eyes at Virgil. She'd had to blow the operation to get the journalist out of there and they'd be lucky to have much to show for it. The boss wasn't going to be pleased, for one thing.

'We can't use a covert recording that wasn't authorised. That's why we'll need your full witness statement.'

They passed two area cars, on blues and twos, heading for Hollywood Park, as they got nearer to the station. Jezza hoped they would manage to round them all up. She was desperately hoping to have something to show for all the time and effort that had gone into the operation to date. The DCI was the best and fairest boss she'd ever worked with, but even he would be expecting something positive to put on his reports to justify it all.

Chapter Twenty-two

Jezza signed them in at the front desk and got a visitor pass for Penny.

'Sarge, I want to interview this witness, but not down here in an interview room. I'll take her upstairs. I don't want any of the three of us to be around when Uniform bring in the little charmers they've gone out to get. There's still a chance I can keep my cover if they don't see me here.'

Bill looked at her ironically.

'You're working undercover, DC Vine? I would never have guessed. I'll call upstairs to warn you when your guests arrive. They sound delightful.'

'Can you come this way, Penny? Virgil, can you see if I can use Jo's office for the interview? I'd better just let the boss know what's happened. I'll be with you as soon as I can, Penny. I'm sure someone will make you some tea or something while you're waiting.'

Ignoring the comments of the team members who were in about her appearance, Jezza headed straight for the boss's office and knocked, waiting for a response before she went in.

Ted looked up from his desk over the top of his reading glasses. He was surprised to see her back in the station, especially still dressed in character as she was.

'Boss, it all went a bit pear-shaped just now. The reporter turned up in the park where I was hanging out with the girl gang. I had to get her out of there in one piece. But I've got uniform rounding the girls up now and so far I don't think my cover is blown ...'

'Jezza, slow down, sit down and tell me calmly exactly what happened while I put the kettle on.'

'But I've got the reporter waiting for me, boss, to take her statement.'

Ted went to his door and put his head out.

'Can someone please make a drink for Ms Hunter and tell her that DC Vine will be with her in five minutes.'

He made green tea for them both then sat back down.

'Right, Jezza, quick debrief, please.'

He knew she wasn't worried about his reaction to what she had to tell him. She knew him well enough by now to know that he was a reasonable boss. But Jezza set herself high standards and hated it when things didn't go as she'd hoped. They would certainly have enough to charge Tara and some of the others with what had happened earlier, but she would have liked a more positive result.

Ted listened without interrupting until she had finished and was looking at him, still clearly anxious, waiting for his reaction.

'It sounds as if you put yourself at some degree of risk, Jezza. But, as the rest of the team will no doubt tell you, I'm probably not best placed to lecture you on that at the moment. It's still a good result, even if you were hoping for more. Get all the paperwork sorted out, let's charge whoever we can, and see if we can get some TICs from them. That'll improve our crime figures. Good work, but you can wind up the operation now and report back as normal tomorrow, minus the hardware.'

If defendants admitted earlier crimes and asked for them to be Taken Into Consideration, it looked good on paper. Some officers tried to get them to admit to anything to improve statistics, but Ted would have none of it under his command. He was only interested in genuine ones.

Rob O'Connell came upstairs to find the boss shortly after

Jezza had left. They were into their twelve-hour extension on holding Bacha. They were still waiting for anything else forensics could give them but, having now spoken to CPS, Ted was happy enough for them to go ahead and charge Bacha with the murder of Vera Ashworth, in addition to the serious charges arising from the arrest the previous day.

'He's just on a refreshment break, boss, so I thought I'd come and update you. We've presented him with the forensics evidence so far and he's asking for some sort of deal in return for him giving us information. I've tried, and his solicitor has, to explain that he's facing a mandatory life sentence for murder but he still seems to think there's some leeway.'

'Has he given any indication of why he stabbed her, rather than just collecting the watch and the laptop, as he was supposed to?'

'And the car, boss. It was always the intention to take the car as well. They'd been watching her when she met Kateb so they knew what it was and that it was worth a few quid to them.

'Another gang member, driving the Astra, dropped Bacha off near where he was to meet Mrs Ashworth in Wilmslow. He was supposed to get the watch then ask to see her phone and give her a receipt. As soon as she opened the car to get the laptop, he was meant to push her out of the way and drive off in it to where the other man was waiting with false plates.

'His solicitor has clearly advised him it can't hurt to be cooperative, so he's started to talk a bit. He says it was all going well. His fake ID was flawless, and the woman had spoken to Kateb on the phone to check he was who he was supposed to be when they met up.

'Mrs Ashworth was clearly no fool, though. She started asking him questions, saying he looked young to be a detective and asking where he did his training and where he'd served in uniform. That was what threw him. He had a good cover story, except for that, and he didn't really know anywhere which would sound convincing. It wasn't his first visit to England, but he doesn't know it well. He said Manchester, because that was where he'd flown in to, but once she started trying to pin him down on a particular area, he just lost it and pulled the knife. It's clear from talking to him that as he comes off whatever it is he uses, he gets very flaky and unpredictable.'

'Such a shame Mrs Ashworth didn't get suspicious before it got that far, although from her diary entries, Kateb had done his homework very thoroughly and his back-story would have been completely convincing. Right, let's get him charged with everything we've got and I'll make sure you're kept updated on anything else that comes from the lab.'

Ted was interrupted by his desk phone. The Super, asking if he knew there was another briefing scheduled for five o'clock at Central Park, in preparation for rounding up the rest of the gang early the following morning.

'Drinks are off this evening, I'm afraid. Yet another briefing for me. It would be good to do it tomorrow though, if we can, especially now Jezza is back with us and has also had a good result.'

Rob got to his feet and risked a comment. He knew Ted wouldn't allow any hint of disrespect about a senior officer but he couldn't help remarking, 'He does love his briefings, Mr Marston, doesn't he, boss?'

The ACC was at the briefing, which explained Marston's unexpected opening remarks.

'Before we begin, I'd just like to congratulate DCI Darling on his arrest yesterday, although it was somewhat unorthodox, and on the commendation nomination which followed it. Perhaps, DCI Darling, you could bring us all up to date with what you have so far on the suspect Bacha?'

Ted had already sent through his reports, which had been circulated, but he began on a concise summary. There was a quiet knock at the door and a uniformed sergeant appeared.

'Yes? What is it? I said no interruptions,' Marston barked at him.

Unperturbed, the sergeant headed unerringly for the senior ranking officer in the room, the ACC.

'We've just had this report in sir. I thought you should see it straight away.'

The ACC scan-read it then looked up and spoke.

'The surveillance car watching Kateb's house has been rammed by another vehicle and the officers inside sprayed in the face with pepper spray. Unsurprisingly, there is now no sign of Kateb.'

Marston appeared momentarily at a loss for words, before starting to assume command.

'We're going to need an APW out, let's try to stop Kateb leaving the country ...'

'Already in hand, sir. We've started by alerting the most likely points of exit, Manchester, Liverpool and East Midlands airports, Port of Liverpool, in case he heads for Ireland first, plus all the mainline railways stations.'

Then, in a tone which was only just on the right side of insolent, he continued, 'And don't worry about the injured officers, sir. They called it in first, asked for the APW, then called an ambulance. They're both being treated on site. They can't see much at the moment but early reports suggest they are both going to be all right.'

Even the ACC didn't pull him up on it. Apart from Marston, the first thought of most of the officers in the room had been for the welfare of the injured surveillance team members. It didn't go unnoticed by anyone that their first reaction had been to call for the All Ports Warning.

'Right, well, yes, good,' Marston blustered, then recovered his stride. 'So now we need to bring forward the operation to round up all remaining gang members, with immediate effect. I've already circulated the assigned roles, so let's move on this as quickly as we can.'

'Before anyone goes anywhere,' the ACC's voice instantly halted the ensuing shuffling of papers and movement to stand. 'I think, Mr Marston, that at this stage, we must consider the likelihood that the gang were in possession of detailed information about the planned raid. The timing of this incident is too coincidental for it to be ruled out. For that reason, ladies and gentlemen, please ensure that your teams are aware that their arrival may not be unexpected. Body armour on for everyone. Now go and get as many as you can.

'Superintendent Caldwell, are you and DCI Darling directly involved in this stage of the operation?'

They checked their lists. They weren't.

'In which case, perhaps we can just sit down together, with Mr Marston, for a brief discussion, before you go back to Stockport. Up in my office, where we can at least get a decent cup of coffee.'

They followed him upstairs. He asked his secretary to bring them coffee and the tea which Ted asked for.

'So, a likely leak of information from an officer, do you think?'

'Sir, it's hard to draw any other conclusion at this stage,' Marston told him. 'It might also suggest how Kateb got away from the surveillance team the last time.'

The ACC bowed his head and rubbed his temples with his fingertips.

'Damn. Just when I think this operation can't go any worse, we get the possibility of a bent copper on the inside. I'll need to talk to the Chief, of course, but my instinct is to go in hard, dig out any hint of corruption, root and branch. And that means involving CCU. Personally, I'd prefer to find the culprit myself and string him up by the ... Sorry, Debra, that was inappropriate.'

'But understandable, sir, in the circumstances.'

No one liked the idea of a police officer being behind the leaked information which could potentially have cost them the operation, not to mention putting officers' lives at risk. The force's Counter Corruption Unit would do a thorough investigation but it would take time. Potentially, every officer involved in Croesus would need to be interviewed, each in the presence of their Federation rep, all of it taking them away from the case.

'Right, Ted, I know I don't have to tell you how to do your job, but Bacha needs to know that he's already toast. He's likely to go down now whatever he says or doesn't say. Get your interviewing officers to try to tease anything at all they can out of him that might help us find Kateb, or at least know where he's likely to head for.

'I'm mentioning this to you three as I think – I hope, at least – that I can trust your discretion. It goes without saying that this goes no further than these four walls. People will know soon enough what's happening when CCU arrive and set up operations.

'I badly wanted this Kateb bastard before this. Now I want him even more, and I want the piece of filth in the force who's feeding him information.'

'Delightful bunch of young ladies your DC Vine inflicted on us this afternoon, sir,' Bill greeted Ted formally, for the benefit of two young PCs who were within earshot. 'Their turn of phrase even made some of our officers blush.'

'All processed now?'

'Charged, bailed and released into appropriate adult care. Where are you up to with your operation? I heard on the grapevine that it's not going well?'

'The grapevine is over-active. It might have lost us a prime suspect. If you hear anything on that, I'd been grateful for the heads up, Sergeant.'

He went in search of where Rob and Sal were still questioning Bacha and pulled Rob out for an update on their progress.

'Nothing new, boss, and we are trying. He says he's had no contact at all with Kateb since what happened and I'm inclined to believe him. He says the numbers he had for him are now out of service. I think they've effectively dumped him and are distancing themselves.'

'So why hasn't he just gone home? Or tried to? There are plenty of ways he could have got out of the country undetected. He must know that. Or why not contact his father and get a ride back on one of their lorries?'

'No money to try by himself. His father paid his fare over, one-way, expecting him to do some work and make the money to go back when he was ready. His credit cards have been blocked long since because he's in so much debt back home. Unsurprisingly, Kateb hasn't paid him what he was promised for the pick-up job. Now he's scared, not knowing what to do. Jo's kept me up to date with the interviews with the family. The father says Bacha kept asking him for money but he had none to give him. Everything he earns goes on his family. It's plausible, boss.'

'All right, good work. Get what else you can then call it a day. Put him up in front of the magistrates in the morning for remand. We need to make sure that it's a remand in custody because of the risk of him leaving the country if not.'

The rest of the team had knocked off long since. The main office was quiet and dark. Ted wondered fleetingly whether he should start writing up reports then decided he was more in need of food. He gave Trev a quick call.

'I was just on my way back and wondered if you wanted a takeaway?'

'That would be great. I've not even started anything yet. I'm busy prepping English lessons. I'll tell you all about it when you get back.'

'Indian? Chinese?'

'Surprise me.'

Ted opted for an Indian, from a restaurant they both liked.

225

He found his stomach was rumbling in anticipation as he drove the short distance home from there.

Trev was tidying up his paperwork and setting the table. Queen was helping him, sitting on each pile of paper in turn as he tried to move it, purring contentedly.

'I put the oven on to keep it warm in case you wanted to shower before we eat. And Skype Annie. She's getting worried about this court case.'

'I'm starving. I could do with eating soon.'

'Talk to your mother first. Just five minutes. I'm going to the centre again tomorrow and the local press are coming to do a feature on us, so I'll be getting my face in the paper. Here, use my laptop to call Annie. I was talking to her earlier.'

Ted sat down obediently, opened the Skype app and called his mother. She was clearly concerned about the court case and he felt guilty that he hadn't spent more time talking to her to reassure her. He was busy spouting platitudes when Trev leaned over him from behind and rested his chin on the top of his head so they were both in shot.

'Tell your mother about your commendation.'

Ted turned to glare at him but his mother was already asking delightedly, 'Oh, Teddy, you got a commendation? What was that for? Is that why your face looks so sore? Did you get hurt?'

'It was nothing. I just had to arrest someone. The black eye was martial arts training that got a bit exciting, that's all.'

'So he's getting a Chief Constable's commendation and we get to go to a black tie reception to collect it,' Trev told her proudly. 'And he'll be in the paper. So will I tomorrow, for these English classes I've started doing.'

'Your dad would have been so proud of you, Teddy.'

'D'you think so?'

'I know so. He always was. From the very moment you were born. He couldn't do enough for you.'

A catch in her voice made her stop.

'I'm proud of you, too, *bach*. I hope we can Skype again soon. And I'd love to see you all dressed up and with your award.'

'I'm dragging him off to another fancy affair on Saturday, Annie, so I'll make sure you see him looking his best. He's praying for a nice grisly murder to get him out of going, but I'm going to confiscate his phone if I have to. And he's promised to sing.'

'Oh, I wish I could hear that. You always had a lovely voice, when you were little.'

Ted was subdued after the phone call, picking at his food, finding his appetite had deserted him.

'What's wrong? You said you were hungry.'

'What she said about my dad. I wasn't very nice to him, at the end. You know that. I told you about it. You know I used to be out on the lash with the team when I should have been at home, doing more for him. I wanted to make him proud, but I let him down.'

Trev put his own fork down and took hold of one of Ted's hands.

'You didn't. You did the best you could in difficult circumstances, and you turned your life around after he died. Look at you now. I never met him but from what you've told me about him, I know he would have been proud of you. Just like Annie is. And like I am.'

Queen took advantage of the pause in eating to jump back on to the table and investigate their plates with interest.

Trev put his hands over her ears before saying, 'I'm going to need the car one day this week. I have to take the cats for their booster jabs. Well, half of them, at least. I'll take the girls first, then go with the boys next week.'

Ted hesitated, lifting Queen gently off the table and putting her back on the floor.

'It might be better if you get a taxi. I'll leave you the money.'

Trev started to laugh then broke off and stared at him, hard.

'Oh my God. I thought you were worried that I might scratch the new paintwork after you got it fixed. But you think someone might still be after you, so you don't want me out in your car. I'm right, aren't I?'

Ted's meal suddenly became magnetically attractive again. He looked down at his plate and began pushing chicken pieces round with his fork.

'Ted, you told me that was all sorted. You said you knew who was behind it and it had been dealt with. But that's not true, is it, or you'd let me take the car?'

Ted lifted his head, trying to hold Trev's gaze and to sound reassuring. It was true, as Trev always said. He was useless at lying to anyone, especially to his partner.

'I think it's fine. I think he got the message and will leave me alone now he's been formally interviewed. I just don't want to take the risk, not for the moment. I'd never forgive myself if anything happened to you because of my work.'

Chapter Twenty-three

'Right, Océane, anything from Bacha's phone or computer?'

'Nothing of any use yet, boss. It's like he's already said. The numbers he had been contacting Kateb on are now out of service.'

'Any way of tracing who they were registered to?'

'Unfortunately not. They're unregistered pay as you go. He's been trying to contact several numbers since Mrs Ashworth's death but he's not got through to any of them. I do have what might be contact details for his drugs dealer, if that's of any use? I assume that's who it is. It's a UK mobile he's been calling every couple of days since he first arrived, and it's still in service. Could be worth following up?'

'Yes, why not? Might as well mop up anything we can while we're at it. Now, early reports are encouraging. Almost all the gang members who were targeted have been arrested, apart from Kateb, of course. There's just a couple still to be found and brought in, but they're small fry, down at the bottom of the chain. That means a lot of suspects to be interviewed and processed, so it's likely we'll be involved in talking to at least some of them.

'There's also all the contents of the various houses to be gone through now, including the one where Kateb was staying. Océane, again, because of the volume of stuff, it's likely some of the phones and computers found will come your way. And you may well need Steve helping on that.

'The other thing we need to look at is the likelihood that

wherever Kateb is now, he'll be on a different ID. We know he's been using a good forger for false documents so it's highly unlikely he's still using his own identity.'

'What about the forger, boss? Has he been identified and questioned?' Jo asked.

'I'm waiting on the daily update from Mr Marston to see if anyone has done so yet. We're wasting time with the APW if we don't know what identity he's travelling under. He could already be out of the country and long gone.

'Again, if any of you have contacts who might be able to supply a name for the forger, that could help us a lot. Ask around. It's just possible I may know someone who might know. I'll see what I can find out. There's a couple of names in the frame but this is very particular, skilled work. We need to make sure we're going after the right one.

'In the meantime, I need your reports on interviews with the family as soon as possible, everyone, please. And let me know if there's anything from those which might help with finding Kateb. Any hint of where he might have gone. Maybe more extended family we don't yet know about, either here or back in France. He can't simply have disappeared. Someone, somewhere knows where he is, and we need to find him. There will be press appeals now, of course, and leafleting, but don't overlook any avenue.

'And let's not neglect the paperwork on our own cases. We could have a decent result or two to celebrate with that drink, when we can find time to go for one. Jezza, you stay with your happy slappers, get that wrapped up. Mike, can you help with that? And Jo, can I have a quick word with you, please?'

Ted headed back to his office, Jo Rodriguez following behind. Ted nodded to him to sit down.

'I just wanted to ask if you wouldn't mind talking to Kevin Turner, just to see how things are going with the assault on my mother. I don't like to keep pestering him. I know he's all over it. It's just, you know ...'

'She's your mother, boss. Yes, I know. How is she now?'

'Recovering, slowly, but she's decided to move back to Wales, permanently. Because of what happened. Because of being attacked for speaking her own language. A British language, in Britain. She's finding that hard to deal with.'

'I'm really sorry to hear that. Has she made a VPS and put that in it? That should have quite an impact when it comes to sentencing.'

Ted knew his mother would have been told she had the right to make a Victim Personal Statement when she was interviewed and gave her account of the facts of the assault. He was ashamed to realise he didn't know if she'd done so. A Victim Statement would give her the chance to talk about how the attack had affected her, how it had made her feel. It would be put to the court before sentencing. She could either read it herself or it would be read by the Crown Prosecutor presenting the case. The fact that she had been affected enough to move from her home of nearly forty years could be a powerful factor in deciding the length of sentence handed down on her assailant. With his record, a custodial sentence was a strong probability. The only question was the length of it.

'I'll talk to her about it. I just wish there was something we could do with the people who just stand and film incidents like this instead of helping.'

'I can understand people being afraid to wade in, though, in case they get injured themselves. I'm not the most courageous person in the world. I'm not sure I'd be brave enough to do anything much, to be honest. But just to walk on by without doing anything, or to film it and then post it online, like some of them do? Now that just makes my blood boil.

'Boss, can I ask you something? About Croesus? You know Neil Smith and I go way back. We were chatting last night and of course he's worried sick that there's been a leak and that it might be one of his. Is there any hint of anything?'

'Jo, you know that even if I knew anything, I wouldn't be

at liberty to discuss it with you. And you also know that's not because I don't trust you. Far from it. You've never given me reason not to. But there are already enough internal enquiries going on into what went wrong the first time Kateb gave them the slip, so there needs to be a tight lid kept on everything now.'

'Of course, boss, understood. Neil himself is as straight as a die, though, I'd bet money on it.'

'But would he? Bet, I mean? You know as well as I do that if someone is leaking information, they're not likely to be doing it for free. They'll be getting a nice little back-hander, so the most likely suspects are anyone with financial problems. Like gambling. If there's anything you know, even if it goes against the grain, it would be helpful if you'd tell me.'

Jo shook his head emphatically.

'Not Neil. He doesn't gamble. Not at all. He's a Quaker. Won't even buy a lottery ticket, or a raffle one, although he sometimes gives money to the charity running it. Hardly drinks, either. Keeps quiet about it because you can imagine what a hard time he's had about the whole thing in the past in our wonderfully inclusive service, especially back in the days when he and I were starting out. It was bad enough for me, with a Spanish name, getting called a spic all the time.'

'The three of us should get together one evening over a jar and compare the insults we've had thrown at us. I should warn you, though, that mine is usually the winning hand.'

After Jo had left, Ted went downstairs to talk to the Ice Queen to see if she had any updates. He wanted to crack on with lines of enquiry but nothing had yet come through from Marston informing him of who was pursuing what angle following the arrests.

'I agree that starting with the forger should be a priority now. I haven't yet seen or heard mention that anyone has been questioned in connection with the counterfeit documents.

Would you prefer me to telephone Mr Marston to raise the matter, or will you do it?'

'I don't want to let any history between me and Mr Marston get in the way of this enquiry. But knowing how obsessed he is with chains of command, it may well be more diplomatic, coming from you. Perhaps you can let me know? I'll just try one line of my own, to see if I can get a name of who the gang might have been using for their documentation. It was clearly of high quality. We don't want to be wasting time going after a small-timer if they weren't the one involved.'

Ted was texting as he went back up the stairs. He wasn't sure of a response but it was worth a try. If anyone knew the best forger in the area, it was likely to be Green, with his connections. He'd suggested one or two but warned they were unlikely to be of the right calibre.

'Best forger Greater Manchester?'

He would have liked to be out doing something positive but for now, he would be at his desk wading through the statements his team had taken from the family members, about Bacha's stay with them. He doubted there would be much there to take them forward, but he couldn't assume that without checking.

It was mid-morning when his mobile announced an incoming message. He opened it to find himself looking at a photo of a beach scene. A small cove, sheltered by a backdrop of cliffs of layered rocks, intensely blue sea lapping on to white sand, with not a soul in sight. There was no covering message. The phone number it had come from was hidden. Other than knowing it obviously wasn't anywhere in Britain, Ted was none the wiser as to where it was or what it meant. He went out into the main office to find Océane. He held out his phone to her, showing the photo.

'Océane, is there any way to find out where this was taken, please?'

She looked at it and smiled up at him.

'I can do better than that, boss. I've actually been there,

believe it or not. It's Diaz Beach, near Cape Town. Definitely not on the tourist trail. It's a bit of a hike to get there, and you're advised not to swim there as the ocean can be dangerous. Oh, and you take food at your own risk, otherwise you get mugged by the baboons. Other than that, as you can see, it's a beautiful place, if you want peace and quiet, solitude, communing with nature, that sort of stuff.'

So Green had returned to South Africa. His situation had clearly not yet calmed down sufficiently for him to stay in the country. Ted didn't think him the type merely to take a holiday. He interpreted the message as a very definite 'Do not disturb' notice being hung up. He hoped, at least, that he would be safe there, for the time being.

His desk phone interrupted him.

'Mr Marston says he would like your team to go and question the forger whose name has come up as the most likely to be behind this operation. Bring him in, if you think it appropriate, but for now our main interest is what new identity he's provided for Kateb, if any.'

The Super gave him the contact details before adding, 'Ted, you will talk to me, if ever the situation between you and Mr Marston stops you from doing your job effectively, won't you?'

There was seemingly genuine concern in her voice as she said it. Ted made reassuring noises before he hung up and went back into the outer office. He'd already decided to take this one himself, with one of his team as back-up. He felt a need to be out there, doing something. Proper policing, rather than endless paperwork and Marston's constant briefings.

Virgil was still at his desk. He would be perfect for what Ted had in mind. He went over to him, pulled up a spare chair and sat down next to him.

'This announcement may contain items which could be interpreted as having racist overtones,' he said ironically before he began.

'Wassup, bro?'

Ted laughed. He could always rely on Virgil to take things the right way.

'I want to set up a meeting with the forger we think may be behind the fake documents Kateb and the others have been using. At the moment, there's probably not enough to arrest him on and he's small fry in comparison to some of the others. What we do need from him is the new name Kateb may now be travelling under. It needs someone who sounds convincing to phone him up and arrange a face-to-face meeting to see what, if anything, we can get out of him.'

'So, you needed a gangsta and you immediately thought of me. I'm touched, boss. What do you need me to do?'

'Here are his contacts. I would like you to phone him and convince him you need to see him urgently for a new ID. Arrange a meeting as soon as you can. I'll follow you there, then we can both talk to him. Nothing too heavy, just mark his card for him and suggest it's in his best interests to cooperate. At the moment, I'm only interested in finding out Kateb's new identity. And letting the forger know we're on to him.'

'On it now, boss. Just don't watch me while I'm talking street-talk, you'll make me laugh.'

It wasn't long before Virgil came to find Ted in his office.

'Meeting all set up, boss. This evening, six o'clock, in a pub car park near Ancoats.'

'Ancoats, eh? An upmarket forger? I thought that was the height of trendy now?'

'Trendy or not, we're on, boss, and he seemed to swallow what I told him. I'll take the Beamer. It looks more the part than a service vehicle and that's what I've told him I'll be driving.'

'I'll follow behind in my trusty little Renault. That certainly doesn't look like a vehicle which any self-respecting police officer would be driving.'

'Are you planning on arresting him, boss?'

'Not at this stage. Not unless he refuses to cooperate. All we need from him at the moment is Kateb's new ID, if he is the one who supplied the documents. If not, he can probably tell us who did. Just a friendly chat, at this stage, not a formal interview, which might scare him off.'

Steve was on the sandwich run at lunchtime for those who, like Ted, were planning a quick bite at their desks. Ted had gone through all the witness statements from the family, more than once, and circulated anything relevant via Marston. He also told him he would be interviewing the suspected forger later that day.

It was mid-afternoon when he was summoned downstairs to the Super's office. She already had coffee on the desk for them both.

'Mr Marston's just informed me that Bacha has been assaulted whilst on remand,' she told him. 'He's in Forest Bank, or rather, he was, briefly, but he's now been admitted to hospital. He was assaulted by another remand prisoner. A serious sexual assault. Not, sadly, that unusual, but given the speed with which it happened, it does raise the question as to whether or not this was pre-arranged.'

'Whoever the informant is, they're up to speed with everything and moving quickly. I don't suppose many people would have known yet where he was taken on remand. And I agree, it seems suspicious, so soon after his court appearance. How is he?'

'Not in a very good way. If this was intended as a warning to him not to say anything, it's probably been very effective. We don't have all the details yet, but it would seem, from early reports, that he was deliberately put with someone with a history of this sort of thing, who was supposed to be kept separate from younger male inmates. Especially attractive ones.'

'So does this mean we're possibly looking at corrupt prison

officers as well, if they allowed this to happen? That means the gang's reach may be wider than we thought.'

'That's something CCU will be looking into. They've already begun, and now they're a visible presence at Central Park, it should hopefully make it harder for the informant to get at sensitive information.'

Virgil's black BMW purred into the pub car park and pulled up next to a dark-coloured Ford. Ted parked his Renault a short distance away. Virgil got out and swaggered over to the front of the Ford as its driver got out. He was completely in character, his movements more like those of a boxer on his way to the ring than how he usually walked. The other man was almost as tall as him but thin as a lath. Vigil did the whole dap greeting thing. There was nothing about him to arouse the other man's suspicions, much less to suggest that he was a police officer.

Even as Ted walked towards them, the other man paid him no attention. He saw simply a short, insignificant bloke in a suit, no doubt heading for a pint after work before he went home to the missus. He was busy talking to Virgil, though he paused as Ted drew level with them.

'Mr Jackson? I'm a police officer. I'd like to have a word with you, if I may?'

Jackson's eyes darted from Ted to Virgil, who flashed him his widest smile as he said, 'Yeah, me too. Shall we sit in my car?'

There was nowhere Jackson could go. They had him effectively cornered. Virgil saw him safely installed in the front passenger seat of the Beamer then got in behind him. Ted sat down in the driver's seat. Virgil slid onto the middle of the back seat, his elbows resting on the front seats, chin on his hands, a silent, looming presence.

Ted produced his warrant card, then took out a photo of Kateb and showed it to Jackson.

'I believe you may have supplied this man with false documentation, Mr Jackson. It would be helpful to our enquiries if you could tell me the new identity you arranged for him. Not the one as Inspector Galton, but the later one.'

'Never clapped eyes on him before,' Jackson said, scarcely glancing at the photo, then added. 'He's making me nervous, sitting behind me like that.'

'He makes me nervous too, sometimes,' Ted replied pleasantly. 'But I'm his senior officer. He has to do as I tell him. Now, could you take a proper look this time, Mr Jackson?'

He looked at it, warily.

'If I tell you anything, I'm dead. Or at least finished in this town for good. I want Witness Protection or something.'

'All I'm asking you at this stage is if you know this man and if you've provided him with false documentation at any time.'

He shook his head adamantly.

'Never seen him before.'

'Fair enough. In which case, I'll be on my way and leave you to enjoy the rest of your evening.'

Ted made to get out of the car. Jackson's voice went up half an octave in panic as he squawked, 'You can't leave me alone with him!'

Ted paused in his movements, appearing to consider the situation.

'If you've nothing to tell me, then there's no point in my hanging around.'

'All right, all right. I have done stuff for him.'

'Anything recent?'

'A new passport. And a driving licence. This last weekend. He sent someone to pick them up yesterday. He doesn't … didn't come in person.'

'Thank you. Now, think very carefully, Mr Jackson, because this next question is the most important one. What was the new name on those documents?'

'I don't know. It was something French. I can't remember. I had to get him to spell it for me.'

'Think very carefully. It's important. I'm a patient man, but DC Tibbs ...'

'Antoine. I remember that. Antoine something.'

Virgil shifted slightly in the back seat and cleared his throat with a menacing rumbling noise.

'Wait! I've got it written down. I remember. It's in my notebook. He printed it for me so I got the spelling right. It's in my pocket.'

Ted made a gesture with his hand as he said, 'Slowly, Mr Jackson. Very slowly, when you're putting your hand in your pocket. You don't want to make DC Tibbs nervous.'

The man's hand shook like a leaf as he reached in his pocket, then fumbled his way through the pages of a small notebook.

'Yes, yes, here it is,' his voice was showing relief. 'Antoine Fournier. Here, look.'

'Thank you, Mr Jackson. You've been most helpful. We'll be in touch if we need anything else. We know where to find you.'

Ted leaned across to open the door as the man all but fell out of the passenger seat and scuttled back to his own vehicle in evident relief.

'You have a pleasant evening now.'

Chapter Twenty-four

Once Virgil had gone, anxious to get home to his wife and baby daughter, Ted took out his phone to call Marston. Much as he disliked his temporary boss, he needed to keep him informed as soon as possible of Kateb's new identity. It was an important breakthrough, although Ted wasn't after any credit or praise. From Marston's tone, almost polite, he was clearly not alone. Ted suspected it may have been the ACC he was with.

'Sir, DC Tibbs and I have just got the name Kateb is likely to be travelling under now. It's Antoine Fournier. F-O-U-R-N-I-E-R. Will you circulate it, sir, or do you want me to?'

'Good, thank you, DCI Darling, that's good work. You can safely leave that information with me.'

Ted smiled to himself as he started his car and pulled out of the car park. He could imagine what Marston would have liked to say to him.

He decided to go back to the station and tackle paperwork before he went home. Trev was going to teach his English learners so would be back later. Ted thought he might as well profit from a quiet hour or so to catch up. The more hours he put in during the week, the more he would feel justified in his absence on Saturday evening. Even if it was the last thing in the world he wanted to do. Standing up in public to sing, making a fool of himself, was right up there with the idea of streaking naked through the Merseyway precinct, as far as he was concerned. But Trev was tolerant of his work and seldom asked a lot of him, so he felt he owed him this. And he'd made a promise.

At least he was highly unlikely to meet any of the guests again, which was a small consolation, as they would be the Beautiful People with whom Willow and Rupert mixed in their professional lives. He'd have to face the two of them again in the future, having made a complete prat of himself, but he could live with that. They had become good friends. He just hoped he wouldn't let Willow down. Trev had no doubt built up her expectations of his partner's abilities, but, being totally tone deaf himself, his judgement on the matter was hardly reliable.

He thought he'd better show willing and practise a bit more on his drive back, so he slid the CD into the slot and tried his best to match his voice to the mellow tones of Kenny Rogers. At least the range suited his voice, but that was about all he could say about his performance.

Bill wasn't on the front desk when Ted arrived at the station. He was doing shorter hours until he was fully recovered. Sergeant Wheeler was on duty and greeted Ted when he signed himself in.

'All of your team have knocked off, sir, but the Super's still in. She asked me to tell you to go and see her if you came back in.'

Ted knocked briefly on her door then went in. The Ice Queen was looking tired, working at her computer. She seemed almost pleased at the distraction.

'I know you won't have coffee in the evening but can I offer you a cup of tea? I'd welcome the excuse, if I'm honest. I'm trying to balance budgets yet again and going under for the third time.'

She didn't often let her guard down to become a mere mortal in the workplace, so he sat down and accepted her offer, then told her of their latest lead.

'Have you informed Mr Marston?'

'I have, and I'll circulate it round everyone, just as belt and braces. Part of me hopes Kateb's found on Saturday evening. Trev's dragging me to a black tie affair I'd rather not go to and I'm looking for a good excuse.'

She made drinks and sat back down. She was smiling now, more relaxed.

'Oh, dear. We'll have to have a special signal. Send me a text if you need rescuing. Seriously, though, you should go. Heaven knows, we get to spend precious little time with our nearest and dearest in this job.'

It was a fleeting moment of her showing her human side, then the professional mask was back as she asked for details of ongoing cases, including the assault on his mother.

Ted had promised to pick up another takeaway on his way back, knowing Trev was busy. He opted for Thai food this time and put it in the oven on a low light to keep it warm until they were ready to eat. He was assaulted by cats as soon as he got in, shamelessly lying about being starving, despite the evidence that Trev had already fed them before he'd gone out.

He wanted to take the time to Skype his mother, without being prompted by Trev for once. Knowing that he hadn't even discussed her VPS with her made him feel guilty. Despite Trev's assurances, he still lived with the guilt of having let his father down badly. He wanted somehow to make a better job of things with his mother.

She was, as ever, delighted to hear from him. She was certainly looking better for her time away, now she was back in what to her was and always had been her home country.

'I'm so pleased you called, *bach*, I've been so worried. I've had a letter about appearing in court and saying if I don't, I could go to prison.'

'It's fine, mam, it's just a standard letter. You do have to attend, but it would never come to that. Just let us know when the court date is and one of us will come and pick you up.'

'Don't worry, *bach*, Aldwyth is going to drive me up. She's never been to Stockport. We can stay at my house, before I sell it. Did you manage to talk to an agent? I know you're busy.'

Ted made a mental note to go and check there was no sign of Green's presence there, although he knew there shouldn't be.

'I spoke to one, but that's all I've done so far. Are you sure about this? You definitely want to sell up and stay in Wales? You do know that Trev and I will miss you, don't you? And the cats will.'

'Aldwyth has said you can come and visit me here any time you want to. There's plenty of room. And I can always get on a train from Ammanford to Stockport. It doesn't take that long. I'm not going to be in Timbuktu.'

Ted smiled to himself as he ended the call. He remembered her using that phrase. It made him think of the happy times before she had left him and his father, when he was a small boy. When they had been a family. He promised to call her again soon, to go through everything she needed to know. He'd talk to her then about the statement, and he'd do everything in his power to make sure he was at court on the day of the trial to support her.

He started clearing and setting the table as soon as he heard Trev's motorbike turn in to the driveway, and the noise of the garage doors opening. Trev always made an entrance. This evening he erupted into the room, smiling broadly, and engulfed Ted in a bone-crushing hug.

'Hey, you, I hope you've been having as much fun as I have. Honestly, I wish I'd thought of doing this ages ago. It's really rewarding. The reporter came and took loads of photos. It's going to be up online tomorrow and in the paper next week. I'll get a copy for Annie.

'Supper smells good. You remembered a takeaway, then? I'm starving. Tell me how your day was. Did you catch the bad guys?'

Trev sat down as Ted started to dish up the meal, absent-mindedly lifting cats off the table and putting them on the floor. It was a never-ending task, with six of them, each as eager as the next to get a sniff of what the humans were having for supper and to see if it was more appetising than their own food.

'Not all of them,' Ted told him as he put their meal in front of them. 'The ringleader is still at large, but I did get a good lead on him today.'

'Well, make sure you have him safely behind bars before Saturday, so you can't use him as an excuse for avoiding your public engagement.'

'Public humiliation, more likely. I'll probably have to go in during the day on Saturday, to be sure of getting away in the evening.'

He saw the expression on Trev's face and went on hurriedly, 'But I have said I'll do it and I will do, if it's remotely possible.'

'It better be, because I swear, if I have to, I'll get Jim to suspend you. And if you do this for me, I will be very, very appreciative.'

He shot Ted a suggestive smile. Ted changed the subject rapidly, knowing that otherwise, supper would get forgotten about.

'I spoke to my mother. She said Aldwyth is going to drive her up for the court case, so they'll stay at her house.'

'Has your squatter gone? What sort of state did they leave it in? Do you need me to go up there and get things ready for her?'

'It'll be as spick and span as a barracks, but if you could just check it over for me at some point, give it some homely touches, that would be great. I'm not sure when I'll have the time. I put the keys back on the hall table.'

'I spoke to Shewee today.'

Trev still used his younger sister's nickname when talking

about her, but no longer when speaking to her, since she'd said that her boyfriend Henry didn't approve.

'She's worried, poor lamb. She thinks Henry doesn't fancy her because he's not even tried to kiss her yet. He says it's because he has too much respect for her and doesn't want to rush things. She still doesn't get it, that he's unlikely to do anything, no matter how much he tries to get her to look like a boy. Bizzie, on the other hand, had a wonderful time with Douglas Campbell, with much snogging and even some tongues.'

Ted looked at him in amazement.

'She told you that?'

'Of course she did. Women tell me their innermost secrets. I'm a gay man, in case you've forgotten. The perfect confidant. The only person who doesn't open up to me is you. How is this case, really? You look tired.'

'I'm fine, please don't fuss. I'll just be glad when it's all over and I'm back with Jim and the Ice Queen as my bosses. When it is finally wrapped up, we should try to go away somewhere, just for a few days. A bit of a break.'

'We should go to Wales to see Annie, in her new home.'

'We'll see her when she comes up for the trial. I meant a bit of time to ourselves.'

'We can do both. We could go to Wales, spend some time with your mother then do some walking somewhere. I've never been to the Brecon Beacons. You could show me where you've done your training marches, see how I would fare on one of those. Maybe even do some riding, now you're getting the hang of it.

'We could find a nice little B&B where they're not too chapel to allow two men to share a bedroom. Or we could have separate rooms and take turns to sneak along the landing. That would be fun.'

Ted smiled at him. His enthusiasm for everything was infectious. It was moments like these that balanced out the difficult side of his job, brought some domestic normality into his life.

'And is this one going to be a dangerous one to wrap up?'

'For me? No. You know I'm just a glorified pen-pusher these days. We may need armed response, but I'll be snug in a command vehicle. That's the closest I'll get to the action.'

Trev reached across the table and took hold of Ted's left hand, turning it over, palm uppermost, to show the livid scar which ran up his wrist, from a knife injury.

'I know you, you like to wade in when you can. Just promise me you won't take any risks this time. You know how much I worry about you.'

'You should see the risk assessments I have to do before I can do anything. I know you worry. That's why I gave up Firearms for you.'

'But you must have done something a bit risky to get that bravery award. Just promise me you won't do anything else like that. Will you be able to get to the dojo tomorrow?'

'I'm certainly going to try. I need a good workout, if I'm going to be wrestling a bunch of murderous, armed gangsters single-handed.'

Seeing Trev's expression, he laughed and raised both hands in a gesture of appeasement.

'Just kidding. Honestly.'

Ted did make it to the dojo, both for the self-defence club and the adults' judo session. Things were relatively quiet on the work front, apart from the mundane, methodical side of any big enquiry. Even with his new identity, Kateb was still lying low. There was no sign of him anywhere, no plane tickets booked in his new name. All his known haunts were being kept under close watch, so far without result. He'd simply faded into the background and been swallowed up somewhere in the city, or even further afield.

None of the other gang members would say anything about

him or his likely whereabouts. It was obvious that they had all heard what had happened to Bacha, who was still in hospital, and wanted, at all costs, to avoid a similar fate.

Ted and his team had been given the task of interviewing the gang member known to be Kateb's deputy, a man called Hamid. Ted let Rob and Sal have a go at him first, as they were on a run of success, but they got nowhere, so Ted tried himself. With his infinite patience, he could often make some degree of progress. Not with Hamid.

Like many of the gang members, he was pleasant, well-spoken, plausible, the perfect front for a conman. He also must have broken the record for the number of times a suspect could say 'No comment' during an interview. But that was all they got from him.

'Going through this stuff on their phones and computers, there's not a scam I can think of that they've not been at, boss,' Océane said at the last morning briefing before the weekend. 'It reads like an expanded copy of the Little Book.'

She was referring to the Little Book of Big Scams which the Greater Manchester Police published on their website and other places to warn members of the public of the dangers of ignoring the maxim, 'If it seems too good to be true, it usually is.'

'There's everything here from identity fraud, through bogus lottery wins, investment scams, bogus speeding fines, and lots of banking and credit card scams. The other geeky types are telling me much the same. Some door-to-door stuff, too, phoney pollsters, collecting personal information.'

'That's why the members like Hamid are ideal. They look perfectly presentable,' Rob put in.

'I wonder if the Book hinders more than it helps? I know we need to warn the public, but does it also give the scammers new ideas, perhaps?' Ted speculated. 'If they're into identity theft, does that mean that somewhere there is an Antoine Fournier who might be surprised if someone suddenly buys an airline ticket in his name? And I still don't quite understand why Kateb's not yet made his move, or seems not to have.'

'Giving himself time to change his appearance, boss?' Steve suggested. 'Grow a beard, perhaps?'

'Nice one, Steve. Océane, can we find if there is an Antoine Fournier on our patch and what the real one looks like?'

'Will do, boss. But there's a simple explanation of why he would choose to create a fake ID from scratch rather than travel on a stolen one. We all know, from this line of work, that bizarre coincidences happen all the time. It could create all sorts of problems if he used the ID of someone who just happened to be flying somewhere on the same day he decides to make his getaway.'

All they really knew so far about Kateb was that he wasn't married but he did have two women on the go, one with a small child. They had both been blissfully unaware of the existence of each other until officers questioning them had casually let slip the facts. They'd hoped that by angering them, one or other might decide to start talking for vengeance. But although clearly furious at the news, both had stayed tight-lipped.

Counter Corruption officers were slowly working their way through checking everyone involved in Croesus. They'd begun by going through the files of all the senior officers who'd been present at all the briefings then interviewing them all, asking probing questions of each of them about members of their team.

Although Ted knew he had done no wrong and doubted if anyone under his command had either, he still felt uncomfortable being interviewed by them. He didn't like the idea that someone within the force was in the pay of a gang who would take money from sometimes vulnerable people.

The mere presence of CCU was making people nervous, closely watching colleagues they would usually trust unreservedly. There was a lot of bad feeling about what had happened to the surveillance team members who had been sprayed, although both were doing better. Whoever was responsible was probably hoping that if they were discovered, it would be by CCU and not their fellow officers.

Ted decided, despite the lack of a satisfactory conclusion to the case, to finish up the week with a drink for the full team together after work. He wanted to get the first round in, as he usually did, but the team wouldn't hear of it. They were determined to get him a drink to toast his commendation. It was good to spend a bit of down time with them. Ted always appreciated it, although the sessions sometimes stirred uncomfortable memories for him.

'Neil's got his interview with CCU tomorrow, boss. He's worried sick.'

Jo was sitting next to Ted, talking quietly so none of the others could hear. They were busy chatting amongst themselves, letting their hair down, gearing up for the weekend.

'If he's done nothing wrong, he should have nothing to worry about.'

Jo took a long swallow of his lager.

'You know how it can be though, within the force. Like I said, Neil's a Quaker. That means he stays away from the funny hand-shake brigade, as well as the gambling and the drink. And I think we both know they have a way of protecting their own.'

'Not everyone in the force is a Mason. It's no secret that I'm not and never would be. But the leak came from somewhere, Jo, and two officers were injured as a result, not to mention our prime suspect getting away. Twice. Stones need to be overturned until we find out who the mole is. Then, whoever they are, they'll be hung out to dry. Very publicly, with any luck.'

Chapter Twenty-five

'Oh, you both look so handsome. You do make a lovely couple,' Ted's mother was beaming with pride as she spoke via Skype, looking at her son and his partner, dressed up to the nines for their black tie occasion.

'You should smell his aftershave, Annie, it's nearly knocking me out. I'm sure he's only put that much on so he can have a coughing fit to stop him from singing.'

'I wish I could hear you sing, Teddy. I taught you to sing in Welsh when you were little. I don't suppose you remember any of it now. You always had a lovely voice.'

She began to sing herself, softly, a gentle Welsh lullaby, her voice full of nostalgia. She too had a good voice.

Huna blentyn ar fy mynwes
Clyd a chynnes ydyw hon.'

To his own amazement, Ted joined in, hesitantly at first, the words long forgotten.

'Breichiau mam sy'n dynn amdanat,
Cariad mam sy dan fy mron.'

His mother's eyes were suddenly bright with tears. Trev's were the same.

'Stop it, you two. That is so beautiful, you're making me fill up here. I am so going to film the two of you singing together one of these days. But right now, I'm going to drag him away with me and make him sing some country. Bye, Annie, love you.'

Try as he might, Ted still couldn't tell his mother that he

loved her as easily as Trev did. He did love her; it was just that there were too many years of feeling abandoned by her which still formed a gulf between them, from his point of view.

'Bye, mam, see you again soon.'

'Have you got your lozenges?' Trev checked as they went out to the car. 'I don't want you crying off with a sore throat at the last minute. I know you'll be looking for any excuse.'

Ted patted the pocket where his Fisherman's Friends were. His go-to comforter for the bloodiest of his murder cases. As far as he was concerned, the coming ordeal was likely to be worse than any of them. He'd never before wished for another murder to occur on his patch. He did now.

Trev had been right about not wanting to tell Ted their destination in advance. He simply directed him where to drive. When Ted saw the imposing Jacobean style building, one of Cheshire's most sought-after wedding venues, he nearly turned the Renault round and made a break for it. He would probably never feel he belonged in such a place. He certainly didn't feel he should be singing in public there. But more than anything, he wanted to make his partner happy.

Willow and Rupert were waiting to greet their guests. Trev hugged and kissed both of them. Ted, always more reserved, gave Willow a peck on the cheek, for which she had to bend down slightly, and shook Rupert's hand.

'I'm so pleased you could both come,' Willow told them warmly. 'And Ted, I really am looking forward to singing with you later on . Trev tells me you're very good, so I do hope I won't let you down with my efforts.'

Ted didn't think he could feel any more sick, but he did. The buffet was amazing, possibly the best he had ever seen, but his stomach was too full of butterflies to contemplate putting much else in it. It had been a long time since he had felt as desperate for a drink, too.

Trev was clearly in his element, eating like a horse, drinking plenty of good wine, posing tirelessly for photos with

Willow and Rupert and the others for the many society and celebrity magazines which had photographers there. He even managed to drag his partner into a couple of shots, though Ted refused to give his name for any of the captions.

When the time came, Trev had to practically drag Ted on to the small, raised stage at one end of the dance floor. Ted felt even more ill with nerves, if that were possible. Trev's suggestion of imagining the audience naked didn't help one bit. It made it worse, somehow, as if he had no business being up there, staring down at them, blinking in the glare of spotlights pointed his way.

Trev was on fire. He grabbed a microphone to introduce Ted and Willow for their first duet of the night. Ted fervently hoped it would be their only one. He couldn't imagine what had persuaded him to agree. Except that he was not entirely joking when he said he loved Trev beyond reason. He would do anything legal for his partner.

'So please put your hands together for our very own Kenny and Dolly – Ted and Willow.'

He finished with a flourish, backing away, whistling enthusiastically through his fingers. He looked like a big kid, so excited and bursting with pride in his partner.

The main lights dimmed, leaving just a couple of spots pointed at Ted, towards the front of the stage, and Willow, standing further back. They'd decided between them to work it like the real thing, with Willow walking forwards to join Ted after the first verse, which he would sing alone.

Ted's stomach started turning cartwheels as he heard the piano introduction and realised he was shortly going to have to sing in public for the first time in his life. And the last, if he had anything to do with it. He silently cursed himself for picking a duet which left him singing the first verse solo.

His eyes desperately sought out Trev in the sea of faces in front of him. He sometimes sang to him when they were alone together. The only way he was going to get through this ordeal was if he pretended to himself that this was just like any of those times, with only the two of them.

His first few notes were hesitant but the whoops of encouragement from Trev got him through the verse, then he could at least pause for breath while Willow did her solo. He'd never heard her sing before and was stunned at how good she was. Despite no practice together, the harmonies worked seamlessly when they came together and suddenly, despite himself, Ted found he was almost enjoying the experience.

They'd planned to do one number as a try-out, *We've Got Tonight*, then have a break while someone else took a turn at the microphone. The crowd were having none of it. At the end of the first song, they were baying for more. Ted and Willow launched straight into their next number, *Islands in the Stream*.

Willow was good. But somehow those present took Ted completely to their hearts. Few knew who he was, other than a friend of Willow and Rupe. Fewer still knew what he was, otherwise the steady stream disappearing regularly outside, Trev included, would probably have dried up. But they couldn't get enough of the self-effacing small man with the easy-listening voice and clearly no idea of how good he was.

Whenever Ted tried to take a break, they called him back for more, until his voice was straining under the unfamiliar effort. They loved him even more when they discovered he could sing Queen numbers as well as country songs.

He managed a quick break, with Trev plying him with iced drinks for his throat.

'I'm not sure I can wait for carriages at six. It is so incredibly sexy watching you up there performing. I might just have to drag you away earlier and have my wicked way with you. I've never seen you let your hair down so much, especially not in the middle of a big case. I like it.'

Ted was part of a quartet, belting out Bohemian Rhapsody, when he felt his mobile phone vibrating in his pocket. He backed away from the microphones and lights, read the text message and groaned, then made his way through the crowd to Trev. He was disconcerted to discover his voice had now almost gone. Those last falsetto notes had about finished it off.

'Got to go. Sorry. Urgent briefing. Do you need money for a taxi?'

His voice was barely above a whisper and Trev had to lean in close to hear what he was saying, his face falling in evident disappointment.

'Go carefully, and thanks so much for doing this for me. I was so proud of you, up there. I'll show you how grateful I am when you get back from work. And hurry back. A husky voice makes you sexier than ever.'

With any luck, it would take Ted less than an hour to get to Central Park at that time of the morning, even if he played it cautiously and kept within the speed limit. He just wished he had time to go home and change out of his DJ. He was going to get some odd looks and some wisecracks, turning up like that for a briefing. He had a spare set of clothes in the boot, as always. They were casual wear, but at least it would be better than turning up as he was. He didn't dare stop until he got there, but if he made good enough time, he could slip into the gents to change quickly before putting in an appearance in front of Marston and everyone else.

Even when he saw a police car lying in wait as he drove through a built-up area, Ted was not concerned. He was keeping an eye on his speed, driving impeccably and hadn't touched a drop of alcohol, despite feeling like breaking his long, self-imposed ban. He'd stopped drinking in time, before it had become an addiction instead of just a way to relax. He didn't want it any more. He certainly didn't need it. Most of the time.

He groaned aloud when the car pulled out of its place, the headlights came on and the blues started flashing as it drew up behind his car. He hated doing it, but he reached for his warrant card before his driving licence, as he indicated and pulled in close to the kerb to stop. Needs must when the devil, in the shape of Marston, called.

The area car stayed where it was for some moments, its lights still flashing. Ted knew they would be checking his registration number before approaching the vehicle. He drummed his fingers impatiently on the steering wheel. He really didn't need this, not right now.

Eventually, the passenger got out and walked slowly up to Ted's vehicle, straightening his hat as he did so. Ted let his window down and waited for him.

'Did you know you have a rear light out?' the constable asked him without preamble.

'No, I didn't know that, constable. I have spare bulbs. I can easily replace that,' Ted replied, although his hoarse voice was barely above a whisper.

Ted reached towards the glove compartment for his driving licence but the officer stopped him with a brusque, 'Leave both hands on the steering wheel, where I can see them. Driving licence.'

'It's going to be hard to hand you that without moving my hands from the steering wheel,' Ted said reasonably. 'My licence is in the glove compartment. Do you want me to pass it to you?'

'Have you been drinking?'

'No, I haven't. And you have no valid reason to suspect that I have. Do I smell of alcohol to you, officer?'

'Hard to tell with that aftershave, mate. It's a bit strong.'

Ted was rapidly losing patience. He didn't like the other man's attitude at all, especially as he was chewing gum the whole time he spoke. He would have liked to mark his card for him. But he certainly didn't want to risk being late for Marston's briefing. His throat was getting increasingly sore and he wanted to get on his way.

'I'm going to pass you my driving licence now. Together with my warrant card. Mate.'

He reached carefully for both, handed his licence to the officer and made a pointed show of looking at his number as he badged him.

'Now, I need to be at a briefing at Central Park. I have your number, constable. You and I will talk again. In the meantime, I suggest you lose the attitude. And the chewing gum.'

As Ted put his car in gear and pulled away, the constable spat out his gum with a resounding, 'Fuck.'

Even the slight delay had robbed Ted of the time in which to change. He was only going to make the appointed hour by the skin of his teeth if he sprinted all the way from his car, pausing just long enough to sign in. The duty sergeant on the front desk had clearly seen it all in his time and did no more than raise an eyebrow as he directed him to the right room. Clearly the sight of a senior officer arriving for a briefing still in evening dress and reeking of expensive aftershave was not as novel as Ted feared it might be. As he took the stairs two at a time, he ripped off his bow tie and stuffed it in his pocket. He might as well feel comfortable.

It was a much reduced selection of senior officers, gathered around a table in a smaller room. Ted's own Super was there, as was Alex Porter, from Armed Response. But Ted noticed immediately that Neil Smith from Fraud was conspicuous by this absence. He wondered if his interview with CCU had not gone well or if Marston was just being paranoid.

Ted slid into a seat next to Superintendent Bill Wilson, Commander of the division responsible for policing Manchester's busy international airport. His presence gave Ted a clue as to the reason for the hastily summoned briefing.

His voice now barely above a whisper, he leaned closer to him to say, 'Hello, Bill, fancy seeing you here. How are you, and how's Pat?'

They'd known each other long enough to be on first name terms in private, and with Ted's voice now so faint, no one else would be able to hear him.

'Not too bad, either of us, thanks.'

He was interrupted by Marston's voice, sounding as tetchy as ever.

'Ladies and gentlemen, if we can make a start, please. This is not a social occasion, although clearly, DCI Darling, we have called you away from one.'

'Sorry, sir,' Ted responded, or tried to.

Marston looked increasingly irritated as he leaned forward in his seat to catch what Ted was saying to him.

'Are you sure you should be here, Darling? We're on the brink of a breakthrough in a big operation. We don't want you infecting everyone here with some sort of virus.'

'Just voice strain, sir. Nothing serious. Or catching.'

'Shall we get on, Mr Marston?' the ACC asked. 'Ted, I think it would be a good idea, in the circumstances, if you said as little as possible. Has some coffee been ordered? I'm sure we could all do with some at this ungodly hour of the morning, and certainly DCI Darling sounds in need of something.'

'It has been ordered, sir. Now, may I proceed?'

It was pompous, at best. An implied rebuke to a senior officer. Luckily for him, the ACC was more interested in getting on with the case than putting Marston down in public. He inclined his head in assent towards the Chief Superintendent. Ted strongly suspected that it was not the end of the matter, though.

'Right, we finally have Kateb in our sights. A certain Antoine Fournier is booked on an easyJet flight to Marseilles via Paris Charles de Gaulle leaving this afternoon at 17.35 from Terminal One. His seat was booked using a cloned credit card, so I think we can be certain that this is our man.

'So now we have to decide on the best way to proceed to bring him in. There are already armed officers at the airport, on routine patrol, of course. I would suggest, therefore, Superintendent Wilson, that officers are deployed to observe the check-in area and to be ready to approach the suspect as soon as we get a positive ID.'

'Sir, can I say something, please?' Ted put in, straining to make himself heard.

'Is it essential? Only I agree with the ACC. It would surely be better for you to conserve what remains of your voice for emergencies.'

'Knowing DCI Darling's experience of such operations, I'd be more than happy to listen to what he has to say, sir, if he can manage it,' Wilson responded.

'I agree. Ted, if you can do so, tell us what you think of that idea,' the ACC told him. 'And can someone get on the phone and hurry that coffee up. I think we all need some, especially you, Ted.'

What Ted would really have liked was some of his green tea with honey. He was prepared to settle for anything liquid to ease the soreness in his throat. He was surprised that it was the Ice Queen herself who stood up to use the phone to ask for the coffee and for some bottled water.

Ted decided to address the ACC directly. He'd given up trying to get through to Marston.

'Sir, Kateb is going to be more nervous than ever now and therefore potentially dangerous. If he sees too many firearms officers about, he might even turn tail and not bother checking in. Superintendent Wilson can correct me if I'm wrong but it is theoretically possible for him to get inside the terminal with some sort of a concealed weapon.'

Wilson was nodding in agreement.

'The one place we can be one hundred per cent sure he can't get to carrying anything at all which could cause harm is on board the aircraft. He'll have had to pass through security, metal detectors and everything else. I suggest we let him get as far as boarding, then send someone onto the plane to arrest him there and remove him. For me that's minimal risk, maximum chance of success.'

The door opened to allow a young constable to enter with a trolley containing the coffee, water, and some dubious-looking croissants of uncertain vintage. Everyone fell instinctively quiet, not wanting to continue a closed briefing in front of anyone not cleared to attend. It made the young woman look decidedly uncomfortable, but she pushed the trolley over to a table near the window and parked it there. Marston ignored her. It was the ACC who thanked her and said she could safely leave them to serve themselves.

Superintendent Wilson and Inspector Porter were nodding their heads in unison at what Ted had been saying.

'Sir, that makes sense to me,' Wilson said.

'I would suggest, sir, that it should be an AFO in plain clothes, carrying a concealed weapon, who goes on to the plane to make the arrest,' Porter added. 'Just in case.'

'Even though we can be almost sure he can't smuggle on a weapon of any sort on board, we don't know what his capabilities are otherwise. Could he, for instance, grab someone from a nearby seat as a shield and threaten to break their neck if approached?' the ACC speculated. 'I'd be happier if we had someone like an SFO, in plain clothes, with a concealed weapon, and with proven close combat skills.'

Chapter Twenty-six

All eyes were on Ted. He made an elaborate show of looking behind him, although he knew he was the only former serving Specialist Firearms Officer in the room. He addressed the ACC.

'Sir, remember I am ex-SFO.'

'But as you were quick to remind me the other day, you've done recent update training. Is your firearms training up to date?'

'Yes, sir, always.'

'And can you do this job? Get Kateb off the plane without risk of injury?'

'Probably, sir' Ted said guardedly.

'Probably? That's no use,' Marston spat. 'We can't put "probably, sir" on a risk assessment.'

The ACC gave him a stern look over the top of his reading glasses.

'I think DCI Darling is right to be cautious. There is still much about Kateb we don't know. For those present who don't know you, Ted, could you please remind us how many black belts you hold in martial arts?'

'Four, sir.'

Ted had the satisfaction of seeing Marston look taken aback.

'The important thing, as I see it, is to arrest Kateb swiftly and discreetly, without causing any panic, especially to passengers on the plane. So the last thing we want to do is to send visibly armed officers on board. If we can do it this way, I think the risks are minimal and therefore justifiable.

'We can presumably find out from the airline which seat Kateb has reserved and make sure the one next to him is kept free for you, Ted. Bill, I imagine your people can get Ted through security, even armed. The question is, do we put him on first, or wait to make sure that Kateb definitely boards the flight?'

'Sir, if I was in Kateb's shoes, I'd want to be last on. That way, they'll be moving the steps and getting ready to taxi, so he'd expect to be away fairly promptly. I'd prefer to be first on and in my seat when he boards. Just please don't let them take off with me still on – I don't much like flying.'

The ACC looked at his watch and took a large swallow of his coffee, grimacing at the taste.

'Right, Ted, you certainly need to go home and change ...'

'Sir, I have a change of clothes in my car.'

'You interrupted me,' the ACC said, but there was no note of reproach in his voice. 'I was going to say change your clothes and also change into an officer who is at least capable of speaking enough to make an arrest and issue a proper caution. Go and grab a couple of hours' sleep. You look as if you need it. And try gargling with TCP.'

'Aspirin's better,' Alex Porter put in. 'Gargle with it, then swallow it.'

'I always swear by hot lemon and honey for the boys,' the Ice Queen put in.

'I'd put a measure of Balvenie in it, but I know you won't, Ted,' Bill Wilson added.

'All right, everyone, can we please get back to the matter in hand. It's starting to sound like a medical phone-in programme,' Marston said impatiently. 'Darling, certainly, go and get yourself sorted out, but I want you back on duty at 2pm. In the meantime, we can sort out the logistics of seating and access.'

'I'll sort you out a side-arm too,' Porter told him. 'You can sign for it when you get back. Any preference?'

'M&P40 from choice, Alex, if you can. Nothing too bulky, and as safe as possible.'

If he didn't encounter any delays, Ted would have four hours before he needed to be back on duty. He was already sucking his lozenges on the drive back, hoping to appease his throat enough to let himself at least be heard by Kateb.

It was a long time since he'd been on a similar operation, a pre-planned one. Not since he'd given up his firearms service to stop Trev worrying about him too much. He'd never told his partner how much he missed those days. He recognised, with hindsight, that it was the right thing to do. He could never have stuck by his decision to stop drinking altogether if he'd stayed in that role. A drink with the team at the end of the shift had been such a part of the culture.

He left his car on the driveway. He'd need it to go back out. He'd already decided to stop off at the station and pick up his service vehicle as he was going to be on duty. The little Renault hadn't let him down yet, but he didn't want to risk it not cooperating for such an important operation.

He was hoping to find Trev back and knew as soon as he went in that he was. He could also guess, from the trail of clothing negligently dumped everywhere between the front door and the bedroom, that he had arrived home stoned and somewhat drunk.

Ted carefully gathered up Trev's DJ, trousers and shoes to put away neatly, as well as his own, and put their evening shirts and underwear into the laundry basket. True to form, Trev was spread-eagled across most of the bed, sleeping the sleep of the innocent. Even the cats, who usually worshipped him and lay as close as they could, were keeping their distance from the smell of cannabis and alcohol.

Ted smiled indulgently as he watched him fondly for a

moment. He didn't like to cramp his much younger partner's style. They had a tacit agreement. Ted would turn a blind eye to a bit of blow, but never to anything more than that.

He suddenly found he wanted nothing more than to slide into what little space remained in the bed and hold his partner in his arms. He didn't anticipate any real danger in the operation which lay ahead of him, but he needed the reassurance. He knew his chances of waking him were somewhere close to zero, but just to hold him close would be enough.

He set the alarm on his mobile phone and put it on the side table next to the bed. Then he slipped cautiously under the duvet, trying to make enough room for himself without waking Trev. It was certainly easier without having to navigate his way between six cats as well. Trev stirred only slightly before burrowing down further under the duvet with a contented sigh.

Ted closed his eyes and managed to sleep fitfully. It seemed no time at all before he was snapped awake by the muted buzzing and flashing lights of his mobile phone. He planted a gentle kiss on the back of Trev's head, the only part visible above the bedclothes, then got soundlessly to his feet to start getting ready.

He was glad Trev was still asleep. He would need to dig his shoulder holster out from the back of the wardrobe's top shelf. That was going to take some explaining if Trev happened to see it. He opted for his poplin field jacket rather than his suit. He didn't want the loaded holster to be bulky and noticeable.

He had a shower then started on some of the remedies which had been recommended, gargling with aspirin, then going downstairs to make hot lemon and honey. Whilst he was waiting for the kettle to boil, he scooped a spoonful of honey out of the pot and sucked on it greedily. He was sure he'd heard somewhere that opera singers took honey to help their throats.

He scribbled a note to let Trev know he was going back to work and had no idea what time he'd be back. Unusually for him, he finished it off with 'Love you xxx'. Then he drove by the station to pick up his service vehicle before heading out to Ringway.

The pre-op briefing was taking place in a police control room at the airport. The same officers as earlier were all there, some of them looking as if they envied Ted the short break he'd taken, although they understood that he, more than any of them, would need his wits about him. There was fresh, hot coffee, which smelt decent enough, and a plate of sandwiches on a side table.

Marston was, as ever, in his element, directing operations. Ted had to concede that he was good at that aspect of his job. Personnel management skills were not something he seemed to bother with, however. He had a diagram of the seating plan of the type of aircraft on which Kateb had booked his flight. As soon as Ted arrived, he went straight into his description of how things would unfold, as long as everything went according to plan and there were no surprises in store for them.

'Kateb's booked a window seat here, on the wing,' he jabbed a pointer at the diagram. Ted wondered fleetingly if he thought any of those present might not know what a wing was, without his guidance, but he kept quiet, his face neutral. 'The airline has freed up the two seats next to his. As you can see, on this aircraft, the seating is arranged in two lots of three, one on each side of the aisle. Luckily for us, the flight is not completely full.

'As is often the case with these budget airlines, the turnaround time between this plane arriving, being cleaned and refuelled and sent back on its way to Paris, is very short. We've therefore arranged for DCI Darling to go on as the cleaners are finishing off and before any of the other passengers start to board.'

'What if Kateb is watching from the gate and gets suspicious at seeing someone boarding early?' Ted asked. His voice was still weak but at least his throat wasn't quite as sore after all his ministrations.

'We already have that covered. You'll be taken to the steps in a wheelchair, by a member of the airport security staff, who will then assist you on board. Perhaps if you could limp convincingly, or something? Then if anyone is watching, you're a disabled passenger and it's not unusual for such people to be boarded before anyone else.

'Now, I know this type of work is more in your area of expertise than perhaps any of us,' Marston couldn't quite keep the grudging note out of his voice, 'but I do want to stress one thing. The last thing we want to happen is for you to have to produce a gun and frighten the living daylights out of the rest of the passengers on board. It's for that reason I would have preferred uniformed officers, perhaps with Tasers. But I accept that would also have involved risks. So we are in your hands, DCI Darling, for a successful outcome. Do you have any questions?'

'A couple, sir. Who knows I'm a police officer under cover?'

'Just in case of anyone seeing your weapon, we've had to inform some of the airport security staff, those who will have direct contact with you, as well as the flight and cabin crew of the aircraft you will be boarding.'

Ted addressed the ACC as he posed his next question.

'And are we happy about the risk of leaks from any of those sources to Kateb or anyone he might be in contact with?'

'CCU have not yet completed all their enquiries but we are as happy as we can be, between us, that the source of the previous leak was internal, within our force, and that those likely to be behind it have been kept out of this phase of the operation.'

Ted nodded and had a drink from the bottle of water which was next to his seat. He wondered if his Super had made arrangements for those, as he saw there were plenty on the table.

'The next thing is, at the moment I can't see a way to get a pair of handcuffs on board, without that being very obvious.'

'Already been thought of and sorted,' Marston put in smugly. 'We've arranged one of those carry-on meals for you, in a brown paper bag. The handcuffs will be underneath a sandwich. If you keep the bag handy, you should be able to access them easily enough.'

'Right, sir. Nothing with mustard for me, though, please.'

There were some smiles at Ted's attempt at humour, although Marston was clearly not impressed.

'And there's plenty of surveillance in place, so we know if and when Kateb is on the way?'

'All of that has also been anticipated and organised, I can assure you, DCI Darling.' Marston again, showing his impatience. 'We've slightly upped the number of armed officers on duty, though not enough for it to be suspicious, and there are plenty of plain clothes officers also dotted about.'

'Thank you, sir. And, excuse me if this sounds as if I'm telling anyone how to do their job, but has it been double checked that Kateb is not, in fact, booked on to another flight leaving today? Perhaps one from another terminal? Because if it was me, I'd want a belt and braces. I'd want to do a thorough recce of Terminal One and then, if I didn't like what I saw, I'd want to go to another terminal and slip away that way.'

'Good call, Ted,' the ACC said appreciatively. 'We've got the railway station, the bus stops and the taxi ranks covered, but it's certainly worth checking other airlines. Mr Marston?'

Ted could see from the furious look on Marston's face that he'd been caught flat-footed.

'The APW is still in force, of course, sir, and should be

covering that, but I'll see that someone follows it up to be doubly sure.'

The ACC leaned back in his seat and looked at Ted.

'So now we wait, and hope that the flight inbound isn't delayed so long it starts to make Kateb jumpy. If he shows up at all. Then it's all down to you, Ted.'

It felt strange to be carrying a handgun again operationally, for the first time in years, although Ted always kept his training up to date. The weight was reassuring against his side. He was fitted with a discreet earpiece and a hidden microphone, so he would be in constant contact with the control room, in case of any problems. Even close to, it would just look like someone listening to music for the flight. He was as ready as he could be.

He'd signed for the firearm Alex Porter had sorted for him and spent a few moments balancing it in his hand, getting the feel of it once more. He'd opted for one with a safety mechanism which meant it would not go off if there was a struggle and it happened to get dropped. He fervently hoped he would not need to use it. It would all depend on how much of an attempt Kateb put up to resist arrest. He'd come so far in evading capture that Ted doubted he would roll over meekly at the end.

Next he checked his pack-up, in its brown carrier bag, to make sure he could access the handcuffs fast enough. He was waiting with Alex Porter and Bill Wilson for company. Both burst out laughing like mischievous schoolboys when Ted studied the sandwich and found it was ham and mustard.

'I'm not wasting what remains of my voice on dignifying that with a response,' he told them, but he was smiling.

The inbound Paris flight touched down only minutes behind its scheduled time. They were nearly ready for action. Ted had been informed that Kateb had arrived and checked in, right at the last minute, as he'd suspected.

Once it was time to get Ted on board, Bill Wilson escorted him to find the security staff member who would wheel him out to the waiting plane in a chair. It felt alien to Ted not to be independently mobile, but it was a good cover, just in case Kateb was watching. He made a point of going slowly and laboriously up the steps, one at a time.

The flight attendant who greeted him launched into her usual spiel, although Ted thought he detected a hint of nervousness about her eyes. He imagined it wasn't every day she had to welcome an armed undercover police officer onto the flight. He also guessed from her expression of slight surprise, that he looked nothing like whatever mental image she had of someone in that role. His hair was a similar colour to Daniel Craig's, but there any resemblance to James Bond or other secret agents ended.

He smiled at her in his most reassuring way. The last thing he needed was any suggestion of anything out of the ordinary when Kateb boarded. He didn't waste time trying to say anything. If she heard how weak his voice was, she might worry that he was ill and not up to the job.

He made his way down the aisle and sat in the first seat in the row in which Kateb had reserved. Once again, all he could do was wait, listening to the disembodied voice in his ear, keeping him up to date. The plane was filling up, the last of the passengers straggling on after the first rush. Ted never understood the initial stampede when everyone could have a reserved seat these days.

Then he got the alert. Kateb was on his way.

'Now sporting a full-face beard and with much shorter hair than in the photos we have so far, but this man has definitely checked in as Antoine Fournier and he matches the suspect for approximate height, build and age.'

Then Ted was getting his first view of their target, Samir Kateb, as he made his way down the plane. He certainly looked like a match, apart from the slight changes to his appearance.

Ted was busy weighing him up as a potential adversary. He was a lot taller than Ted, athletically built, but not overweight. He was checking the seat numbers and stopped when he got next to Ted.

'Excuse me, please,' he said politely. He looked relaxed, calm, but his eyes were alert, assessing. Ted saw an expression in them he had seen so many times before. Kateb's gaze travelled over Ted and instantly dismissed any threat in this small, insignificant-looking man.

'Yes, of course,' Ted replied, getting to his feet and stepping back to allow Kateb through. He saw that he was carrying a cabin bag, which suited his plan ideally.

As soon as Kateb reached up to open the overhead locker to store his luggage, Ted stepped up close beside him, effectively preventing him from moving anywhere. Not making any attempt to raise his voice, he simply said, 'Samir Kateb? I'm a police officer. I'm here to arrest you.'

Kateb moved quickly. He whirled as much as the confined space allowed and a straight-edged hand shot out in a chopping motion aimed at Ted's throat. He had no way of knowing what he was facing. Ted's speed was legendary. Trev knew to his cost that when Ted was on form, it was impossible to anticipate his moves and certainly to defend against them. They simply happened too quickly.

He effortlessly knocked Kateb's feet out from under him and had him face-down across the seats and in handcuffs before the other man had worked out quite what was happening to him. It all happened so fast that apart from a few curious looks from the passengers in the row directly behind, nobody seemed to have realised what had just taken place.

Ted hauled him upright by his cuffed hands and said, still making no effort to try to raise his voice, 'Let's go quietly, Mr Kateb. I am armed, so I strongly recommend you just cooperate and don't try anything further.'

He pushed him into the aisle and directed him along the

passageway towards the still-open door. He smiled at the same flight attendant who had greeted him and said, as he shoved Kateb towards the exit, 'There's an unopened ham and mustard sandwich on my seat, if anyone wants it. I hate mustard.

Then, into his mike, 'Suspect arrested and secured. No weapons visible. We're on our way out.'

Chapter Twenty-seven

As soon as Ted emerged from the plane with his prisoner, Armed Response Officers came running across the tarmac to surround Kateb and take him away. One or two of them nodded their appreciation to Ted. It was a job well done and they respected that.

Ted sauntered off to find Porter and Wilson where he'd left them. Both were grinning their pleasure, thumping him on the back and congratulating him. Ted was surprised to see Marston walking towards him. The other two tactfully withdrew at the sight of him.

'Well done, Darling,' he said, although it was clear it cost him an effort.

'Thank you, sir. I must have got lucky. Again.'

Marston's face darkened as he retorted, 'Don't push it. I haven't changed my opinion of you just because of a couple of good arrests. I still think you're a cocky little sod who knows he can do no wrong in the eyes of the top brass.

'Now get yourself back to Central Park, straight away. I've called a debriefing for all officers involved, and the ACC will be there.'

Marston pivoted on his heel and stalked off. Ted wished his voice was stronger so the Chief Super could have heard the contempt in the 'Sir,' which he threw at his retreating back.

Once he'd signed his firearm and ammunition back in, he made his way out of the terminal and found his service car, pausing, before he started it, to send a quick text to Trev:

'Mission accomplished. Just debriefing now. Home when I can. T xxx'

He was surprised to find quite a crowd at Central Park, assembled in the large conference room, for the end-of-operation briefing. He spotted straight away that Neil Smith was amongst those present. He took that as a good sign. He'd hopefully been cleared. Ted would try to catch a word with him at some point.

There was a relaxed air about the gathering. Everyone was standing, drinks in hand, celebrating the closure of a complicated operation with a successful result. As soon as the ACC saw Ted, he raised his glass in acknowledgement.

'Here he is, the man of the moment, once more. Bloody good job, Ted. Well done. And well done to all of you. Good result, well worth celebrating. Get a glass, Ted. We remembered and got some fizzy pop for you. There's food too, of sorts, some of which might even be edible. This has been a good outcome, just the way we wanted it to finish. All the gang members safely rounded up and I'm pleased to tell you that the mole within has also been exposed and arrested. So we have a good excuse to raise a glass.'

'Sir, with respect, should we perhaps complete the debriefing first, before we start to relax?' Marston asked him.

'I think we all deserve to relax now, Mr Marston. I know I do. Everyone, please ensure you put your reports through to Mr Marston no later than first thing tomorrow morning. There, that's the debriefing taken care of. You'll have all the reports you need tomorrow. After that, I imagine, you'll want to get on your way back to London, as soon as possible? And I'm sure the rest of us want to get back to our families as soon as we can this evening.'

It was so close to a public put-down that Ted had to hide a smile in his glass of sparkling apple juice. As there was clearly going to be no formal agenda, he made his way over to Neil

Smith.

'All sorted now, Neil?'

'Yes, sir, thankfully.'

'Sir? Behave yourself. It's Ted, now we're all letting our hair down. So, who was our informer in the end?'

'Luckily for me, not one of my team. One of the extras who were drafted in early on for the surveillance. It was a DS with a serious gambling habit. He'd been in the gang's pocket for years, as well as that of several others. Such a relief for me to know it wasn't one of my own. Anyway, congratulations to you. Good result.'

Ted had to put up with a lot more back-slapping and congratulating. In the end it was his own Super who came to his aid. She could be supportive and sensitive when the occasion called for it.

'Ted, you look rough. You need to go home. I'll make your excuses while you slip away. Go and get some rest, and I'll see you at work tomorrow. Standing around making small talk isn't helping what's left of your voice and I know it's not your thing. Go. I've got you covered. It's my job.'

Trev had clearly been listening out for him coming home. As soon as Ted put his key in the front door, it was pulled open and he found himself engulfed in a warm hug, at the same time as being pulled bodily into the house.

'How did it go? Did you get the bad guys? Are you all right?'

Then he pushed Ted back to arm's length, frowning.

'Why have you got a shoulder holster under your jacket? Have you been doing armed and dangerous stuff?'

Now he'd been rumbled, there was no chance of Ted returning his holster to the wardrobe without Trev noticing. He took off his jacket and undid the harness, putting it on the hall table.

'Nothing dangerous. They just needed an SFO to go on

board an aircraft and arrest someone. The suspect wasn't armed or anything, but I just had to carry a concealed weapon as a precaution.'

Trev was still looking at him suspiciously.

'Really. It was all just routine. Nothing for you to worry about. It won't even get me another commendation.'

Ted was trying to make light of it. If Trev hadn't noticed the holster, he wouldn't even have mentioned it to him.

'I promised you I'd give up Firearms and I have. I'd do anything for you, you know that. Surely you believe it, after last night?'

Trev was softening in his attitude.

'I was so proud of you, last night. And your poor voice. But my god, it makes you sound sexy, talking husky like that. Almost as sexy as seeing you wearing your holster. Put it back on. I like it.'

He picked the harness up off the table and thrust it towards his partner, taking his hand and pulling him towards the stairs.

Ted was sitting with his mother between him and his partner, with her friend Aldwyth on the other side of Trev. They were in the witness area of the Crown Court in Manchester's Crown Square. His mother's attacker had opted to exercise his right to ask for a full jury trial at the Crown Court, rather than a hearing in the magistrates' court with sentencing in the higher court. It meant it could go on for some time.

All four were holding hands, Annie clutching tightly to those of Ted and Trev, her face pale, drawn and anxious. Because the accused had stated his intention to plead not guilty, she would have to face him in court and give her evidence. She was dreading it.

Ted was still hoping for common sense to prevail and for the accused man to change his plea to guilty at the last minute. He had no doubt that his barrister would be strongly recommending him to do so. The sight of a man of his size and bulk, in comparison to Ted's small and slight mother, would be likely to sway a jury. He could face a stiffer sentence for not admitting the offence, amounting to wasting the court's time, and for not showing any remorse or accepting responsibility for his actions.

They were early, as Ted usually was for everything work-related. He'd explained to his mother that someone from the CPS would come and find her soon to explain the procedure. He'd also warned her there was a chance that she might come face to face with her attacker outside the courtroom, but that he and Trev were there to see that she was not intimidated in any way.

It was some time before one of the Crown Prosecutors, whom Ted knew well, came hurrying along the corridor, accompanied by a barrister, in wig and gown, who would present the prosecution case to the presiding judge and members of the jury.

'Hello, Ted, I didn't know this was a case you were involved in,' Suzy Lewis said as Ted stood up and shook her hand in greeting. 'I think you know Evan Hughes?'

'This is Mrs Jones, the victim in this case, who also happens to be my mother.'

'Ah, that explains it,' Suzy smiled. 'We've just heard from the defence that they're changing the plea to one of guilty. The jungle drums must have been at work with news of your involvement and that perhaps made common sense prevail. This is good news for you, Mrs Jones, as it means you won't have to give evidence in court, although Mr Hughes here will still read your Victim Personal Statement to the judge before the defendant is sentenced. The jury will be released, now there's a guilty plea. It will just be the Recorder who will listen to the presentations and pass sentence.

'And on that subject, I have even better news. We have the Hanging Judge today and he is more than a little annoyed at having his nice smooth schedule disrupted for the day by a change of plea at the very last minute. Oh, and I heard on the grapevine that the defendant turned up wearing a Britain First T-shirt. His barrister sent out for something to cover it up. I do hope someone mentioned that in His Honour's ear.'

Ted knew that the Crown Court Recorder in question, a man by the name of Shield, had gained his nickname through his zero tolerance and fondness for maximum sentences whenever possible. It looked as if his mother's attacker was going to be spending quite some time at Her Majesty's pleasure.

All four of them were now on their feet as the barrister spoke.

'Mrs Jones, I'm so sorry you've been put through all the stress and anxiety of anticipating the trial. I will now do my most persuasive best to see that your attacker gets sent down for as long as possible. And he really has done himself no favours at all in already incurring the wrath of His Honour, who is now likely to want to make an example of him.

'Now that you're no longer required as a witness, you are perfectly at liberty to leave. Or, if you prefer, you can take a seat in the public area of the courtroom to witness justice at work.

'Please excuse us now, while we go and prepare to do battle on your behalf.'

Annie looked anxiously towards her son for advice as the two prosecutors walked away.

'Up to you, mam. If I was you, I'd want to see him sent down. Trev and I, and Aldwyth, will be right there with you, supporting you.'

She smiled at them all.

'Well, let's go and do it, then. Then we can put the matter to bed and go and get a cup of tea somewhere. My treat.'

'Mam, if you want a cup of tea near Crown Square, it better be my treat. It's daylight robbery.'

The four of them sat together, still holding hands, as the

brief proceedings unfolded. Annie's attacker was looking unconcerned, smug even, clearly expecting nothing more than a light sentence and a rap on the knuckles.

Hughes was a good prosecuting counsel, with the perfect voice to sound compelling and sincere, capable of putting meaning and emotion into his words. Ted had helped his mother to write her Victim Statement and to hear the barrister read it was a moving experience. Annie had to take a hand back from Ted to wipe her eyes at one point.

The Hanging Judge had the perfect poker face. It was impossible to read him. Ted knew him well and guessed he would not be at all impressed at the idea of a physical assault on a smaller, older woman by someone as oafish as the defendant in front of him. Once he'd listened to all the submissions, he asked for the defendant to stand.

'Owen Davis, you have admitted to making a totally unprovoked attack on a woman going about her own business and posing no threat whatsoever to you. As has been described to this court, you are considerably taller, a lot younger and much heavier than your victim.

'You claim, in mitigation, that your intention was never to cause her any harm, simply to push her because you were annoyed with her. You were annoyed because you believed, wrongly, that she was speaking Polish, rather than her native Welsh tongue, and you blame Polish immigrants for having taken your job, although you yourself have acknowledged that they are prepared to work longer hours for less money than you.

'You have not once, at any stage of this enquiry, expressed the slightest remorse for your actions, nor offered any form of apology to Mrs Jones, your victim. On the contrary, you have continued to protest your justification for your behaviour. Furthermore, you have wasted a considerable amount of court time by your determination to plead not guilty, only changing that plea at the last possible minute.

'We have heard that, because of your unjustifiable actions, your victim, Mrs Jones, has decided to leave her home of nearly forty years to move back to Wales, where she can at least feel safe when speaking her own language. This has resulted in her losing close contact with the son who has only recently come back into her life after a long absence. And still you have shown no remorse, nor made any apology.

'In light of all of the above, and particularly after having heard your lamentable existing criminal record, I am sentencing you to the maximum amount of time which the law permits. You will go to prison for five years.'

Suzy Lewis turned her head slightly to flash a beaming smile towards Ted and to make a discreet fist-pump gesture, before the court was ordered to rise as His Honour the Hanging Judge swept out, no doubt pleased with his efforts.

Ted's mother was in tears of relief, now it was all over. Ted put an arm round her as he guided them all out of the court building.

'I'm so pleased it went well, Annie,' Trev told her, giving her a hug and a kiss. 'I really do need to get back to work now, though. Ted's taken the day off, so you make good use of him. Don't let him go sneaking off back to the station. Get him to take you somewhere nice for lunch, and I'll hopefully be seeing you again very soon. He's promised to take some time off so we can get away and we're going to come down to Wales to see you. Mind you, he doesn't always keep his promises, where work's concerned.'

'Hey, you,' Ted laughed in mock offence. 'I sang in public for you, didn't I? And that was worse than any arrest I've ever made.'

'Why don't I cook us all a nice meal tonight? You three go and have a lovely trip out somewhere and a light lunch, then Ted can pick the two of you up again later to bring you to supper.'

He kissed all of them then went on his way to the bike

dealership which he now owned jointly with a business partner, thanks to Ted funding the bank loan to buy into the concern.

'You are so lucky, Teddy, *bach*. He is such a lovely young man, and it's obvious how much the two of you love one another.'

'I know. I don't deserve him. Right, ladies, where shall we go? What about Lyme Park, mam? We can get a decent lunch there at the hall.'

It was another week before Ted felt he had made sufficient inroads on all the paperwork for the various cases to risk asking for time off. He was hoping to take five weekdays and to include the weekends at either side, but he knew it was asking a lot.

His Super was surprisingly supportive of the idea.

'You've been working some extremely long hours over the course of this operation, Ted. And with two excellent arrests to your credit, not to mention a commendation coming your way, I think it would be churlish in the extreme to put any barriers in your way with regard to taking some time off at this point.

'Your team have once again proved their worth, and now that Jim Baker is a bit more mobile once more, I'm sure that, between us, we can manage to hold the fort in your absence.'

Jim was getting back to his old self, now the plaster cast was off and he had a lighter support on his injured ankle, making him more mobile. The pain was less, too. He and Ted had caught up over lunch one day in The Grapes. Ted was pleased things were back to normal between them.

Jim had laughed to hear of Ted's encounter with the traffic officer with attitude and chewing gum, on his way back from the big night out.

'And will you follow it up? Speak to his boss, or see him yourself?'

'Oh yes,' Ted told him. 'I don't like behaviour like that. It gives us all a bad name. But not yet a while. Might as well let him sweat a bit longer.'

'You can be a bit of a sadist sometimes, Ted. Did you know that?'

Ted had invited his team members to have a drink with him in The Grapes on the Friday evening before he was due to go away. He wanted to let them know they were appreciated. He'd suggested Trev should come over later to join them, and that they should have a bite to eat there together afterwards, to save either of them having to cook.

They'd booked a live-in Animal Aunt to look after the cats while they were away. She would arrive first thing on the Saturday morning, so they could get away in good time. They would take the car, rather than the bike. Going for a full week, and knowing how Trev loved to change clothes every day, sometimes more than once, they'd never manage to transport everything they needed for that long on the bike. They also wanted to take their riding gear, in case they could find somewhere suitable for both their levels of ability.

Unusually, it was Ted who had made time to sort out all the arrangements. He'd booked them a guest house, not all that far from where his mother was staying with Aldwyth, where the management hadn't turned a hair at the booking for two men in one double room. Trev was surprised when Ted insisted they each pack a decent suit. His usual preference was for casual clothes for everything, especially when on holiday.

'I just thought, with Annie moving away, it would be nice to splash out and take her and Aldwyth out somewhere really special for a meal. Somewhere they wouldn't normally choose for themselves. I know we'll still be in touch, but it's not going to be the same as having her living not far away. A nice evening out for us all to remember, all dressed up to the nines. She'd like that.'

He was rewarded with a hug from his partner.

'That's a really lovely thought, especially as I know you don't like dressing up. Annie will love it, and so will I. Which means I'll have to show my appreciation, again.'

Chapter Twenty-eight

The team were enjoying the get-together, relaxing, laughing, forgetting about work. Ted couldn't resist talking shop with Jo, making sure he covered all eventualities before he took some time off. It wasn't that he didn't trust his team, especially now he had Jo to deputise for him. He was just a good copper, who found it hard to switch off.

'You can always call me, at any time, Jo, if you need to double-check anything. I'll have my phone with me all the time.'

'Boss, seriously? I have a feeling your Trev might kill me if I do. We'll be fine. The Super is actually quite approachable, surprisingly, and the Big Boss is getting back on his feet. I'm touched that you'll miss us so much but there's no need. You go and have a good time. You've not seen much of your Trev with Croesus taking up so much of your time. The two of you deserve a break.'

Ted looked across the bar-room to where Trev was talking and laughing with Rob and Sal, no doubt about big bikes, as usual. He felt the usual sudden emotion, almost like a physical pain in his chest, whenever he looked at his partner. He was going to make this holiday the best time they had ever spent together. He was determined not to let anything spoil his plans.

Once the team members started drifting away, Trev joined Ted at the bar and draped a possessive arm around his shoulders.

'Are you ready to eat now? I'm starving. Shall I grab a

table? What's the special tonight, Dave?'

'Steak and ale pie with chips. How does that sound, gentlemen? And Ted, your table's all ready whenever you are.'

'Sounds good to me,' Trev told him, looking round the bar. 'Have we got a special table, then?'

'Come with me,' Ted told him, taking his arm and leading him through to the small private room at the back, where he'd met up with Green.

It wasn't much of a place, not very glamorous, but Dave had done them proud. There was a clean white linen cloth on the only table in the room laid up for service, and he had carefully arranged the three red roses Ted had ordered, in a glass vase as the centrepiece. Ted guided his partner over to the table and pulled a chair out for him to sit down.

'This is nice. Is it a special occasion that I've forgotten about? Or are we celebrating your commendation in advance?'

Ted suddenly felt awkward, uncertain, not sure if he was about to make a complete idiot of himself. He had invested so much in this moment.

'I thought it would be nice to have a bit of a romantic meal together, just the two of us, to start our holiday. Besides, I wanted to try again.'

'Try again?'

Ted took one of the red roses out of the vase and moved closer to his partner. Then he got down on one knee.

'Trevor Patrick Costello Armstrong, will you do me the honour of marrying me? Please?'

'Ted, I love you, very much. I just don't want anything to change.'

'It won't, I promise you. We'll go on as we were, as we've always been. I'll need to update my personnel file, so you get my pension, but that's confidential. We won't tell anyone else. Well, except my mother. She's coming to the wedding. With Aldwyth.'

Trev was looking at him suspiciously.

'The wedding? You mean you've planned it all? That's why you wanted us to take suits? Ted, for goodness sake get up, you'll ruin your good work trousers.'

'Say you'll marry me first. Before Dave comes in with our food. Please?'

To his intense relief, Trev burst out laughing and said, 'Yes, all right, then, you soppy sod. Get up, for the love of all that's holy. I will marry you, but only in secret. I don't want it broadcast. And I want you to promise that it really won't change anything between us. You do realise Shewee is never going to speak to us again if she's not invited to the wedding?'

Ted got up and kissed him, handing him the rose, before sitting down opposite him at the table.

'It's fine, I've invited her and she's coming. I phoned her school and arranged the time off for her, and Henry is driving her up. It's nothing very exciting, just a hotel reception room, us two and the four guests, with a nice meal afterwards. And nothing will change, I promise, except on paper. We won't tell anyone else, unless you want to. No rings or anything, except just for the ceremony. But it does mean that you will be provided for, if ever anything happens to me, and that puts my mind at rest. Thank you.'

'And you've arranged all this, without a word to me? You devious little detective. I'll never be able to trust you again. Does Dave know?'

'Heck, no. He just thinks we wanted a romantic dinner at the end of a long and difficult case. I sorted it all out with mam when we went to Lyme Park after the court case. She's over the moon.'

'What if I'd said no again?'

'Then I'd have looked like a proper dickhead.'

They were interrupted at that moment when Dave appeared, carrying their food, steaming hot pies which gave off an inviting aroma, with a side order of chips. He placed them on the table with a flourish, together with a decent bottle of

French wine for Trev and a soft drink for Ted.

'Here you go, gents, enjoy your meal. Just shout if you need anything else.'

Ted poured his partner's wine then raised his own glass in a toast.

'Thank you. You've made me very happy. And I promise you'll never regret it.'

It was a week of behaving nothing like a policeman. It was a week when Ted felt happier than he could ever remember being in his life before. Their guest house accommodation was charming, the Dutch couple who ran it warm and welcoming.

After the first weekend, even Ted had stopped checking his mobile phone every few minutes. He could never completely forget about work, but he was managing to push it to the back of his mind. Trev had banned him from bringing his laptop so he couldn't keep an eye on the local news for his patch. Sneaky looks at his mobile phone were too obvious. Trev had his laptop. He'd wanted to show Annie and Aldwyth the local newspaper coverage of him teaching English at the refugee and immigrant centre. The pictures looked so much better on the laptop than on his phone. He was photogenic, so the photographer had included him in all the shots, with his name in the captions. He'd brought a paper copy for Annie and promised to send her one of Ted when he went for his commendation.

'They'd better not put my picture in the paper,' Ted muttered at the mere idea.

They took Annie and Aldwyth out a few times, to places Ted's mother remembered visiting from her childhood - Carreg Cennen Castle, Pembrey Beach. But mostly, they spent time alone together, walking in the Brecon Beacons, even finding a riding centre which took just the two of them out for a two-hour ride over Llanllwni Mountain. Ted was given a sedate and impeccably mannered Welsh cob, as smooth as an armchair,

285

which even hopped him successfully over a small fallen tree, his first ever jump. Trev and their escort roared ahead on their hunters, sailing over a flight of point-to-point hurdles on their way, which Ted and Missy carefully skirted by mutual consent.

The low-key wedding was perfect. Annie was in tears and even Trev's younger sister Siobhan, the epitome of cool sophistication most of the time, had to borrow Henry's neatly pressed handkerchief from his top pocket to wipe her eyes.

'So, husband, remember your promise. As soon as we get back home tomorrow, we go back to being partners and none of this is ever mentioned again,' Trev told Ted as they lay in bed together on their wedding night, the last night of their holiday. Trev had joked about them breaking with tradition to have the honeymoon before the ceremony.

'That's absolutely fine. I promised you, this changes nothing. Only on paper, and that makes me feel better. If ever anything happens to me, I know you'll be taken care of now. You're entitled to my police pension and I wanted to make sure you could get it. And now you can. So thank you.'

'Just don't go doing anything daft and dangerous involving firearms. I'd much rather have you than your pension. This has been a fabulous week. Thank you. Now, why don't we make the most of our last night of no possibility of being interrupted by your phone?'

'And finally, a Chief Constable's special award for bravery goes to DCI Darling, from Stockport. DCI Darling went in alone against an armed and dangerous suspect who was holding a young girl hostage at knife-point. He negotiated the girl's release, thereby probably saving her life, and successfully disarmed and arrested her assailant. The Chief has warned me to gloss over how he did it, as it wasn't exactly by the book.'

There was general laughter from those attending the Chief Constable's reception. Most of them had heard what had happened at the arrest of Bacha. Nothing like that stayed a secret for long in the force. Trev frowned at Ted and said quietly, 'You can tell me all about it later on. The real version.'

'DCI Darling, where are you hiding? We all know you hate publicity, but come up and get your award,' the Chief Constable ordered, peering down from the raised stage of the hotel reception room where the event was being held.

Reluctantly, Ted moved forward and went up the three steps to join him.

'About bloody time, Ted,' the Chief said quietly. 'We've been trying to get you to accept an award for ages. I was beginning to think we'd never succeed'

He was speaking through his teeth as he smiled at the cameras, shaking Ted's hand and passing him his award, a framed certificate and a piece of engraved Perspex on a wooden plinth. Unless Trev got to them first, both were going into the furthest dark corner of the loft as soon as he got home. He did his best to smile, as instructed, then escaped with relief as soon as he decently could.

His ordeal wasn't over yet, though. Trev was enthusing over the award, saying the trophy was going on display as soon as they got home and that Ted should put the certificate up in his office. A press photographer came over to them, all insincere smiles.

'Inspector Darling? I'm doing some photos for the local papers. You're from Stockport, right? Can I get one of you with the awards? And is this your Significant Other? Perhaps he could be in the shot as well?'

'I'd prefer not to. It makes my job easier if people don't know I'm police when they see me and I like to keep my private life private.'

'It'll be on the GMP website, Mr Darling. Anyone can see it there.'

'Oh, come on, Ted, you know I love having my photo taken. What harm can it do?' Trev said persuasively. 'Just think how proud your mum will be.'

'That's perfect, close together like that. Perhaps you could hold an award each? That's lovely. Could you smile a bit, Mr Darling? Look as if you're pleased with it. Perfect, great, keep smiling. Thank you. Can I just take your name? Are you his husband, partner, boyfriend? What do you like to be called?'

'I'm Trevor Armstrong. I'm his ...' he hesitated slightly, then went on, 'his partner.'

'Why are you sulking?' Trev asked, as they headed home in the car after the reception.

'I'm not sulking. I just don't like fuss, you know that.'

'Why didn't you want me to be in the photo? You're not ashamed to be seen with me, surely?'

'Don't be daft,' Ted put one hand on Trev's arm and gave it a clumsy, apologetic pat. 'I just worry that with some of the types I have to deal with, being seen with me in public could make you a target for abuse.'

'I love it that you're so protective of me. But you know I can take care of myself.'

It was a laughing, happy group of people who came out of the building at the end of their English lesson with Trev. He was at the centre of them, clearly enjoying himself immensely. With his love of languages and natural flair for learning them, he had already picked up a few words of greeting and farewell in Polish, Romanian, Arabic and a few others. They paused outside the building to chat a bit more before going on their separate ways, already looking forward to their next meeting.

None of them paid any attention to the man standing on the pavement directly opposite them, watching intently, his eyes locked on Trev. There was a chilly breeze and he drew his broad, rugby-player's shoulders up to his thick neck for protection against it. He was wearing an old fleece jacket, his hands pushed deep into pockets made shapeless by repetition of the gesture. A faint feminine fragrance still clung tentatively to the fabric.

THE END